SUMMER'S HEART

Suzanne Cass

Summer's Heart

Storm Cloud Press, Perth Australia

Copyright © 2025 by Suzanne Cass

Cover by Vikncharlie

All rights reserved.

ISBN: 9780648643074

To protect all the endangered wildlife around the world—it is surely our responsibility to save them.

CHAPTER ONE

Summer hurried past the shop windows and café doors, all closed up for the night, her sneakers tapping a quiet tattoo on the concrete path. Glancing behind her, she let out a tight grunt of relief when she saw the street remained empty. She chanced a quick peek at her watch—just past nine p.m.—then silently cursed herself for getting too carried away photographing the gorgeous sunset over Lake Union and not concentrating on the time. Even this early in the season, the nights in Seattle were staying lighter for longer. Which was great, because it allowed her to take some amazing photos. But it also meant that temptation had prompted her to break her own self-imposed curfew—never walk alone after dark.

With a sigh of relief, she reached the front door that led to her block of flats, checking behind her before punching the entry code into the keypad. Taking the stairs two at a time, Summer began mentally ticking off her list of things she needed to complete tonight. Tomorrow she was due to head out on a three-day field trip with a group of photographers from Wildlife Defenders, going to the Flathead National Park in Montana to see if they could document a small population of an endangered large cat, the lynx. Their work would help in the preservation efforts of this beautiful animal, and

Summer was excited to have been chosen. Almost packed, she had all the stuff she would need on this excursion already neatly laid in her large backpack on the floor next to her bed. She was planning on taking her Nikon, of course. And her Canon—currently slung around her neck—as a backup. But even now she was debating whether to take her Hasselblad film camera. This project required still photos only, and her Hasselblad was heavy, adding to the weight she'd have to carry.

Summer reached the landing of her fifth-floor apartment, puffing only slightly. Taking the keys out of her jeans pocket, her movements automatic and familiar, she was still considering the pros and cons of what equipment to pack. If she took her Hasselblad and recorded the Lynx on film, that could be priceless. It would be the first time she'd ever captured this graceful, elusive creature on film. But if…

Summer drew up short as she went to put her key into the lock. The door was ajar, and on closer inspection, it looked as if the bolt had been broken.

"What the…?" Summer stepped back and surveyed the landing, eyeing the three other apartment doors on this level, which were all closed up tight. She shifted her focus to the elevator doors in the far corner, but they too were shut, the digital readout next to the button displaying that the elevator car was all the way down on level one. There was no one up here, and she'd seen no one on the stairs either. But that didn't mean they hadn't used the elevator to make their getaway when they'd heard her coming. She returned her gaze to her door, unsure whether to go inside or hightail it back down the stairs. Who would want to break into her apartment? No one should be able to get into the building without a code. Did that mean it was another resident? She cast a sideways glance at Tad's door, opposite hers in the far corner. No, even he wouldn't stoop to that.

All her cameras were in her flat. Had some thief broken in and stolen them? She had to go in and find out. Gingerly, she pushed the door until it swung open. Her hand flew up to cover her mouth as she gasped at the destruction laid out in front of her. Her once-beautiful apartment looked like a bomb had exploded inside it. Chairs were tipped over, the glass coffee table had been smashed, and books and knickknacks had been swept from shelves, forming piles on the floor beneath. The bunch of daisies she'd bought only yesterday were shredded and strewn all over, the water from the vase leaving a wet puddle in the middle of the rug. Her bicycle, which had been sitting on its training stand in the corner window, had been overturned, the spokes on the front wheel twisted and bent as if they'd been stomped on. Even her sofa hadn't been spared, the cushions thrown across the room, scattered heaps of stuffing creating small white clouds on the wooden floorboards.

This wasn't just a break-in. Someone had gone to a lot of trouble to trash the place. Or they were looking for something and were in an extreme hurry.

But why? What had she done to provoke such wanton destruction?

She had no enemies. Everyone liked her, didn't they?

Careful not to step on the broken glass shards from the coffee table, she edged her way past the upturned furniture and detritus of her life to where the door to her darkroom stood open. She always left that door closed. Always. Which meant only one thing. Whoever the thief was, they knew what they were after. Her cameras. Carefully, she poked her head around the doorframe, expecting the worst, but was surprised to see most of her equipment still in the room. They'd been taken down from their cupboards and scattered on the bench top, but all were here and intact. With a single notable exception. Her big Nikon was missing.

A thought struck her, and she swiveled on her heels, heading for her bedroom. Oh, please let it still be there.

She barely registered that her room had also been wrecked as she dropped to her knees next to the far bedside table, pushing the baseball bat she always kept under her bed out of the way, and placing her Canon and backpack on the bed as she did so. Opening the small cupboard door, she let out a sigh of relief when she saw the safe hidden inside, untouched and unopened. With lightning-quick fingers, she punched in the code and peered in. Lifting her head to the sky, she touched the tiny cross at the base of the throat and sent up a silent prayer. Thank the Lord they hadn't found her Hasselblad. The old film camera had cost her a pretty penny and was her pride and joy; it was almost irreplaceable. Unlike a lot of photographers, she wasn't a collector of camera paraphernalia, but she had a few curated pieces. And this was the pinnacle of her collection. Her newer Hasselblad, the one she was contemplating taking on her field trip, was also an expensive item of equipment, but nothing compared to this beautiful old piece.

A sudden noise made her lift her head to peer over the top of the bed. The door to the wardrobe that filled the wall on the other side of her room was open. Hadn't that been closed when she came in? Then she heard the unmistakable sound of booted feet crunching across broken glass.

Someone was in her apartment.

The thief was still here.

Had they been hiding in her cupboard all along? Her hand clasped the baseball bat. This was the exact reason she kept it under her bed. Everyone told her she was crazy, that she lived on the fifth floor and no one was coming in here. And yet... Leaping to her feet, she gave a banshee yell, brandishing the bat above her head and sprinted around the end of the bed, getting to the doorway just in time to see a figure in a dark hoodie clutching her Nikon to his chest, run through her front door.

"Hey, stop!" she shouted. "Give that back." She launched herself after the dark figure.

But when she reached the exit, he'd already vaulted down the first set of stairs and was on the fourth-floor landing. "Stop, thief," she yelled over the railing at him. For a split second, the tall guy looked up at her, and she glimpsed a large, hooked nose and two beady, almost black eyes staring at her. Then he was taking the steps three at a time, sprinting downward.

Not thinking, Summer took off after him. No way was this bastard getting away with her camera. Especially after he'd just trashed her apartment. Gripping the railing, she flew down the stairs after him, hoping she didn't misstep and break her ankle. But all her years of running, and swimming, and biking stood her in good stead. She was fit and athletic, and could most likely outrun this guy in a race. If only she could overtake him. In her haste, she dropped the bat on the third-floor landing but continued the chase without it.

The man barreled through the front door and took off down the street while she was still descending from the first floor. Determined to catch him, she put on an extra spurt of speed as she made it to the entryway and pushed the double doors with all her might, stumbling out onto the pathway.

Straight into a solid wall of muscle.

The air left her lungs, and she gave an involuntary grunt of surprise. She and the man who'd appeared from nowhere went down together like a sack of potatoes. Somehow he maneuvered himself in mid-air, so that he was the one who landed on the concrete first, with her on top of him. Which caused *him* to give an involuntary grunt of pain.

"He stole my camera," she yelled. "I have to catch him." She struggled to untangle her legs, to get up so she could give chase. The stupid idiot, what was he doing standing in front of the door? Now the thief was getting away.

By some miracle, the man managed to disentangle himself and stand up, reaching a hand down to help her up. "Are you okay?" His tone was terse, worried frown lines crisscrossing his forehead as he did a clinical perusal of her body, presumably looking for injuries.

"Yes, I'm fine," she snapped, then turned to stare down the now empty street. "But that bastard stole my camera." She took off in a half-hearted dash in the direction the thief had been running.

"No." A hand landed on her shoulder, and she came to an abrupt standstill. "You wait here; I'll see if I can find him." His deep voice held such an air of authority that Summer found her feet coming to an automatic halt, and then she watched him jog smoothly away down the street, her mouth opening and closing like a goldfish, unable to come up with a retort. Who did he think he was, ordering her to stay as if she were a trained show dog? She was of half a mind to follow him. But the gap between her and the stranger was widening quickly as his tall form flitted between the intermittent pools of light cast by the street lamps, and she knew that even on her swift feet, she wouldn't be able to catch him now. She'd have to come to terms with the fact that the thief and her camera were long gone.

Retracing her steps, she retreated to the well-lit area in front of her building to stand and wait, on the slight chance the stranger might return with her precious possession.

If he wasn't some kind of accomplice, that was.

The sudden thought jolted her, and she backed up against the glass door, welcoming its solid feel against her spine, head swiveling at every real and imagined noise. That man could've been standing guard on the street, waiting for his thieving friend to appear, and now he'd gone off to join him, both of them laughing at her gullibility. Maybe that's why he hadn't stopped the burglar, and instead stepped in to slow her down.

Blast, she was a pea-brain. Now, as she digested the ramifications of what she'd just done, her hands began to shake. What the hell had she been thinking? She'd chased a felon out into the street. Would've kept chasing him if that big lug hadn't got in her way. It would've been her alone, running down the deserted roadway after an intruder, perhaps with another criminal hard on her tail. What a stupid, stupid thing to do. She'd acted on instinct, white-hot anger driving her on. But now… In the light of her adrenaline withdrawal, she could see how foolish she'd been. Not even her Nikon was worth putting herself in that kind of danger.

Summer startled and almost let out a scream as the tall stranger materialized out of the darkness by her side. Blast, where had he come from? She'd been so caught up in her own self-recriminations, she'd forgotten to keep watch. Either that, or he was good at moving quietly. She shrank away from him, toward the safety of the doorway, her fingers already reaching for the access panel.

"Sorry, I could find no sign of the man who stole your camera." He had a strong accent that she couldn't place, with a stilted way of speaking.

Summer lowered her hand from the keypad, tilting her head to look up into his face, and was arrested by the strange color of his eyes. They were so light blue; they were almost silver. A tad disconcerting. Together with the prominent touches of gray at his temples and forehead in his otherwise dark hair, it made a compelling combination. Her friend Bianca might've called him a silver fox, but then he surely wasn't old enough to fit that category. He looked to be Summer's age, perhaps a few years her senior.

His mouth tilted down as a concerned frown hovered on

his brow. He didn't strike her as a criminal, but that meant nothing; she was often a poor judge of character. He was smartly dressed in dark blue jeans, black trainers, and a simple black T-shirt that stretched over impressive biceps. Now that she took the time to study him, the rest of him was impressive as well. Tall, with lean hips and broad shoulders.

"Are you okay?" he asked again as he leaned in to search her face for signs of shock or hurt.

But she tilted away, and replied curtly, "Of course I am. I'm just pissed that guy got away with my camera. And he trashed my apartment," she added with a sour grimace.

The man's features hardened. "You need to call the police."

"I left my phone upstairs," she responded, not letting on that she didn't really want the law involved. In her experience, they weren't to be trusted and were next to useless when it came to tracking down the perpetrators of a crime.

He pulled a cell from his back pocket. "What is the number you American's use? 911, is that it?"

"Wait, no…" she grunted in surprise but was too late; he was already making the call.

"My name is Mårten, by the way," he said as he handed the phone over and she took it from him reluctantly. "I'm a police officer from Sweden," he added just as a tinny voice asked what her emergency was. So that's why he'd been so keen to chase down the thief, and then report the theft. It would be second nature to a cop; he was just following procedure. She eyed him suspiciously as she spoke into the cell, wondering what he was doing so far from home, and his reasons for standing out the front of her building at that time of night.

After Summer had related the robbery and ransacking of her apartment, and been told a unit would be there soon, she handed him back his phone, strangely tongue-tied. A stab of shame coursed through her when she remembered she'd thought he might be connected to the lowlife who'd robbed her, when he'd genuinely been trying to help. But now that she knew he was in law enforcement, she still couldn't bring herself to regard him with anything more than a flawed distrust.

"Umm, thank you," she said, then stared up at him, unsure what to do next. Annoyingly, her hands continued to shake, and she tucked them into the pockets of her leather jacket, hoping he hadn't seen.

"I think I should wait with you until the police arrive," Mårten said as he replaced his cell in his back pocket.

Damn, maybe she hadn't been as good at hiding how rattled she was as she'd hoped. Summer bit her lip, then shook her head and opened her mouth to speak, but he interrupted before she could decline his offer.

"Break-ins like this can be quite shocking. I know; I deal with the victims of crime all the time. You should have someone with you when you return to your apartment. Trust me."

She hesitated. Oh, she knew exactly how it felt to be the victim of a violent crime. And this was nothing compared to what she'd experienced back when she was seventeen. But she wasn't about to tell him her life story. However, now that she thought about it, the idea of facing her wrecked apartment by herself *was* a little daunting. Perhaps having someone with her, even if it was a stranger—a foreigner and a cop moreover—might be better than the alternative. An officer of the law would be used to dealing with these kinds of situations. And although she didn't trust most cops, he did seem to be sincerely concerned.

"It's the least I can do, seeing as how I stopped you from catching your thief," he said with a lopsided half-grin.

Summer considered him for a few seconds before deciding.

"Thank you, that would be nice. My name is Summer, by the way," she added, before ducking her head and pushing open the doors, leading him upstairs, her need for moral support overcoming her need to keep this handsome stranger at arm's length. She just hoped she was making the right choice.

CHAPTER TWO

Mårten followed the woman up five flights of stairs to the top floor, watching with interest as she retrieved a baseball bat from the third landing. Had she chased the man using that as a weapon? His respect for her went up a few notches. Now, she hovered by the open doorway; her determined footsteps faltered. He'd seen enough cases of people in shock to know what it looked like, and this woman was definitely suffering the effects, even if she was trying to hide it. She'd been as white as a ghost after he'd returned from chasing the felon, and her hands had been shaking badly before she tucked them in her pockets. Reality might be setting in now, but a few moments ago she'd shown just how kick-ass she could be when she'd run after that guy down the stairs and out into the street without a thought to her own safety. Courageous as well as a tad foolish. He wondered what she would've done if he hadn't stepped in her way. How long would she have hunted the thief down the street? And what would've happened if she'd caught him? He shuddered to think. That robber could have been carrying a knife, or even a gun. Perhaps it was destiny that he'd been on the street at that exact moment.

Mårten had been taking an evening stroll, checking out the

neighborhood, and giving his friends, Jacob and Nikki, some time to themselves. Even though they continued to tell him how welcome he was in their house, their love affair was still fresh, and they could barely keep their hands off each other, although they tried to hide it whenever he was in the room. Jacob had given him an appreciative tilt of the head when Mårten had said he needed some fresh air and that he'd be back in a couple of hours; he could just imagine they'd made a beeline for the bedroom as soon as he'd shut the front door.

His visit was almost at an end, and he was due to fly back to Sweden in four days. This was his first trip to the US, and the three of them had had a great time doing the tourist thing, even flying down to Las Vegas for a quick weekend jaunt. Mårten had been surprised at how beautiful and unaffected the state of Washington was.

The real reason for Mårten's visit was never discussed, however; to check out this woman who'd lured Jacob away from his family, friends and career. But he could find no fault in her. As a matter of fact, Mårten was trying not to be jealous of his friend and ex-police partner's good luck. Nikki was an amazing person, and Jacob was lucky to have found her, even if he'd had to move halfway across the globe to be with her. Less than six months ago, Nikki had been the target of two hitmen, who'd been trying to stop her testifying in a court case against Diàoyú, a Chinese fish farming company. Thanks to Jacob's heroics, she'd survived to give her evidence, but they still hadn't tracked down the ultimate villain responsible for ordering the hit on her life, which was both frustrating and annoying. But after all they'd been through together, it wasn't surprising they'd discovered love along the way.

So, it was indeed mere coincidence that Mårten had been walking down this exact street at this exact time. He'd seen the man in the hoodie dashing out of the door right in front of him and had stopped and turned to see what he was up to when the woman had careened into him, both of them ending up in a heap on the pavement.

He disliked being taken by surprise. Being a trained cop, he looked unprofessional at the very least. And it was one reason he'd offered to go upstairs with Summer, to atone for his lack of awareness and reaction to a sudden threat. A reason, but not the only one. She might've been putting on a brave face, but he could recognize vulnerability and fear when he saw it. She was in need of protection right now, and he was just the guy to give it. It didn't matter that she had an alluring, sultry pout to her mouth that intrigued him. Nope. That had nothing to do with why he followed her pert, jean-clad backside up the stairs. Nothing at all.

"I'll go in first, if you like," he offered, seeing her hesitate.

"No, it's fine." She squared her shoulders and lifted her chin, tossing her long ebony ponytail over her shoulder. She was petite, small and slim, the top of her head not quite reaching the middle of his chest, dressed casually-hip in a black leather jacket over blue jeans and white Adidas. Downstairs, she'd stared up at him with dark, haunted eyes. But even in the face of her trauma, he'd noticed how sensuous those eyes were, causing his heart to kick like a mule behind his rib cage. He'd heard her give her name to the police on the phone as Summer Pérez, and he guessed she was of Latino heritage. He liked her determination. Liked that she was prepared to chase a criminal into the street in pursuit of her property. She seemed distressed at the loss of the camera, and it made him wonder why it held such value for her.

Following close behind, he turned into her apartment and was shocked to see the complete state of disarray. She wasn't wrong when she'd said the burglar had trashed the place. Immediately, his instincts were on high alert. It was unusual for a mere thief to cause this much damage. This person was either looking for something or making a statement. Or perhaps both.

Summer kicked half-heartedly at some of the debris scattered on the rug with the toe of her Adidas and stared forlornly at the mess. She bent down to pick up an overturned plant pot, and he shook his head. "No, leave everything just as it is, so the police can see what happened."

"Oh, really?" She recoiled and stood up quickly.

"I know your first impulse is to clean up, but trust me on this matter."

Her cheeks had regained some of their pink quality on the way up the stairs, but now all color again drained from her face, as she took in the utter destruction of her home for the second time.

Mårten laid a comforting hand on her shoulder, the leather jacket butter-soft beneath his palm. She turned to stare up at him.

"Thanks," she said. "I didn't know."

"Of course you didn't," he replied as he raked his gaze across the ruined apartment. It was compact. He noted the floor-to-ceiling corner windows would let in copious amounts of light during the day, and even at night still afforded a lovely view over the rooftops and down the street all the way to the bay and the city lights twinkling in the distance. This large room comprised what would have been a cozy sitting area, decorated with natural fibers, and muted, warm colors. But now, all the cushions were scattered haphazardly around the space, smashed glass trinkets lay on the floor, and upturned plant pots had spread dirt in every direction. In amongst the mess he could see a bicycle on a stand had been tipped over.

A full kitchen filled the section to his left as they walked in the door, with state-of-the-art appliances and stone countertops. He also noted a corridor and assumed it led to a bedroom and a bathroom. "Come on, let me make you a coffee," he offered, steering her behind the kitchen bench, and flicking the switch on the machine. "Where are your mugs?" he asked, opening a cabinet next to his head.

"Up there." She pointed to the second cupboard along, but didn't move to give him a hand. She had a glazed, vacant look that so many victims took on. Shock turning to dismay as she processed everything that'd happened. Mårten knew that a hot, sweet drink often helped in cases like this. A dash of something harder also wouldn't hurt, but after opening a few more cupboards he gave up looking for alcohol. He busied himself making them both a coffee, monitoring her in his peripheral vision.

When he and Jacob had worked together, Jacob had accused Mårten of being the good cop in their partnership. The one who kept a cool head and was always easygoing, while Jacob was the brash, reckless one. Mårten wasn't sure he agreed with his friend's assertion; Mårten could be just as uncompromising and even violent if the situation called for it. But he also understood that compassion and empathy got you equally as far in the long run. It was one reason he'd joined the police force, wanting to help people who were in trouble. Wanting to right the wrongs in this world. His older brother, Erik, had once told him he had an unhealthy compulsion to fix other people's problems, but he preferred to think of it as having a strong moral compass.

He liked to be of service. But really, it was just a nice thing to do—make this poor woman a hot drink and try and take her mind off the terrible catastrophe that was her apartment.

She was still staring blankly out the window a few minutes later when he put a coffee on the bench next to her. "Here you go," he said. Wrapping his palms around his own mug and leaning back against the countertop. A glint of gold caught his eye from a delicate cross on a fine chain sitting in the hollow of her throat beneath the collar of the leather jacket. He'd noticed that she'd touched the necklace just before she'd stepped through her doorway earlier; a habit or an entreaty to God to protect her, he wasn't sure which. She wore no other jewelry that he could see; no rings adorned her fingers. She had her hands clasped in front, but she repeatedly rubbed her right thumb across the palm of her left hand in an unconscious movement that hinted at her agitation, even as her gaze finally focused on him.

"Thank you." For a fleeting second, he was trapped within the depths of her dark eyes as she regarded him seriously. Equally dark lashes framed her eyes, giving them a sensual vibe that was hard to ignore.

Forcing his gaze back to his cup, he took a careful sip, before asking, "Is there someone I can call for you? To come and be with you? Family perhaps?" No one should have to go through this alone. And he knew he must be a very poor second to having kin or perhaps a boyfriend here.

Summer shook her head. "My family all live in San Jose. I moved up here to go to uni, and well..." she gave a delicate shrug that made him wonder if there was more to the story.

"Blast it! I have to get that camera back," she said, placing her mug on the countertop with a bang. "It's my primary camera; I need it to carry out my work."

That piqued his interest. It sounded like she was a photographer of some kind. "Was it expensive? Is that why they stole it?" he asked.

"Yes," she agreed. "It's a top of the range Nikon, worth over $5000." Her shoulders slumped. "I was scheduled to leave on a research trip to Montana tomorrow to help document a population of lynx cats. They're very rare, practically endangered. I'm going to have to tell them I can't make it now." Her eyes became hard and brittle as she stared down at the mess on her floor. "I guess I'll be cleaning this up instead. And sourcing a new camera."

"So you're a wildlife photographer?" he asked, hoping to redirect her anger, but also genuinely interested. "And you earn a living from it?" The only photographers Mårten knew captured weddings or portraits. Not animals in the wild. And they often struggled to make ends meet.

Her focus returned to him, and some of the heat went out of her gaze. "Yes, I generate a good income, actually." Looking around the apartment, he decided she must be right. He was no guru on rent prices in Seattle, but even he could tell this was a nice place. Perhaps someone targeted her for that reason? Had the thief tried to break into other apartments in this block? He made a mental note to ensure the police checked that out when they arrived.

"At least I had my computer in my backpack with me, so they didn't have a chance to take that. My life's work is on that laptop," she mused. "And I'm insured, so I can replace the camera he stole, but..." she tapered off at the sound of footsteps on the stairs. At last, the officers in blue had arrived. Mårten placed his cup on the countertop and turned to greet them. He wished he'd thought to put his police shield in his pocket before he left the house this evening, so that he might prove beyond a doubt his credentials. As it was, the Seattle cops would just have to believe him.

A female dressed in the traditional dark-blue uniform knocked on the open door and stepped through without waiting for an invitation, an older, more rotund male following close on her heels.

"Are you Miss Pérez? The owner of this residence?" the woman asked in an efficient but not unkind tone that Mårten recognized. He adopted a similar approach when he was attending to victims of crime.

"Yes," Summer confirmed.

"My name is Constable Susan Moreland, and this is Senior

Constable Downy." She gestured to the middle-aged man behind her.

"And is this your boyfriend?" Moreland asked when Summer looked at her expectantly, forgetting to introduce him.

"Oh, gosh, no," Summer spluttered. "I only met him half an hour ago. He was on the street when I chased the guy outside. His name is Mårten," she added.

Mårten wasn't offended by Summer's vague description; she was still coping with the traumatic situation. Leaning forward, he offered his hand to the constable. "Mårten Viskten. I'm an inspector with the Swedish police. I'm over here on holiday, and just happened to be standing in the street when everything went down. I pursued the thief, but he eluded me. Then I offered to accompany Ms. Pérez upstairs and waited with her until you arrived."

Mårten stood up to his full height as both officers turned to stare at him, evaluating him in a new light now they knew he was one of them. He seemed to be acceptable to both, because Constable Moreland reached for her small writing pad and pen in her top pocket, and the senior constable inclined his balding head in Mårten's direction by way of acknowledgement, then said, "Sounds like it was a good thing you were there."

Mårten stood out of the way while the constable took down Summer's statement, and Downy perused the room, his sharp, blue gaze missing nothing. The guy might be overweight, but that didn't mean he wasn't skilled at what he did. Mårten had met his kind before in the Swedish force, and they always made up for what they lacked in physical prowess with mental astuteness. Mårten waited until the officers had finished collecting their evidence, and the constable was talking quietly to Summer just outside the front door, making sure she had an appropriate description of the thief, before he approached Downey.

"Have you had many home invasions in this area recently?" he asked.

"No, this is a good suburb normally," Downey conceded.

"So, do you think this might be a targeted break-in?" He kept his voice low, not wanting to spook Summer any more than she already was.

The senior constable met his gaze with his own steady one. "It's a distinct possibility," he answered quietly, lifting an eyebrow. "The amount of damage done would suggest this is more than just a break-in. Also, Ms. Pérez has a lot of expensive items in this apartment. That bicycle over there, for instance, is specialized for triathlons and is made of titanium, worth over $10,000. And she told me some of her other cameras are much more valuable than the one he stole." Mårten let out a low whistle as Downy stopped and drew in a breath. "If I were to hazard a guess, it seems as if they were looking for something in particular," Downy added. Funny, because Mårten had decided the same thing. He pursed his lips in agreement, but said nothing as Summer turned a quizzical look in his direction. "I don't think she should stay here on her own tonight," the senior constable muttered out of the side of his mouth. Mårten liked the way this officer thought. He was careful in his collection of the fine details, but also considerate of the victim's feelings as well as their personal safety.

"I agree." Mårten nodded thoughtfully. "I'll see what alternatives I can come up with." But what was he to do if she rejected all of his suggestions? Summer struck him as not only a kick-ass woman, but a decidedly stubborn one too. He gave a heavy sigh. If she refused to leave, then he might just be spending the night in her apartment. Because one thing was for sure, he wasn't leaving her alone.

CHAPTER THREE

Summer closed the door behind the two police officers with a sigh. She didn't hold out much hope that they'd find the thief. He'd disappeared like a ghost into the ether. She'd never get her camera back now. The young female constable had seemed compassionate, as though she wanted to be of assistance, but Summer knew through harsh experience that was most likely just a front. They weren't going to help her. They'd smile and say the right things, but in the end it would all come to a big fat nothing.

Why had the burglar targeted her apartment, though? And why had he taken only one of her cameras? Was it because she'd caught him in the act and it was all he could get away with? It was strange and surreal, and she could barely wrap her head around it. To top things off, Senior Constable Downy had knocked on all the nearby doors, but no one had heard a thing. At least not until she'd started shouting and chasing him down the stairs, but by then it was too late. Convenient. Also highly unsatisfactory, as well as quite unsettling. How had the guy even got into the building? Someone must've let him in. Either that or he had the code, and both options were equally disturbing.

She turned away from the door to see Mårten's tall frame

lounging against the kitchen countertop, and her heart did a silly little flutter. He was good-looking; she'd give him that much. But it was high time to send him home so she could deal with this mess.

She thought she'd got used to the sight of her trashed apartment, but it still stole the breath from her lungs when she turned around and took it all in again. Dirt from her many potted plants was all over the floor and ground into the rug; a lot of her keepsakes and ornaments, some of them precious heirlooms from her grandparents, lay broken and smashed. The thief had even taken a knife and slashed her couch cushions, so they'd need to be replaced. Where was she going to start?

Steeling herself, she tried to put the shambles from her mind and turned her thoughts to getting rid of Mårten. "Thank you for everything you've done for me tonight." She took a few steps toward him. "But you must have somewhere else to go. I've held you here long enough." She remembered now that he was visiting from Sweden, and she was mortified that he might have someone anxiously waiting for him, a girlfriend or a family back in a hotel somewhere. She clapped a hand to her mouth. "Oh blast, I hope I haven't kept you from anything important."

"No, it's fine. I called my friend Jacob earlier and told him what was going on. I'm staying at his place a few blocks over from here, it's all good."

"Oh…great." She sank against the countertop, overcome with heavy fatigue. Then her stomach rumbled loudly, reminding her she still hadn't eaten, and it was now nearly midnight, but she was too tired to bother. There was no way she could cook anything in her destroyed kitchen anyway.

She noticed Mårten had made no move to leave. "Will you be alright to get back by yourself?" she queried, wondering why he was still lounging in her flat and not high-tailing it out of the door like any normal male whose job was now finished might've done.

"Of course, I'll be fine. But…" he hesitated, and she had the distinct impression he was trying to find a way to couch his next words in the best style possible. "But… I don't think you should stay here tonight. Not on your own, anyway." Mårten's disconcerting silver eyes fixed on her. "Do you have somewhere you can go? A boyfriend? Or a friend's place?"

She was about to argue and tell him she'd be fine by herself, but another glance at the mess surrounding her and that cold fatigue settled more heavily on her shoulders, a lump as big as stone forming in her stomach. This chaos felt so overwhelming.

Summer freely admitted that she was a bit of a neat freak, but some of her friends went so far as to joke occasionally that she had a touch of OCD. That wasn't the case; she just liked everything to be in its correct place. And she liked her life to run on schedule. She appreciated routine, and if she couldn't have routine, then she preferred planning, lots and lots of planning. She usually took weeks to plan a field trip or a photo shoot. Like this one to Montana, she'd been asked two months ago to join the team and had been prepping for the trip ever since. Spontaneity wasn't one of her strong suits. So, this upending of her home made her feel as if she'd lost all control over her life. And she needed to get that authority back. She was like a boat adrift at sea without it. But right now she was stuck, as though she were in limbo, unable to move forward or back. Maybe Mårten was right; she needed to get out of here, at least for tonight, gather her wits and return tomorrow recharged.

She twisted her hands together while she contemplated an answer to Mårten's question. "No boyfriend," she acceded, staring out the window. And wasn't that an understatement; she hadn't had a proper boyfriend since Marco. The few times she'd dated in the twelve years since had all ended after only a few weeks. No man was worth the risk. The risk to her heart or the risk to her well-controlled life.

As Marco's name entered her mind, images of him swam to the surface. Of his eager, youthful face, so full of promise and vitality. But more gruesome memories soon replaced them, of blood and screaming and pain. Summer grimaced, then shrugged off the visions, forcing her mental walls to slam back into place, keeping the echoes of that time locked safely away.

Returning to the present, she remembered Mårten's question about friends. "Bianca is in the Arizona desert on location, filming for her next production. She's my best friend," she added when Mårten raised an eyebrow. If she were going to call anyone in an emergency, it would be Bianca. She was the person who understood her the most. It wasn't like she had no one else to call on, however. And so she mentally went through the list of her other close friends.

Josie and Mark were planning their upcoming wedding in three weeks, and while they'd welcome her into their home without question, Summer was loath to impose. Josie's mother had flown in a few days ago to help with the million and one things that had to be finalized, and Josie was already moaning that her mother was driving her crazy with her pathological need to make everything perfect. While Mark had taken to spending more and more time holed up in his study to avoid the two bickering women. The last thing they needed was a distraught bridesmaid on their doorstep. No, she couldn't call them.

Trent would be here in a flash if she asked. He'd take her into his arms and fuss over her, even give up his bed for her if necessary. But he was out on a first date tonight with the hot man he'd been talking about for weeks, and Summer didn't want to interrupt the possibility of new love, fragile as it could be.

There were others, Serena and Mayte, who she knew she could reach out to, but they'd both be busy with their own lives this late on a Friday night. Either in bed fast asleep, or out on the town having fun, and Summer hated to inconvenience them. Mayte often said Summer was too self-sufficient, and she was always reminding her that friends were there to lean on, to care about her and for her to care about in return. But even though she was in a plight, Summer still hesitated to call them.

She'd already mentioned to Mårten that her family lived in San Jose. God, she missed her sisters every day, all three of them, including when they were all talking at once and she couldn't get a word in edgeways. She missed her mother's calm aura, a balm to her sensitive soul. She even missed her father's gruff manner and grizzled face; he was a man of few words, but he had a heart of gold underneath. But it'd been her choice to move away, and she had no one else to blame but herself. So, although she wanted her family right now, they weren't an option.

No, she'd get through this on her own, like she always did. Independence meant freedom. Not having to rely on anyone else for your emotional or physical needs meant freedom. And freedom was what she craved most of all. Freedom gave you control. And when you controlled your own destiny, then nothing could ever hurt you.

"I'll be fine here on my own," she said quietly, but with determination. This was her choice, and she'd get through it unaided.

A sudden twinge of pain made Summer look down at her hands. Her left palm was chafed where she'd been rubbing her thumb over and over the old scar criss-crossing from one side to the other, leaving it inflamed. She closed her hand into a fist, hoping Mårten hadn't noticed. It was a bad habit, a behavior she couldn't seem to break.

"What about a neighbor?" he asked. Summer shuddered at the idea. Of the four apartments on the fifth floor, the only other tenant she knew by name was Tad, across the landing. And that was only because he'd tried to flirt with her on so many occasions when she first moved in, with such determination, that she'd had to say mean things to get rid of him, and he now ignored her. But he was still a creep, and she was aware that he ogled her butt whenever he climbed the stairs behind her.

Summer lifted her chin and looked Mårten straight in the eye. "I'm not friends with any of my neighbors." Why did that sound a little sad, like she was some kind of lonely hermit who had no one special in her life and lived an isolated existence?

"Okay, so not a single person available you can stay with then?" Mårten asked, as if finding it hard to believe she had nobody she could call on.

Summer shook her head defiantly. "I'll be fine, really," she said again.

"Hmm." Mårten closed his eyes and tapped a finger to his forehead. Lifting his head, he fixed her with his silver gaze.

"No pets we should worry about?"

"No." Summer hated to think what the lunatic might've done to any animal she had in her care. "I travel too much," she added, then immediately regretted her words. He didn't need to know that about her. Didn't have to know anything more about her private life than she'd divulged so far.

"Right then, there's one other alternative. You can come and stay with my friends tonight. Jacob and Nikki would be more than happy to have you."

"Nope, not going to happen. No," she repeated more firmly. "I will not impose on you and your friends. You've already helped enough." The idea of staying with strangers wasn't appealing in the slightest.

Mårten placed his feet squarely on the floor, standing up to his full height, looking suddenly imposing. Until now, Mårten had been compassionate and helpful. But in that second she glimpsed Mårten, the hardened cop. And he wasn't a man who was used to being trifled with. "You either come with me, or I'm staying here with you. It's your choice."

"What? No!" she declared, more loudly this time.

He said nothing, merely stood his ground staring down at her, eyes glinting dangerously, his generous lips thinned into a firm line of determination. He looked like he could stand there all night, as if he were made of stone. Oh blast, what a frustrating man. The urge to stamp her foot was overwhelming, but she knew her childish gesture would get her nowhere while he was in *police mode*. Instead, she tried to reason with him.

"There's no place for you to sleep," she said, indicating the ruined couch. And even if she managed to remake her bed with clean sheets, there was no way she was sharing it with him.

He considered her for a few heartbeats. "I'll have to sleep standing up then," he replied, a wicked smile spreading slowly over his face.

Wow, that smile. He could light up a room from fifty feet with that smile, and it set her stupid heart to thumping in her chest. It showed off a set of straight, white teeth and lit up lots of gorgeous crinkles around his eyes. She was so enamored of his smile she almost forgot to be angry at him.

She stared back at him, hands on hips, her mouth forming an unconscious pout as she considered her options. Perhaps she *should* call Mayte. Even though she hated the idea, it might be better than going with this annoying cop. But then —

"Well. What is it to be? I can stand here all night," he said, interrupting her train of thought. In that moment, she believed him. She wouldn't get any peace until she did what he wanted.

"Fine," she spat. "I'll come with you. Give me a second to pack a few things. She stomped off down the hallway toward the bedroom, hoping to make it clear how unhappy she was with his ultimatum. "As long as you phone and make sure it's okay with your friends," she retorted. There was no way she was turning up unannounced on a stranger's doorstep. It was bad enough admitting she needed someone else's help, but she'd at least do it with a bit of decorum; her mother would never let her live it down.

A few minutes later she returned with her computer backpack slung over her shoulder, into which she had stuffed a change of clothes, her running shoes and shorts, and her toothbrush. At the last second, she'd also grabbed her precious Hasselblad camera and put that in as well. It was the one item she couldn't bear to lose. Mårten was talking on his cell as she came into the kitchen.

"See you soon," he said, and returned his phone to his back pocket. "They're expecting us," he added, tilting his head to the side as if daring her to argue.

"Let's go then." She knew he was doing her a favor, and she knew she was being ungrateful in the face of his help, but she hated to be forced to do anything. The way he'd railroaded her into accepting his aid made her blood boil, anger simmering just below the surface, and she couldn't even raise a smile for him, let alone any agreeable words.

Mårten followed her out the exit in silence, then fiddled with the handle for a few moments. "We'll need to call a locksmith in the morning. But there's not much damage. I think I can get the door to at least stay shut until we return tomorrow."

Summer was too tired to argue. The odds of anyone else

wanting to burgle her apartment would be slim to none tonight. Unless the same thief came back... A prickle of foreboding slid up her spine. Was that why Mårten wouldn't leave her alone? There wasn't much she could do about it, so she shrugged.

Glancing around, she noticed the doors to the other three apartments remained firmly shut, telling her everything she needed to know about her neighbors. Until this moment, she'd liked the fact that there were no nosy tenants on her floor, apart from Tad, who also now snubbed her. She valued her privacy and had very much kept to herself, rebuffing any attempts by the people who lived next door to start up a conversation. But in that instant she realized the extent to which she had isolated herself. Kept herself so aloof that not even Tad cared anymore to find out why the cops had been here late at night. It was her own fault, but still the knowledge burned deep in her gut.

She led the way down the stairs, then waited outside the front door for Mårten to guide her to his friend's house. Mårten must've felt her sudden change of mood, because he kept up a light monologue as they proceeded down the dark and quiet streets, not requiring Summer's input as he told her how much he had enjoyed his stay in Seattle so far, and revealing how Jacob, his ex police partner had moved here to be with the love of his life, Nikki. And how it was actually a fortuitous move, because now Jacob was working for the FBI, not that Mårten was jealous or anything. As they walked, her anger faded, but the fatigue returned with a vengeance. She was tired beyond belief, and just wanted somewhere to lay her head and let sleep take over.

True to his word, they'd only walked two blocks, when Mårten turned a corner and then stopped in front of a gate set into a white picket fence, behind which nestled a cute cottage, painted dove-gray, with white trim, a neat yard, and lots of green grass and soft hedging. The porch light gleamed with a soft warmth, giving the place an air of welcoming them home. Summer had passed this way a few times before and been envious of the gorgeous wooden cottages and well-maintained gardens. The streets here were wide, leafy and cool, and if she could afford to buy a house, this was probably the area she'd choose to stay.

She followed Mårten through the gate, along a pebbled driveway, and up a small set of stairs onto the veranda. Mårten unlocked the front door and held it open, ushering her into a long hallway before closing it behind them. Light spilled from a doorway about halfway down a darkened passage, and she could hear the murmur of quiet voices. Suddenly uncertain, Summer indicated Mårten should go first, then drew in a breath and trailed after him through the door and into a kitchen.

Sitting at a small table were a couple who must be Jacob and Nikki. A tall, dark-haired man with a close-cropped beard rose to greet them.

"You didn't need to wait up for us," Mårten admonished lightly. Even in those few words, Summer could tell Mårten was fond of his friend; there was a strong bond between them.

"We were worried about you," he said, giving Mårten a quick tap on the shoulder in greeting. "Hi, I'm Jacob. Welcome to our home." He held out a hand for her to shake. She was a little taken aback by his chiseled features and broad shoulders. He was as handsome as Mårten, but in a darker, more dangerous way. Were all Swedish men this good-looking?

"Thank you…for letting me stay. Mårten said it was okay, but I…" she stammered, unsure how to thank these strangers for their kindness.

"Hi, Summer, I'm Nikki." The blond woman surprised

Summer by taking her into a warm embrace. "I'm so sorry to hear what happened to you...to your apartment. That must've been terrible. And very scary. You're welcome to stay here as long as you need."

Summer felt undone in Nikki's arms. Perhaps it was the human contact, so simple, yet something Summer rarely received, that hit her in the solar-plexus, but she had the feeling she might burst into tears.

"Thank you," she stammered again, drawing back and ducking her head to hide the unfaithful shimmer of tears glazing her eyes.

"No problem," Nikki replied with a soft laugh that lit up her face. "Come and take a seat. I'll make you a cup of tea. And are you hungry? I'm going to cook us all grilled cheese. We all need a bit of food in our bellies," Nikki chatted as she led Summer to a chair and then turned to put the kettle on.

Summer liked Nikki immediately. Which was surprising, because Summer didn't trust easily, and it often took her months to warm to a person. This gorgeous woman with the honey-colored hair and the heart-shaped face didn't seem as if she had a mean bone in her body. And the way she put Summer at ease, so effortlessly and without resentment, warmed Summer's heart. Nikki reminded Summer of her youngest sister, Riviera, who was enthusiastic and vivacious, but also sincere and compassionate, ready to drop everything and help someone in need.

Mårten took the seat next to Summer, a quick look passing between him and Jacob that she couldn't decipher.

"What did the police have to say? Do you think they have any chance of catching this guy?" Jacob asked, his gaze sliding between herself and Mårten before settling on Mårten. Summer left Mårten to answer, feeling unable to form words anymore. They began discussing the details of how the criminal had jimmied the door and then methodically trashed the place, as if looking for something specific. It wasn't anything Summer hadn't heard before, and so she tuned out, letting the two men take on their cop personas and talk shop.

The classic smell of grilled cheese sandwiches filled the kitchen, and Summer's nose twitched as her stomach growled. She watched Nikki flit between the stovetop and the cupboards, getting down plates and then flipping the sandwiches over in the pan. Now that she looked more closely, and the shock of the immediate introductions was over, Summer thought something about Nikki was familiar.

With a jolt, Summer realized she knew this woman. Of course, this was Nikki Winter; she worked at the Marine Conservation Institute. The institute had commissioned Summer to do a few projects over the past few years. She'd never had an assignment from Nikki, but she'd met her more than once. Perhaps she hadn't recognized her earlier because her long hair was cascading around her face and over her shoulders, whereas she usually wore it up in a high ponytail at work.

Then she remembered the terrible tragedy that had befallen Dr. Tammy Pittman, a friend and colleague of Nikki's. It'd been in all the newspapers about four months ago. Summer had met Tammy once; they'd worked together for three weeks last year on a video highlighting the effect on orcas from polluting toxic stormwater runoff in Puget Sound. Tammy had been an intelligent woman, passionate about protecting the marine environment, and Summer knew her loss was a great one in the fight to save the oceans. She didn't remember all the details of the event that'd ended in her death—it had something to do with stopping unscrupulous practices in the salmon farm industry in Norway—but she did remember that Nikki had been working on the same project with Tammy when she'd died. It must've been devastating to lose a friend like that.

Quietly, Summer stood and walked over to where Nikki was plating the sandwiches. Mårten and Jacob were still deep in discussion, heads bowed as they dissected each minute detail, hoping to find some clue to help capture the thief.

"You worked with Dr. Pittman," Summer said softly. "I didn't put two and two together initially. I'm a freelance photographer, and I did some videography work with her last year. I'm so sorry for your loss."

"Oh." Nikki's mouth formed a soft O as she looked up in surprise. "You knew Tammy?" Summer watched Nikki's face as first pain, then confusion clouded her gaze, before sudden comprehension dawned. "Yes, of course, now I remember you. We met a few times in the previous year. I'm sorry I didn't recognize you. I'm usually good with faces." Nikki's beautiful countenance was lined with self-reproach.

"It's not a problem," Summer replied. Then she laid a gentle hand on Nikki's arm as she leaned in, wanting to keep their conversation private. But she needn't have worried; the two men were still deep in discussion, and not listening. "Tammy was a wonderful lady," Summer added. "I'm sure the marine conservation family is mourning her loss greatly."

The pain returned to Nikki's face. "Yes. She was a great champion of our oceans." Her eyes glazed over as a memory seemed to take hold. "I was working with her in Norway when she was murdered. It was terrible."

Nicki recoiled. Murdered? She hadn't realized that someone had taken Tammy's life. That was a bit intense. The media had never mentioned homicide. But Nikki must know the truth, if she'd been there. "Gosh, that must've been hard for you," she stuttered, unsure what to say to this woman she barely knew, who'd lost a good friend and colleague in dire circumstances.

"Yes. I got dragged into some pretty precarious situations, too." Summer's hand was still on Nikki's arm, and so she felt the slight shudder run through the other woman's body. Wow, something dreadful must've happened while they were on that Norwegian field trip. She wished she knew Nikki a little better, as it was she couldn't very well ask a stranger any of the questions that were clamoring in her mind. It would be impolite.

"I don't like to think about it too much." Nikki continued, her gaze clearing. "But there was a silver lining, if there can ever be a silver lining to anybody's premature death." Nikki lifted her head to stare at Jacob's back, her gaze softening, her lips parting in a smile. "I met a handsome Swedish cop. He saved my life. Protected me."

Summer turned to stare at Jacob as well, putting a few more of the puzzle pieces together. From what Mårten had said, Jacob had followed Nikki here to be with her. Which was kind of romantic, if you were into that sort of thing.

"So I know what it's like to need a place of sanctuary," Nikki said, standing a little straighter, then grabbing a plate in each hand. "And you couldn't be in a safer place right now. With Mårten being a cop, and Jacob working with the FBI, no one would dare break into this house. And if they did, they'd get a nasty surprise," she added with a wink. "Which is why you're welcome to stay here as long as you want."

Summer was left standing like a stunned mullet, staring after Nikki. That was a hell of a lot to digest all at once. Mårten had mentioned that Jacob now worked for the FBI. At the time, she hadn't been sure how to feel about the news. Her natural skepticism made her wary. She'd never dealt with the FBI before. But they were simply another form of law enforcement, and with no proof to show her otherwise, she decided they were just as bad as any uniformed police officer.

At least she now had an insight into why Jacob and Nikki were so eager to have her stay with them, and she looked at

Nikki with added respect. The woman had evidently been through a terrible ordeal and come out the other side with Jacob's help. They were a very interesting couple.

"Come and eat," Nikki called over her shoulder, galvanizing Summer into action. Grabbing the other two plates, she ferried them to the table before sitting next to Mårten, keeping her head down as she tried to process everything she'd just learned, her hand resting on the small gold cross at her throat.

Jacob was already taking a huge bite of his grilled cheese, but Mårten turned to look at her, leaving his sandwich untouched. "You okay?" he murmured, as if perceiving the confusion and disquiet in her eyes.

Gratitude welled in her chest as she stared back at him. Summer knew she'd treated him unfairly and was suddenly remorseful. She was safe and had a place to sleep tonight because of his compassion. He'd cared enough to help her, a complete stranger, after she'd been robbed and traumatized. Not only was this man gorgeous, with his silver eyes and silver hair, but he had a heart the size of a house. He was proof that there were good men out there. A tiny flame ignited within her as she stared into his eyes, melting a fragment of the ice she'd surrounded her soul with for so long.

She smiled at him, this time a genuine smile, and said, "I'm alright, thanks to you." Dropping her hand from her necklace, she lifted half of the grilled sandwich, dripping with gooey, melted cheese to her face and inhaled deeply. "And I'll be even better once I've got this in my stomach."

"Cheers to that," he replied, lifting his own sandwich, his eyes crinkling with smile lines as he took an enormous bite.

Oh, God. There was that smile again. The one that made her heart do stupid pitty pat things. She should rein in her disorderly emotions. There was no place in her life for love.

Not even for a dalliance. Maybe because she was tired and distraught and her defenses were down, she'd let herself feel the attraction, just this once. She was sitting in a cozy kitchen, eating grilled cheese sandwiches next to a good-looking man, and at least for the following few moments she could indulge herself in his company. Tomorrow was soon enough to get back to reality.

CHAPTER FOUR

Mårten entered the kitchen, still rubbing the tiredness from his eyes. He hadn't slept as well as he would've liked, his mind worrying over the details of the break-in at Summer's apartment. He hated to use the term gut instinct—he believed it was his police training and time spent on the job that gave him enough wisdom and knowledge to feel when things weren't right—Jacob was the one who'd always followed his gut. But something was telling him that things just didn't add up with this case, and he wasn't sure why. Yet.

It seemed he was the first one awake; there was no sign of Jacob and Nikki. It'd been a late night. They hadn't gone to bed until after two a.m., and the couple deserved a lie-in on a Saturday morning.

He flicked the coffee machine on and got himself a mug down from the cupboard. It wasn't until he turned around that he noticed a note on the table, tucked underneath the sugar bowl. It was short, but to the point. Summer had gone for a run and would be back in an hour or so. A frisson of unease ran through him. How long ago had she written the note? He stared out the window, hoping in vain to see her come jogging up the driveway, but it remained stubbornly empty. Darn. He wished he'd heard her get up. She must've crept through the house like a dormouse. He hadn't even caught the sound of the front door giving its normal loud squeak as it clicked shut.

Summer was a grown woman, he reminded himself. Allowed to go on an early morning jog if that's what she wanted. But he couldn't budge the tight feeling in his chest, and knew he wouldn't feel at ease until she returned.

Senior Constable Downey had been suspicious of the thief's motives, and Mårten had agreed with him, which was why he hadn't allowed Summer to stay alone in her apartment last night. But surely she was safe now? Even if it had been a targeted attack, the burglar was long gone, and there was no way anyone could know she'd stayed in this house overnight, either. Summer could carry on with her life unhampered. But he continued to stare out the window, waiting and watching, while the coffee machine bubbled to itself. He could call her; they'd exchanged phone numbers, but he knew she wouldn't appreciate that, so he waited.

Twenty minutes later, his coffee sitting cold and forgotten on the countertop beside him, he gusted out a low release of breath as Summer let herself in through the gate. She was back. Unharmed and unaffected. She walked up the driveway, checking her watch as she came, taking long easy strides. She hardly seemed to be breathing heavily at all, and Mårten wondered how far she'd run.

His gaze traveled up her body, from her sneaker'd feet to the crown of her head, verifying she was okay. But his perusal turned to something else entirely when he noticed how well the brief pair of black running shorts and crop top showed off her lithe figure to perfection, and he became transfixed, unable to drag his gaze away. She had an athletic body, thighs tight and toned, stomach flat and ridged with muscles. As he continued to stare, he was hit with a sudden shot of lust so strong he had to grip the edge of the countertop to keep himself from swaying. God, she looked fucking hot in her running gear, like she'd just stepped off the front cover of one of those sports magazines. Long hair pulled in a high ponytail, which flicked jauntily over her shoulder, and golden-brown skin glowing with perspiration. Mårten had observed how gorgeous she was last night; he was a red-blooded male, of course he'd been aware of her allure, even admitted there might've been a moment of heat between them. Dressed in her jeans and leather jacket, she'd had a cool vibe that he'd found appealing. But today, with all that flesh on display, he knew he found her much more than just appealing. She might even be his perfect woman.

He clutched the countertop harder, trying to banish this sudden, crazy attraction. She was a woman who'd needed his help; needed his protection. The last thing she wanted was for him to be ogling her as if he were an infatuated teenager with raging hormones he couldn't control. He was a cop, and she was a victim of crime, and he'd do well to remember it.

Actually, so would she. Summer should be reminded that she might not be out of the woods yet. She should be more careful. More circumspect. At least until they caught the thief. And that included not going out on her own early in the morning. A simmering irritation burned low in his belly, possibly fueled by his ill-advised lust. But anger was an emotion he could do something with.

Mårten had the front door open and was standing in the doorway, eyes narrowed, waiting for her as she mounted the steps.

"Oh, good morning," she called with a bright grin when she noticed him.

He didn't reply, merely frowned a little deeper.

"I always feel better after I've run off all my worries. Don't you?"

"I don't run," he declared. Which wasn't the whole truth.

He did sometimes go for a jog, but in Sweden, where winter snow covered the ground for over half the year, it was often hard, if not impossible, to achieve any useful exercise. He'd much rather do his workouts in the gym and get his aerobic fitness from skiing and ice skating, which were common pastimes in his country. "You should have told me you were going out," he added, his voice coming out in a low growl that was terser than he intended.

"What? Why?" She looked genuinely confused. "I run every other morning. I need to stay fit for my triathlons. Did you want to come with me or something?" Confusion clouded her pretty eyes.

So she was a triathlete. Now, her athletic figure made more sense. As did the training bicycle on the stand in her apartment. Triathletes were among the fittest people on Earth. But he couldn't let himself get sidetracked.

"No. Yes. No…I just wanted to know where you were. To make sure you were safe." He knew he was sounding like an overprotective idiot, but now he'd started he was unable to stop. "I think you need to take some care. At least until they catch the man who broke into your place. You shouldn't go out alone."

He moved closer, closer than was necessary, glowering down at her. He needed her to know that he was telling the truth. The danger wasn't over yet. He couldn't explain why— not in any way that she'd understand—but she had to believe him.

He was so close he could see the individual beads of sweat glistening on her golden skin. For one traitorous second, he wanted to lower his head and lick that salty droplet right off her shoulder. Taste her. Touch her.

"Oh, really? Mr. Big-shot Swedish cop." She rested her hands on her hips, her beautiful mouth twisting with contempt as she glared up at him. "I came here with you last night because you gave me no other choice, and I needed somewhere to sleep. And I thank you for that. But that's where it ends. I don't need your help anymore, and I don't need you to become some sort of self-appointed protector. I'm perfectly capable of looking after myself, and I don't need to be told what to do. I control my own destiny, if you please."

Her gaze was bright with fury now. He returned her stare, not about to back down either, and their gazes caught and held. Something hot and elemental flashed between them. He saw the way her incredible eyes went even darker. Darker with desire? He leaned in closer. Oh yes, that was desire all right; she was definitely attracted to him. He knew when a woman liked what she saw. His gaze flicked to her lips, then returned to her eyes. It shouldn't have come as a shock that he wanted to lean in and kiss her, but the strength of the urge still disconcerted him. It was all he could do to continue to stand his ground and not sweep her up in his arms, hold that lithe body hard up against his and capture her sweet mouth. He'd been sexually attracted to more than a few women in his life, but this feeling was next level. He was holding his position by the merest thread, using all of his steely self-will just to stay where he was.

Did she feel it too?

Summer broke their stare first, taking a step backward and dropping her gaze. At the breaking of their contact, Mårten drew in a sharp breath and clenched his fists at his side. He should be thankful she at least had the capacity to stop *it* before *it* went too far, because he seemed to have lost his mind momentarily. Whatever *it* was.

"Good morning," a sleepy voice called from behind Mårten's shoulder. Mårten swiveled on his heel to see Jacob standing in the hallway, passing a hand through his short hair and yawning, watching them both on the front porch with interest. "Are you off for a run?" Jacob asked, catching sight of Summer's running gear.

"I've just been for one," Summer replied, barging past Mårten, careful not to catch his eye. "Is it okay if I take a quick shower?" she asked Jacob, who nodded and told her where to find the towels in the linen cupboard. Summer stalked down the long hallway toward the spare room, and Mårten closed the front door and followed Jacob into the kitchen.

Had he noticed how Mårten had been standing so close to Summer, enthralled by her? God, he hated how he'd let his dick take over. It was unprofessional and uncool, and he hoped Jacob hadn't caught the vibe.

"Something going on that I need to know about?" Jacob asked, flicking a quick glance at Mårten before busying himself getting a coffee. Shit, he should've known he wouldn't be able to hide anything from his ex-partner. The man was whip-smart and highly observant, even if he liked to downplay it with his breezy attitude. Deep down, Jacob was astute and could read a room as soon as he stepped into it. It was why Jacob had made such a good cop, if perhaps one with a reputation for being a tad reckless. It was also why the director of the FBI had offered Jacob a job; even he could see how much of an asset Jacob would be to his department.

Jacob lifted a mug out of the cupboard and poured himself some coffee, then sat at the table. But Mårten saw the subtle sharpness in Jacob's gaze as he waited for an answer.

"Not really." Mårten dumped his cold coffee down the sink and served himself another mug. But Jacob pinned him to his chair with his stare when Mårten took a seat, and so he shrugged and said, "I was just reiterating to Summer that perhaps she should take a little more care, and not go blithely out jogging on her own when the perp is still out there somewhere."

"I'm sure she took that well," Jacob said, raising one

eyebrow. It seemed Jacob had already pegged Summer as a self-sufficient woman with a stubborn streak.

"No, not really," Mårten acceded with a grimace, which made Jacob laugh quietly. It was unusual for Mårten to dive in and order people around; he was usually a better judge of character than that. He should've taken a different tack with Summer; he knew that now. But he'd been so… irritated, exasperated, annoyed by her behavior. And he could admit, perhaps a little scared. Worried about her well-being.

"You don't really believe this guy is going to come back for her, do you?" Jacob sat up straighter, all pretense of sleep now washed from his face as he changed the topic.

"No. Maybe. I don't know." Mårten shrugged again with a frustrated sigh.

Jacob stared at him unhappily for a few seconds. "I know you don't like to believe in hunches or intuition," he said at last. "But for whatever reason, if you think there's something else going on here, you shouldn't dismiss it."

"Yeah, but I'm not sure what else I can do," Mårten replied. "I'll keep pushing those cops to make certain they're investigating it properly, but I'm an officer of the law from a foreign country. I have very little sway here in America."

"Hmm." Jacob nodded his agreement. "I wish I could help more. Unfortunately, I don't think there's anything that warrants the FBI getting involved," he added with a frown.

"I know." Mårten raised his palms to show he understood. The FBI never took part in anything as simple as a break and enter. They were concerned about national security, not petty theft.

"I could ask Miller; she'd know better than I if there were something we could do," Jacob offered skeptically.

Miller was Jacob's new FBI partner. Mårten had been introduced to Claire Miller when he'd met Jacob while they were both on their lunch break last week. He liked the woman. She was smart and no-nonsense, a great foil for Jacob's impulsiveness. But Mårten still found it ironic that Jacob had been paired with the same agent who'd shot him in the leg to stop him from escaping custody when he'd been trying to protect Nikki back in February. Jacob had insisted that he was the one who had requested the partnership, saying that he respected her as a highly skilled officer, and knowing Jacob, Mårten wasn't all that surprised. He was always doing the thing that people least expected him to do.

"I'm still the rookie over at the office, and you know what that's like," Jacob added, his mouth puckering as if he'd just sucked on a lemon.

Mårten patted him on the back. "Don't worry, mate, I wouldn't want you to jeopardize your new job." His ex-partner had been recruited by the head of the FBI after he'd discovered the extent of Jacob's skills when he'd fought tooth and nail to keep Nikki safe, while exposing a corrupt agent who'd done everything in his power to stop her from testifying at the court case against the Chinese company. Jacob had been in the job less than three months and was yet to complete the compulsory, rigorous, five-month training regime at the FBI Academy in Quantico—the gunshot wound to his thigh making it impractical until he was declared physically fit enough to endure it. Even though Jacob had been at the rank of inspector back in the Swedish force, he'd returned to the bottom of the pile with the FBI and was now a basic-level trainee agent, with very little—if any—clout. Thankfully, because Miller was his partner, people offered him a certain degree of respect that he might not otherwise have received.

"Thanks for that," Jacob grouched. But then his countenance changed. "Speaking of rookies, have you heard from Aurora lately?" He shot Mårten an impish grin.

Mårten grunted in displeasure. "Don't you start. I've got

enough trouble with one willful woman by the name of Summer right now. I don't need any reminders of the other thorn in my side. Aurora needs to respect that I'm on a break and just get on with the job," he grumbled.

"Yeah, you're probably correct. But you did leave her in the middle of an investigation while you jaunted off on holiday. And she just wants to make sure she doesn't muck anything up while you're away. Besides, I don't agree with Nikki's theory. I don't think her constant need to contact you has got anything to do with the fact she's got the hots for you," Jacob said, but was already on the move as he said it, dodging away neatly as Mårten took a swipe at him.

Nikki had said something similar the first time Mårten had complained about how he couldn't seem to get any peace from the rookie cop, and so he'd kept quiet ever since. It wasn't true. Well, he hoped it wasn't true. She was young, beautiful and very intense, wanting to get everything right. That was all. And Mårten wasn't the slightest bit attracted to her. Not that he'd condone a workplace relationship anyway.

"It's your fault that I've been saddled with the little..." Mårten bit back the word that'd been on the tip of his tongue. He'd been going to say menace, but that would've been unfair. Aurora was just very enthusiastic and motivated. He needed to remember that. If only Aurora would stop emailing him and texting him two and three times a day with so many questions and theories, or requests. Like the one she'd sent him yesterday when she'd asked to be allowed to get a warrant to search an alleged rapist's house. Which was a definite no. She was driving him quietly insane.

"If you hadn't left to move halfway around the world, then we'd still be partners and..."

Footsteps in the hallway announced Nikki's entrance, and Jacob stood up to kiss her good morning, offering her his chair as he poured her a coffee. With silent agreement, Mårten knew their conversation was over.

"How did you sleep?" He asked Nikki instead, reverting to mundane topics.

"Gosh, I haven't slept in this late for a long time," she admitted. "But how is Summer going? Is she up yet?"

Mårten and Jacob exchanged a glance, but Mårten finally said, "Yes, she's already been out for a run."

"Wow, she's keen. But she mentioned something about competing in triathlons, so that makes sense." Nikki tilted her head up to give Jacob a doe-eyed look as he handed her a coffee, not realizing how Summer's safety might have been at risk. "Do you know what her plans are? Perhaps we should help clean up her apartment?" That was so typical of Nikki, always ready to jump in and lend a hand.

They already had an agenda for the day, as it was Mårten's last weekend in town. They were going to catch the light rail into the city and show him around. Afterward, they were hoping to end up at the famous Pike Place Market, where they would buy some fresh fish and vegetables and bring them home to cook a feast for dinner. Mårten didn't want to ruin their schedule, but he knew all three of them would give up their day in a flash to help Summer.

As if summoned by their thoughts, Summer stepped into the kitchen, a towel draped around her shoulders as she dried her hair.

"Good morning, everyone." She smiled warmly at Jacob and Nikki but failed to meet Mårten's eyes. "That has to be the most comfortable bed I've ever slept in. It might even be better than my own bed," she added, heading straight for the coffee. "Thank you so much for letting me stay. You're right, I wouldn't have gotten any sleep if I'd been in my apartment." This bright and bubbly Summer was a different woman from the one who had snarled at him on the front porch only half an hour ago. But the show was clearly for Nikki and Jacob, and he guessed he deserved his treatment.

"That's good," Nikki said, indicating Summer should take the chair next to hers. "We were just talking about whether you'd like us to come and help straighten up all the mess. It'd be no bother; we'd love to be of service. I can't stand thinking of you going back to that place and having to cope all alone." She patted Summer's arm, and something unspoken passed between the two women.

"Thank you, I appreciate the offer…"

Mårten knew what was coming next before she even opened her mouth.

"But I'll be fine. I don't want to put you out any more than I already have. You let me sleep in your beautiful house in your comfortable bed, and I'm eternally grateful."

Mårten held back a grunt of irritation. She was so stubborn, not wanting to accept help from anyone, but he kept his eyes focussed on his coffee, telling himself he shouldn't get involved. It was none of his business if this woman found it impossible to accept support when it was offered.

"Besides, I have friends I can call on. Mayte and Trent will be around in a flash when I tell them what's happened," she continued.

Yes, but she hadn't wanted to call those same friends last night in her hour of need, Mårten thought to himself. But again, he said nothing.

"I don't think you should go into the apartment alone." Nikki persisted.

"No, neither do I," Jacob added, narrowing his eyes over the top of Summer's head in Mårten's direction.

"I'll be fine," Summer reiterated, keeping a smile plastered on her face. "I'm sure you already have plans; it's the weekend after all."

Before Nikki could open her mouth to offer another

objection, Mårten jumped in. It seemed this woman only ever reacted to an ultimatum. "Yes, you're right; we have some things we were going to do," he admitted. "But we all want to make certain you're safe. Surely you can respect that?"

Summer glared at him, but didn't dare argue.

"I propose I walk you back to your apartment while these guys get ready to go out. I'll wait with you until your friends arrive, and then we can continue our Saturday as we planned. Is everyone in agreement?"

He raised his eyebrows and turned to look squarely at Summer, hoping she could see the determination in his face. He wanted her to know that if she didn't comply, there would be consequences. If she refused to phone her friends for support, then he'd stay in her house until she did. Much the same as he'd done last night, he was prepared to stand in her way for however long it took, until this feisty little lady accepted his help. He could see her running through the scenarios in her head as she pursed her lips.

"That sounds fair enough," she finally agreed. But he could see the same hot fury from this morning glinting in her eyes, burning just below the surface. She didn't like his implied ultimatum. Not one bit. But she was smart to know when she'd been backed into a corner. "Give me ten minutes and I'll be ready."

Nikki and Jacob, who'd remind silent during this conversation, turned two pairs of curious eyes toward him as Summer exited the kitchen, both of them feeling the strange undercurrent of the things that remained unsaid between himself and Summer. But right now he didn't need anyone trying to dissect the reasons Summer seemed to push all of his buttons. So he rose from the table and went to his room to get changed.

CHAPTER FIVE

Summer strode along beside Mårten, keeping her head down and not saying anything. It was a beautiful morning, but in her dark mood she hardly noticed the bright sunshine and birds singing in the trees above. She hated being manipulated; being controlled. And this was the second time this man had ordered her around in less than twenty-four hours. She wasn't sure why Mårten pushed her buttons; all she knew was that he did.

They stopped in front of the main door of her building so she could punch in the access code. In the silence, she heard Mårten's stomach rumble, reminding her she hadn't eaten breakfast because she'd been so keen to get this over and done with. And by the sounds of it, he hadn't had anything either. She shouldn't feel bad, but she did. She almost turned and told him there was a little cafe down the street and did he want to grab a pastry? But then she remembered he was forcing her to phone at least one of her friends, and she hardened her heart and kept the words locked behind her lips. He wouldn't be in the apartment very long; she'd make sure of that, so he could wait until he got home.

Mårten held the door open for her, and as she passed by, she caught the aroma of his cologne. Something light, like sandalwood, it reminded her of a fir tree in the middle of the forest in summer. Clean and natural. His small chivalrous action took her by surprise, reminding her that Mårten was a nice guy at heart. Few other men she knew would've tried to chase down a fleeing felon, stayed with her until the police came, and then offered her—a complete stranger—a safe place to sleep. He was only trying to help, and she needed to remember that, even if he was going about it in a manner that rubbed her up the wrong way.

She glanced back at him as they climbed the stairs, and he fixed her with his pale-blue gaze, face serious, and her heart stumbled for a few beats. Why did he have to be so damn good-looking? It just made her more confused. She didn't want to be attracted to him, but she was. Not that he ever needed to know that. She had no room in her life for love. And even if she did, Mårten was a cop. And cops weren't to be trusted. So she had plenty of reasons to wish to squash this unruly attraction way down deep and forget it ever happened.

She opened her front door and let them into the apartment. Nothing had changed. It still looked like a nightmare, even in the fresh light of day. Where the hell was she going to start?

She should be on a flight to Montana right now. Getting ready to track down the elusive lynx. But instead she was stuck here, her life altered forever, in subtle ways she might never fully understand. She'd got in touch with Claire, the US Forest Ranger who'd organized the project, early this morning while she'd been out on her run, to tell her she couldn't make it, and apologize profusely. Summer had met the other two wildlife photographers also engaged on this assignment once or twice before, and was sure they could get the pictures Claire needed. But she hated letting anyone down. And she was also sad she wouldn't be there to capture the moment as well. Summer told Claire that a personal issue had come up unexpectedly, not wanting to go into the details of the break-in, but the ranger had been more than understanding, which only made Summer feel worse.

She refocused on the room, sensing Mårten's presence close behind her as he waited for her to make the first move. She might as well begin by calling a friend. At least that would get Mårten off her back. But who should she call? Bianca was still in the desert and wouldn't be back for a week. Summer settled on Mayte. She dropped her bag on the kitchen island and pulled out her cell, waving it in Mårten's direction. "I'll just call in backup, then you can be on your way."

"Put her on a speaker if you don't mind," Mårten said blandly.

Was this guy for real? Did he not even trust her to make a simple phone call? But when she looked up into his face, she could tell he wasn't joking. *Blast him to hell!* She hit the speaker button with exaggerated force.

Mayte's sleepy voice echoed out of the phone. She was probably languishing in bed after a late night, but Summer plowed on regardless. Her friend's drowsy tone soon turned anxious and then solicitous as Summer told her what'd happened and asked for help. Of course she would be there as soon as possible she said, and did Summer want her to call Trent as well? And perhaps even Serena. Summer decided in for a penny, in for a pound, and if she was going to admit defeat and ask for help, she may as well go big and get most of her friends involved. Mayte made more promises to see her shortly and hung up.

"Happy now?" Summer lifted her chin in Mårten's direction.

"Yes," he said simply. Then he took a deliberate step closer. "But I still don't get why that was so hard for you. That's what friends are for, isn't it? To help in times of need?"

Summer raised one shoulder in reply. For most people that was probably true, but for her...it was a knotty mess of emotions she'd rather not delve into. And his proximity was sending her nerve endings tingling again, exactly as they had this morning on the front porch, when something primitive and sizzling had sparked between them. If he hadn't been such a jerk about her going for a run, she might've even leaned in and... And what? Kissed him? No, she wouldn't have done that. Not in a million years. And yet? Something in her softened as she stared up into his face.

"It's complicated," she answered finally. "I'm used to dealing with things on my own. I don't like to depend on others too much. People have a way of abandoning you right when you need them the most, and then you get left with a giant hole in your life. So it's just easier to be independent." She wasn't sure why she was telling him all this. Perhaps it was her way of atoning for her bad behavior toward him earlier. But she'd already told him more than enough, and so she turned and pretended to busy herself at the kitchen countertop. "Anyway, thank you again for your incredible help." She pivoted and flashed him a genuine smile. "But as you heard, my friends will be here soon, and you're free to go. I hope you have a wonderful day with Nikki and Jacob. Can you please tell them once more how much I appreciated their kindness."

Mårten remained standing in the middle of the room, as if rooted to the spot. Normally, he had a very good poker face. She guessed it was a requirement when you were a police officer not to let your emotions show. But right then the uncertainty in his features was almost palpable. He opened his mouth as if to say something, but then shut it again as a strange vulnerability shone in his eyes.

He said nothing for many long moments, merely stared at her, and she began to regret telling him even that much about her life. "It was great to meet you, Summer," he said at last, his lips twisting upward in an odd version of a smile. "I'm truly sorry someone did this to you, and I hope you get it all sorted soon. Remember, if you ever need anything, I'm only a phone call away." They locked gazes for an instant, but when it became clear she was going to say no more, he turned and picked his way through the debris that was once her home, disappearing through the doorway.

"Goodbye," she called after him. Then, as if her feet had a mind of their own, she raced across the room so that she could watch him descend the first set of stairs. It hit her that this would be the last time she saw him. And part of her wanted to etch him into her memory once more.

As she watched him walk away, a strange feeling of loneliness crept over her. She hadn't felt this alone in years. It was a bad sign. Because it meant she was beginning to need him. Which was unusual. How could she need someone after only knowing them for twenty-four hours? It was preposterous. And best for both of them if she never saw him again.

Hoping to rid her mind of all these traitorous thoughts, she busied herself with the dustpan and broom, sweeping up the spilled dirt from her pot plants. Before she knew it, Mayte appeared in her doorway, her long dark hair tied back in a messy bun, and her shirt buttoned wrong as if she got dressed in a hurry. Mayte lived in the nearby neighborhood of Fremont, so she hadn't had far to come, but even so, she'd made it here in record time.

"*Oh, Dios mío.*" Mayte clapped a hand over her mouth as she took in the mess. "*Ese bastardo. Esto es terrible.*" She often reverted to Spanish to express herself when her emotions became too much. Mayte felt things deeply, and that, along with her Cuban heritage, gave her a passionate and excitable personality. Her friend rushed through the debris, nearly tripping over a small pile of books in her haste to get to Summer. She gathered her into her arms and hugged her hard. "When you said on the phone that you had a break-in, I never imagined anything as bad as this," she said, tears forming in her dark-brown eyes as she surveyed the apartment. "This is terrible… It is beyond shocking. Why would anyone do this?"

"I don't know." The same heaviness that'd settled over Summer last night returned with a vengeance. She wished she knew why she'd been targeted, but this was just as confusing to her as it was to everyone else. Mayte stepped away, not letting her friend out of her embrace, but so that she could search Summer's face with her sympathetic gaze. "*Tu pobre pobrecita.* You poor, poor thing," Mayte crooned, rubbing comforting circles on Summer's back. "This is an abomination."

Perhaps it was the feeling of being held in her friend's arms, or maybe it was because of Mayte's obvious distress, but now Summer felt her own tears forming.

Mayte had seen her fair share of violent acts. She had fled Cuba as a refugee with her mother and older sister when she was only eleven, and they had many harrowing tales to tell of their life in Cuba and their eventual escape to America. So, for her friend to be this shocked by the shambles that was Summer's apartment showed how bad it must be. Summer had met Mayte at university when they both completed the same photography course, and they'd become firm friends ever since. But she rarely hugged her friends. And while Mayte was a very touchy-feely sort of person, she usually respected Summer's need for personal space. Today was different. Today, she must realize Summer's innate need for human contact.

"Come, sit down," her friend directed Summer, tugging one of the kitchen stools upright and placing it next to the island bench. "It's okay," Mayte murmured. "It's okay for you to cry." And even though Summer tried to hold back the tears, that was exactly what happened. She hadn't cried in years, and it was shocking to her that she could be this vulnerable. At least she hadn't cried in front of Mårten. Her tears turned into sobs as Mayte handed her a tissue. Her sobs became louder, until she was sucking in great heaving breaths, the weeping taking on a life of its own.

Somewhere in the middle of her crying jag, Trent arrived, putting his arms around both her and Mayte's shoulders and weeping right along with them. The three of them huddled together next to the island bench, consoling each other for Summer knew not how long. But in the end, she was the first one to pull back from the brink, blowing her nose like a snotty toddler.

"Oh, honey," Trent said, dabbing at his own eyes carefully with a tissue that Mayte passed to him. "When did this happen? Please tell me you didn't spend all night alone in this tragedy. It would be too much for me to bear if I knew I was out having fun while you suffered through this alone." His expressive mouth turned down at the corners, and he looked like he was about to burst into tears all over again.

"No, no," she replied, wanting to allay his fears, not needing another bout of weeping. "I wasn't alone. I was with Mårten." The words were out before she could stop them.

Oh, blast! But it was already too late. Trent's teary gaze sharpened, his bright blue eyes now filled with interest.

"Mårten, hmm? Pray tell, who is Mårten?"

"He's a cop. He helped me when I first discovered someone had broken into my apartment. He chased the guy down the street," she answered quickly, wiping at her own tears, then throwing the tissue in the bin.

"Hmm," Trent hummed theatrically again. "Ooh, I like the sound of that. And what does this Mårten look like? If he's a lawman who isn't afraid to chase criminals, then he sounds pretty hunky to me." Trent moved away from the bench top so he could tilt his head, then caught Mayte's eye and gave an exaggerated wink. "And you say you stayed the night with him?"

"No. Well, yes, but it's not how it sounds. Summer rose from the bench seat, pretending to straighten her hair back into a neat ponytail, hoping to hide the flush of red that she knew was climbing her neck.

"Well, honey, don't keep us in suspense. Tell us how it really was, then," Trent crowed. Even Mayte was staring at her with undisguised intrigue, all tears for her trashed apartment now forgotten. How had this turned so quickly from her friends comforting her to an interrogation of the ninth degree?

"He lives in Sweden," Summer snapped. "So you can both stop thinking what you're thinking, because even if he is extremely good-looking, he's going home in three days." She gave a triumphant little huff, as if that solved everything.

Trent lifted his gaze to Mayte and, ignoring Summer, said, "Did you hear that? He's extremely good-looking." Trent was purring with satisfaction.

"Oh, yes, yes, I did," Mayte replied with an expectant look on her pretty face.

"We need to meet this mysterious Mårten." Trent turned to Summer and raised both his manicured eyebrows in a question.

"Oh, you two are incorrigible. Are you going to lend a hand to clean this up? Or are you going to hijack my love life?" Summer was tired of this conversation.

"Well, admit it, you don't have any love life to speak of, so there is nothing to hijack." Trent pouted his luscious lips. "And you know we're only trying to help. Because we care about you, Summer. We want you to be happy."

"I know. Thank you." Summer demurred, consciously easing her hands open from where she'd been rubbing at her scarred palm again. She was overreacting. This wasn't the first time her friends had played matchmaker. Try as she might, she couldn't seem to get them to understand why she was better off alone. Bianca was the sole person in Seattle who knew the whole truth about Marco, because Summer only had the strength to tell the full story once. And today certainly wasn't the day to discuss how Marco had left an enormous hole in her life, and how handsome strangers were something to be avoided at all costs. So, she changed the subject. "But we have more important things to do, don't you think?" She waved her hand around the room to indicate the mess.

"Yes, sure, honey. We can talk about this later," Trent said, not at all contrite, his smug look telling her he would not leave this alone. But for now, he seemed content to change the subject. "Look, I brought coveralls." He dug into his large shoulder bag and pulled out a pair of blue denim dungarees that looked like they'd never been worn. Trust Trent to always look stylish no matter what he was doing. "Let's do this thing," he said with a flick of his wrist as he cocked his head in Mayte's direction.

Summer smiled at her friends, watching as Trent pointed out Mayte's mis-buttoned shirt, helping her to straighten it up. It was nice to have them here. Nice not to have to do this all on her own. And much as she hated to confess, she had Mårten to thank for pushing her to call them.

"Right, ladies, why don't we start with your poor ruined couch. Once we get rid of all the stuffing, we might be able to see what else is going on underneath there." Trent took command as he pulled his coveralls over his clothes. And so they got to it.

Serena arrived soon afterward, but this time Summer

didn't burst into tears, instead handing her another of Trent's seemingly endless pairs of coveralls, and they got to work, talking as they cleaned. Trent told them about his first date with the scrumptious Zane, and how they'd shared a sizzling kiss goodnight on the front doorstep of Trent's apartment block. He was taking it slow with Zane, which was why he hadn't invited him upstairs, he explained. He was determined not to sleep with his new beau—even though the chemistry between them was insane—until they'd been on at least four dates. The girls all exchanged silent looks. Trent had a reputation for falling hard and fast, then regretting it when it turned out not to be true love. They knew he wouldn't be able to hold back much past the second date.

Mayte told them about her evening she'd spent with a group of Cuban refugees. They'd invited her into their home, preparing a meal for her and allowing her to take photos of their daily lives. Of their daily struggles just to make ends meet. It was a sobering conversation, but an important one. Summer respected Mayte so much for what she was trying to do.

Serena told them about her date with the man she'd been using as the male model in her latest photo shoot. She was just as shocked as they were; she had a bit of a rule about not dating anyone she worked with, but this guy had been so charismatic and charming that she couldn't resist. Serena had also been a model in her teenage years, but now she made a good living from the other side of the camera.

Summer plied everyone with hot coffee and some sweet biscuits she foraged from the pantry—which was decidedly empty; she needed to do some shopping. The locksmith came around mid-morning and replaced her broken lock on her front door, which made her feel much more secure. The cleanup took less time than she imagined. By lunchtime, they had most of the mess tidied up. Books and unbroken trinkets back on the shelves, plants repotted. Two of the couch cushions were still intact, but the rest had to be thrown out, and her couch sat in the corner looking lopsided and sad. Summer wondered if she could get replacements or whether she should just buy a whole new lounge. But the decision was too big to be made today. She straightened her bedroom, remade her bed with fresh sheets, and placed the clothes back in the wardrobe. Anything that was broken was loaded into a large plastic bag, which Trent carried downstairs to the dumpsters around the back. The only thing left to clean was her darkroom, but Summer wanted to tackle that alone. It'd take time and patience to get everything back to rights, check to see if any of the equipment was damaged, and only she knew where all the items lived.

Summer's stomach rumbled loudly; the coffee and biscuits had not done enough to replace the breakfast she'd missed. Mayte flopped down on the two remaining cushions on the couch, while Trent groaned dramatically as he lowered himself into the single armchair, which thankfully was still intact. A surge of gratitude filled Summer, making her chest ache as she went to stand next to Serena, who'd taken a seat at the island bench.

"Thank you," she said, leaning her hip against the countertop. "I couldn't have done this without you."

"No problem, sweetie." Trent waved a weary hand in the air.

"I owe you all lunch," Summer said. "Come on, I'll take you down to Olé on the Ave." It was a rustic-chic little cafe that specialized in tapas and Spanish sweet pastries, great coffee and even better cocktails, and was one of Mayte's favorites.

"Ohhh, that sounds wonderful." Trent was on his feet in a second, dragging off his coveralls.

Mayte and Serena weren't far behind.

"Food sounds good." Mayte patted her stomach. "But you don't have to treat us," she argued, fixing Summer with a steely stare. "We did this to help you, no strings attached."

"I know you did. But I'm starving, and we deserve a reward after all that hard work. And you need to let me show my gratitude. Please," she added in a beseeching tone to her voice.

"Okay," Mayte relented, even though Serena continued to scowl at Summer, but didn't offer a vocal argument.

"Oh, goodie." Trent clapped his hands with glee.

Summer herded them out onto the landing, locking the door carefully behind her, with her new keys. She still had no idea how the thief had gotten into the complex, but she decided that upon her return from lunch, she was going to knock on a few doors to see if anyone had seen or heard anything out of the ordinary. Someone had let him in; that much was sure. Because the alternative—that the burglar lived in the building—was too terrifying to contemplate.

* * *

Summer punched in the code to her building's front door. She'd already bid farewell to her friends on the street, thanking them again for their help. Her stomach was bulging and uncomfortable; they'd eaten way too much food, and the three cocktails Summer had consumed were making her sleepy. They'd spent longer than they intended in the café, and it was now almost dinnertime. But Summer felt far better. The laughter and companionship of eating and drinking with her buddies had lifted most of the terrible weight pressing down on her shoulders.

She climbed the stairs wearily, looking forward to an early night. Hopefully, she could sleep, and thoughts of someone breaking in wouldn't haunt her.

An incoming text beeped on her cell, and she pulled it out of her pocket to see who it was from. Her heart skipped a beat as she momentarily imagined it might be from Mårten. Maybe he was messaging to check how she was going? But it was from an unknown number, and Summer bent her head over her phone trying to decipher the weird message, taking the stairs up to her landing on autopilot.

It was from Peter Macdonald from the United States Fish and Wildlife Service (USFWS) in Yellowstone National Park, asking her to call him at her earliest convenience on a matter of urgency. Summer stood in front of her apartment door staring at her phone, wondering if it was some kind of scam. She'd never heard of this guy before. And he—

Something wasn't right. A prickle of awareness slithered down her spine. This landing was usually well lit, but the section over near the lift was in semi-darkness. Funny, that light had been working when they'd left to go to the cafe earlier, hadn't it?

There was a flicker of movement in the far corner. As Summer stared intently, a figure morphed out of the gloom. A man wearing a hoodie. A tall man. She glimpsed a large, hooked nose protruding from the shadow of his hood.

Oh, fuck!

It was the same guy from last night. He took two steps toward her, an aura of menace emanating from him.

"Hey, bitch." He smiled, showing crooked teeth. "Do you remember me? There ain't no cops around to help you tonight, and you ain't got no baseball bat either. This time I'm going to get what I came for." He took three more steps, and Summer turned and ran. She wasn't stupid enough to want to fight him. This guy was mean and on a mission; to hurt her.

She had a slight head start on him as she sprinted down the stairs, but she could hear him thundering after her. His legs were longer, so he could take the stairs at a faster pace. He was gaining on her. As she rounded the landing on the fourth floor, she thought about calling out for help, knocking on someone's door, but decided he would catch her if she stopped running for even a second. Her breath burned in her throat, and she nearly dropped her phone as she swung herself around the corner using the railing to keep herself upright.

Halfway down the stairwell to the third floor, she heard a cry and then a thud, followed by a string of loud curses. She kept going, but could no longer hear the pounding feet close behind. He must've fallen. She risked a glance upward and saw him struggle to stand on the flight above. He began to hobble down the steps, but he'd hurt himself, because he'd stopped gaining on her.

She had a chance to get away. Her relief was palpable as she dared to take her first full breath since she'd seen him standing there. Not allowing herself to slow down, she continued to bound down the staircase like a rabbit fleeing a fox, until she hit the front door and burst out into the street.

But she didn't stop there. She turned left and sprinted down the road toward the only place she knew she'd be safe. In her panicked state, her mind was telling her to run, run straight to Jacob and Nikki's house. Straight to Mårten. It was stupid and pathetic, but the only thing her adrenaline-fueled body understood right now was that he would protect her. Oh, please, God, let him be home.

CHAPTER SIX

"Cheers." Jacob lifted his glass and saluted Mårten. "It's been great having you here, bro," he added. Mårten clinked his wine against Nikki and Jacob's and took a sip.

"It's been great to be here," Mårten replied sincerely. "I'm starting to understand a little of the attraction of his place," he conceded. America was a country of immense natural beauty, and the people weren't half as bad as he'd first imagined. He was almost sorry he would go home in a few days. "And you're right; this fish is amazing." He set his glass down and lifted his fork, ready to take another bite of the freshly caught lingcod they'd bought at the market this afternoon. A fish native to these northern waters, Nikki had created a crispy skin lingcod dish fried in butter and parsley, and complemented by some boiled baby potatoes and a fresh salad. It was a simple but delicious meal. The flaky flesh had melted in his mouth, and he was eager to taste more. It almost matched the quality of the wild salmon he often snagged in his northern Swedish rivers.

Which reminded him. "Nikki still needs to try our Swedish delicacy, surströmming." Mårten lifted an eyebrow in her direction. "You have not tasted fish until you have tasted that. It's delicious, isn't it, Jacob?"

Both men smirked at each other.

"I'm sorry, but I'm not eating that disgusting fermented stuff, not for anyone. You couldn't pay me enough," Nikki declared, wrinkling her pretty nose. "Jacob let me smell it when I was over visiting his family, and it almost made me throw up in my mouth." Jacob roared with laughter at the look of revulsion on her face. Most Swedish natives learned to love the fish, but it was definitely an acquired taste.

Mårten took a further mouthful and savored the flavor, letting the butter and herb sauce wash over his tongue. He was just lifting another forkful of potatoes to his mouth when a loud knock on the front door startled them all, and three pairs of eyes turned to stare out to the hallway. Who could it be at this time of the evening? He didn't think they were expecting anyone.

"I'll go, Mårten offered; he was seated closest to the door.

He gave his fish one rueful glance before he got up from the table, but was almost shocked into speechlessness when he opened the door. "Summer? What's going on?" She was the last person he expected to see, but he was immediately on edge. Summer was breathing hard, her dark hair fluttering loose around her shoulders. But it was the look of barely controlled fear in her eyes that had him on high alert. He tugged her inside without waiting for an answer, shutting and locking the door behind her.

After he'd bid Summer farewell this morning, a strange melancholy had settled over him as he'd walked the two blocks back to Nikki's house. He knew it was the last time he'd ever see her, but he wasn't sure why that bothered him so much. Mårten had feigned interest in their tour around the city not wanting to offend his friends, but a part his mind had refused to leave Summer's apartment, and he'd found himself wondering how her clean up was going, and hoping her companions would stay, so she wouldn't have to be on her own. Even throughout cooking dinner and his banter with Jacob over who was the better chef, it felt like a piece of him was being dragged down, and he had to remind himself to put a smile on his face. He was on holiday, enjoying a day with his friends, so he should relish every second. But now, here she was, standing in front of him. And he couldn't control the way his chest expanded, as if something had loosened at the sight of her.

In the hallway, she bent over, hands on knees, as she fought to regain her breath. Fixing his gaze on the top of her head, he waited until she recovered enough to speak, a thrum of agitation setting his blood to thumping through his veins. "He came back," Summer puffed finally. "The guy from last night—he was waiting for me on the landing when I got home." Mårten didn't bother to ask if she was sure it was the same person. If she said it was him, he believed her.

Jacob strode into the hallway, his face full of concern, Nikki close behind him.

Mårten already had his cell out of his pocket. "Did you call the police?" he asked Summer.

"No, I ran straight here."

"I'll do it," Jacob said. "You make sure she's okay." Jacob returned to the kitchen, his phone held to his ear, Nikki on his heels.

Mårten grabbed Summer's shoulders, holding her face close to his so he could scrutinize her for the truth. "Are you hurt?"

"No." She shook her head, and another tight knot released in his chest.

"Did he follow you? Does he know you're here?"

"I don't know. I don't think so." Summer shook her head again, her breath still coming in ragged pants, eyes wide as she stared up at him. "He fell and hurt himself as he was chasing me down the stairs. That was the only reason I got away. I doubt he could've run very far."

"Jesus Christ," Mårten swore loudly. He should've trusted his feeling that told him the guy would be back. Instead, he'd just left her there to fend for herself. Alone. He ought to have demanded she stay another night at Nikki's house. He couldn't help himself; he pulled her into a tight embrace. "Thank God you're okay. If he'd hurt you…" he trailed off, leaving the words unsaid, resting his chin on the top of her head for two glorious seconds before he released her again.

"I'm fine," she replied suddenly subdued. "This is not your fault, you know," she added, as a strange mix of confusion, stubbornness, and something else—was it desire—flashed through her eyes. But she was wrong on that count; this was his fault. He was a cop; he should've known better.

"Wait." Mårten's mind swirled with scenarios as he stared at her. "So this man could still be in the area?" If he were, then Mårten was going to find him. Without waiting for a reply, he hunkered down to put on his shoes; it was Swedish tradition to always remove your footwear whenever you entered a house. "I'm not waiting for the cops. I'm going to see if I can locate him."

"No!" Summer shouted, pulling him back by his sweater. The barely controlled fear he'd seen in her eyes earlier flared again, becoming full-blown terror. "You don't understand. He's dangerous. He wasn't scared of me this time. He threatened me. I think he was planning to hurt me."

All the more reason to get him, Mårten thought.

"It might be our only chance," he declared, before gently levering her hands from his sweater and then sprinting out the front door just as Jacob returned to the hallway. He heard Jacob yell something unintelligible after him, but he was already barreling down the driveway.

Mårten was a fast runner when he put his mind to it. And he wanted to catch this guy. Otherwise, Summer might never be safe. How could he go back to Sweden not knowing when, or if, this guy would strike again? But when he made it to the front door of Summer's building in less than five minutes, the street was deserted. Dusk was now settling over the city, dulling the sharp edges of the buildings and turning the sky a soft dove-gray. Mårten swore softly. Only a rookie would've believed the crook would still be in the vicinity. Nevertheless, he set out to make a thorough search of the area.

Jacob caught up to him five minutes later, as he was jogging back toward Summer's apartment, but he needn't have bothered. The felon was nowhere to be found; Mårten had checked all the alleyways and side streets. Perhaps the criminal had a car, and he'd escaped that way. Or perhaps he lived in this neighborhood and had just disappeared off the street through this front door to become invisible. Either way, he was long gone.

A police siren sounded, heralding their imminent arrival. Mårten made a mental note to ask them to check if there were any local CCTV cameras on the street. If the bastard lived nearby, he was determined to find him.

Jacob called Nikki and told her it was okay to bring Summer around. Then the four of them spent the next half an hour talking the police through what'd happened. It was a different unit from the two cops who'd attended last night, which was a shame, as they had to go through the entire story again. They wanted to see Summer's apartment, and they wanted a second statement from her. After the officers left, Mårten didn't even need to say the words; with one look from Nikki, Summer silently went and packed a bag. Mårten was grateful there would be no arguing this time. They all understood this wasn't over. Then they escorted Summer the two blocks back to their house. Nikki and Summer leading the way, with the men forming a vanguard behind them.

"It's unlike you to be so... reckless," Jacob said quietly as they walked, both of them keeping their gazes trained on the surrounding street, watching for trouble. Mårten swung his gaze to the two women striding out ahead, but they were deep in conversation and wouldn't have heard Jacob. "That's usually my job," Jacob added with a smile. "This girl has you a little wound up, perhaps?"

Mårten grimaced, but didn't bother replying. He couldn't even explain to himself why he was acting so carelessly. He knew he was well out of his jurisdiction, had no authority here, and logic told him he needed to leave this to the local police. But they weren't doing an acceptable enough job in Mårten's eyes. And every cell in his body screamed that Summer needed his protection. So that was what he was going to give her. For tonight at least.

He softened as he continued to stare at his friend. Jacob had always been good at stating the obvious. His blunt manner had once complemented Mårten's steadier style of policing. But he'd invariably been able to count on Jacob to have his back, no matter what. It was why he missed him so much now that they were no longer partners. "Thank you," he said, nudging his friend in the shoulder. "For helping her." Jacob might not be as invested in this case as Mårten seemed to be, but even he understood this woman needed their help. Once again, he had Mårten's back.

They stalked the rest of the way to the house in silence, both men turning to check the street was empty before they followed the women through the front door.

"I'm sorry I ruined your lovely dinner," Summer said, as they all filed into the kitchen, looking more than a little contrite.

"Don't worry, I'll reheat it. It'll be fine," Nikki said, touching Summer on the arm, before bustling around the room, pulling their covered plates out of the fridge and popping them into the microwave one by one. "Would you like some?" she asked.

"No, thank you." Summer shook her head, making her dark hair swing in waves across her shoulders. "I had a late lunch with Trent, Mayte and Serena, and we ate until we nearly exploded." She gave a weak smile, the first since she'd arrived on their doorstep. Mårten was gratified to hear her friends had turned up for her. If only they hadn't left her alone afterward. But they weren't to know. He was the one who should've insisted on looking after her.

"Sit down. I think we could all use a drink," Jacob said, retrieving the bottle of white wine from the fridge and pouring everyone a glass. Mårten pulled out a chair for Summer, then took the one next to her. The police had already asked her this question, but Mårten's cop brain lingered on it.

"Are you sure this guy didn't give you any hints about why he'd come back? Even the slightest detail might offer us a clue. He kept his voice low, not wanting to upset her.

"No, I've told you before." Her tone revealed only slight exasperation. "He was wearing the same clothing as last night. There was nothing distinctive about him. No tattoos, no rings on his fingers. He said nothing about what he wanted from me. His last words were, *This time I'm going to get what I came for.*' But I still have no idea what he wanted." Summer's hand shook, and she put her glass on the table. "If only I knew, Mårten. If only I could give you something to work with." Her face was a picture of misery, and he almost wished he hadn't asked her. But that wasn't how he got things done. If they wanted to catch this guy, he needed every single detail, no matter how minor.

"Okay, let's try this from a different angle," he said, leaning back in his chair, taking his glass with him, trying to make this conversation as informal as possible. "You've already told me you don't have any enemies. But I just want to check. There's no one holding a grudge against you? No ex-boyfriend, who wants to seek revenge on you for some sick reason?" Mårten pushed her for answers, part of him hating that he was causing her to look at him with fear in her eyes, her face now pale and drawn.

"No," she said, gritting her teeth at him. "No one like that. I've lived alone for the past four years, ever since I graduated uni and started my photography business. And I haven't had a boyfriend in that time. I'm a normal person, living a normal life. "

She seemed pretty adamant on that front, but something about her life wasn't normal; he just had to figure out what.

"Let's change tack then. Tell me about your work. You said you're a photographer, and you also take lots of wildlife videos," he prompted as Nikki set his re-heated plate of food in front of him. She took her seat next to Jacob, but none of them touched their meal, as they all waited for Summer to answer.

"Mmm hmm. I'm a freelance photographer, and I work on commission, but my passion is wildlife and the environment. I have contacts in lots of government departments as well as not-for-profit charities. People usually reach out to me if they want something done." She nodded her head in Nikki's direction. "For instance, Tammy searched me out to help her on the project because of my special underwater skills, and that's how I met Nikki." Summer narrowed her eyes as a thought occurred to her. "You can't seriously tell me that everyone I've worked with over the last four years could be a suspect?"

"No," Mårten replied patiently. "That's not what I'm saying. I'm asking you to consider whether anyone stands out from the crowd. Or seems a little off. Perhaps they asked you to do something you weren't comfortable with."

Summer lifted one shoulder in a *how am I supposed to know* kind of look, and Mårten had to grit his teeth. She didn't seem to take this seriously.

"Mårten is on the right track," Jacob butted in when Summer's face closed over as if she were withdrawing from the whole idea. "But it seems like a giant task when you suspect everyone. How about you start with your most recent job and work backward?" he suggested.

"Okay," Summer relented after taking a large gulp of wine. Maybe this current gig with the FBI was giving Jacob more of an understanding of how to interrogate a witness without getting them offside. A skill Mårten used to have, which now seemed to have deserted him. Mårten took a deep breath and flashed Jacob a grateful glance; at least one of them was staying cool under pressure.

"My last video job was a few months ago, working for the USFWS—the United States Fish and Wildlife Service," she explained when they all gave her blank looks. "Over in Yellowstone National Park. I was…" Summer trailed off, her mouth forming a thoughtful pout. "Hang on a second." She pulled her phone from her back pocket. "I missed a call from the head wildlife officer in Yellowstone this afternoon. He asked me to call him back as a matter of urgency." They all stopped eating and turned to stare at her. "But when the guy tried to attack me in the stairwell…" she trailed off, her face twisted in consternation.

"Well, maybe you should return his call now," Jacob prompted.

"It might be too late," Summer muttered—it was after eight—but she was already hitting the redial button. Then she put her cell on the table and turned on the speaker.

She gave a surprised start when a deep voice answered the phone. "You've reached Peter Macdonald," he said. Then, when Summer hesitated, he added, "How can I help you?"

"Sorry," Summer stammered, and seemed to collect herself. "My name is Summer Pérez. You left a voicemail on my cellphone."

"Ah, yes, Ms. Pérez, thank you for returning my call." Peter's voice gained an urgent edge. "I was contacting you on the slight chance that you may have heard from Paige Owen. You recall the field officer who helped you with your work on the black-footed ferret last month?"

"Yes, I remember Paige," Summer confirmed, a confused furrow forming between her eyes. "But no, I haven't had any correspondence from her since I returned from Yellowstone? Why do you ask?"

"Ah," Peter Macdonald cleared his throat. "You've not heard the news yet? Her fiancé has reported her missing. Supposedly, she failed to reach her apartment after work on Friday last week."

Mårten's gut tightened painfully as a shiver of foreboding slid down his spine. Mårten didn't know who Paige was, but if she had a connection to Summer, then this was bad news.

"Oh, no," Summer whispered, leaning back in her chair away from the phone as if she couldn't bear to hear anymore of this dreadful news.

"It's very unlike Paige, and her fiancé is distraught," Peter continued. "As you probably already figured out, Paige was a dedicated officer. She loved her job, and she also loved her fiancé, so this is more than a little puzzling. She wasn't home when the fiancé returned from work. They were supposed to be spending the evening with friends; he'd only talked to her a few hours before, and she was excited about going out. They found her car in the parking lot of the building where she lived, but there was no sign she'd made it into the apartment. The police are following up all leads here in Montana, but they asked me to get in touch with anyone she's worked with or spent time with over the past few months."

Summer covered her mouth with her hand, a small squeak

of alarm escaping from behind her slim fingers. Jacob and Nikki cast dismayed glances in Mårten's direction, then Nikki laid a comforting hand on Summer's shoulder.

Mårten took charge when Summer seemed no longer capable of speech. "Hello, Mr. Macdonald, my name is Mårten Viskten, a friend of Summer's. This is very distressing news. Do you mind if I ask you a few questions? I'm a police inspector from Sweden; perhaps I can be of some assistance," he qualified when there was a heavy silence on the other end of the phone.

Could there be a link between Paige's disappearance and the attack on Summer? It was a long shot. The other woman had gone missing in Montana, and Summer had been attacked 2000 miles away in Seattle a week later. But it seemed Paige might have disappeared somewhere between her car and her apartment. Had someone been waiting for her on the landing? Exactly like the man had been waiting for Summer?

He found Jacob's gaze resting intently on him when he glanced up. What could the two women have in common, aside from the fact that they'd worked together for less than a week? He asked the question with his eyes, and Jacob sent him a silent nod of agreement. The coincidence seemed to be too great for there not to be a link. "We may have some information that might be pertinent," Mårten said when the ranger still hadn't replied.

"What do you mean?" Peter Macdonald's tone was grim.

Mårten looked to Summer for her permission to proceed. This was really her story to tell, but by her expression, it seemed she would struggle to do so. When she nodded, he drew a deep breath and began.

CHAPTER SEVEN

Summer stared at the sliver of light escaping into her bedroom through a slit in the curtains, sleep eluding her. After Peter's shocking revelation, she had eventually recovered enough to re-engage with the conversation, and together with Mårten and Jacob had asked endless questions of the head ranger, and answered endless questions in return. But the result had been a big, fat blank. None of them could come up with an explanation for why both she and Paige may have been targeted. They'd all agreed that perhaps some rest might help them finagle out the reason, and so just after midnight, they'd gone to their separate bedrooms. Summer hoped everyone else was doing better at getting some sleep than she was.

Summer had mulled over and over the time she'd spent in Yellowstone with Paige, relating every detail she could remember to Peter, while the other three sat around the table and listened intently. Now, she did it again and again in her head.

Summer had been contacted by a project officer for the Montana Ecological Services Field Office who'd asked if she were available to help with a feasibility study they were running to document how a small population of black-footed ferrets living on the outskirts of the Yellowstone National Park might be impacted by a proposed new gold mine to be built in the area. These diminutive carnivores thrived on a diet of primarily prairie dogs, but they'd been thought to be extinct from the western United States when ranchers cleared them out to make room for their cattle. They were rediscovered in the early eighties, however, and then biologists used a captive breeding program to build up the numbers, releasing some limited populations onto ranches and federal land around Yellowstone. It's very rare for an animal to come back from extinction, and Summer had been thrilled to be invited to join the enterprise.

The project officer had told her the United States Fish and Wildlife Service, USFWS, had a vested interest in the program and so they'd allocated a ranger to accompany her on the field trip. The ranger would help plan and conduct the nighttime catch and release survey. Which was how Summer met Paige. She and Paige had gelled almost instantly. They were around the same age, and both had a passion for conservation and the environment. Paige had an infectious laugh that lit up her bright, hazel eyes and made her cheeks wobble with mirth. Paige was the same height as Summer, but with a lot more curves, and at first Summer had been fooled by her looks, thinking her soft. But she soon discovered that Paige was as fit—if not fitter—than her, and could bound up a rocky incline, a full pack on her back, with the determination of a mountain goat, leaving Summer panting in her wake. Paige was strong and tenacious, and it was only because of her help and guidance that Summer had recorded some amazing videos of this small creature in the wild.

They'd spent five days and four nights traipsing through areas the ferret frequented, carrying all their gear on their backs and camping out under the stars. Paige was also a great benefit when they encountered ranchers or property owners, which they invariably did, as most of the animal habitats were situated just outside the boundaries of the national park. Paige's official uniform lent an air of authentication to their little venture that Summer wouldn't have been able to pull off if she'd been alone, and Paige, who could talk the hind leg off a donkey, sweet-talked them all into allowing them access to their land.

However, none of her recollections had helped her to figure out why Paige might have been abducted—because that was what Peter was afraid of, even though he was loath to voice his concern—and for Summer's apartment to be ransacked and then her possibly nearly kidnapped as well.

She rolled over in bed, then slipped out from underneath the covers, her mind revolving through her and Paige's time spent out in the wilderness. Was it something to do with the project itself? They were looking into how the mine might affect these animals. Could the mining company be hoping to quash the endeavor? The Montana Ecological Field Office was yet to release their report; Summer had sent her photos and videos to the project officer almost as soon as she returned to Seattle, but they were still pulling together all the data and records from other researchers collaborating on the study. Summer knew the outcome would not be favorable for the Gold Mine. Everything pointed to the mine being a huge disruption to the ferret population. Once the environmental report was handed to the Bureau of Land Management, it would have to reconsider its options. Hopefully, it'd stop the mine in its tracks. Or at the very least force them to reconsider the location, reducing the mine in size to leave a large enough buffer zone for the animals to remain untouched; which would also put a large dent in their profits.

Summer flicked on the bedside lamp, pulled a sweater over her head and grabbed her backpack, tugging it up onto the bed next to her. Maybe if she looked at the photos she'd taken on that field trip, they might jog her memory. She withdrew her laptop and waited for it to boot up, giving thanks once more that she hadn't left it in the apartment the other night so the thief could potentially steal it. It took a few moments to find the correct folder. This might take a while. There were hundreds of photos; Summer had documented the entire trip, but she'd only sent the relevant ones of the ferrets to the project officer. There were plenty of other images of the amazing wilderness. A luminous sunset from the top of Pelican Cone, the sparkling ripples of the waters of Yellowstone Lake, and so many other vistas in between. Chewing her lip, she bent her head over her computer and began to scroll.

What felt like only moments later, there was a light tap at the door. Summer checked the clock on her screen and was shocked to see she'd been stooped over the photos for an hour. It was now two a.m.

"Come in," she called out softly. Mårten's face appeared around the crack in the door.

"Sorry, I saw the light under your door. Couldn't you sleep either?"

"No," she consented as Mårten came all the way into the room and shut the door quietly behind him.

She couldn't help but notice how his black T-shirt fit ever-so-snugly over impressive biceps as he raised a hand to run it through his silvery hair. She had heard the term sexy and disheveled before, but never in her wildest dreams had she thought to use it herself on a man standing in front of her. At this particular moment, however, it seemed one-hundred percent appropriate. Mårten exuded that exact air; his hair was sexily sleep-tousled, his silver eyes heavily lidded, his manner unguarded and vulnerable. Something clenched tight in her chest, and then something echoed that clench much lower down, between her legs.

"Whatcha doin'?" he asked as she stared dumbly at him, unable to form a coherent word.

"Um…" She tried to corral her thoughts, but then he raised both his arms above his head and stretched, exposing a wedge of washboard-flat stomach, and her mouth hung open. Oh. My. God. His abs were amazing. Well-defined, his skin ever so slightly tanned, with a faint trail of darker hair leading down beneath his waistband.

Summer shook her head. Blast. He was affecting her again, when she needed to be thinking clearly.

"Um…" she said again. Then, she snapped her mouth shut and pointed at her computer. "I was going through all the photos I took on our trip to Yellowstone. I thought something might jump out at me."

"Good idea," he said, walking over and sitting on the bed next to her without being asked. Like, right next to her. So close she could almost feel the brush of his shoulder through the thick material of her sweater. "Can I help?"

"Um…" God, she sounded like a broken record. *Get it together, Summer.* "Sure." She pointed to the current photo on the screen of a tall metal fence running across a small clearing and then disappearing into the tree line in the distance. "This was taken on day four of our trip, when it was getting late. We were looking for a campsite. We were on federal land by that stage, right where the mining company had already built some preliminary structures." Summer almost laughed at the audacity of the company. "They were so sure they were going to get approval they'd started building roads and set up a whole raft of demountable offices, as well as many large sheds housing all kinds of equipment, and had even started work on a small power plant," she scoffed. "This section of the proposed mine site, where all the supporting infrastructure was situated, wasn't supposed to be considered in the scope of our study. It was the open-pit ore extraction sites, the waste storage areas, and the access routes that would affect the ferret populations the most. But we were passing right by, and so I asked Paige if we could take a look. These large fences surrounded it, so we didn't go in." Oh, but Summer had wanted to. She'd even pleaded with Paige, but the ranger had stood firm.

"We can't be seen to be breaking the law," Paige had said, her normally jovial face serious for once. "We can't give this gold company any ammunition they might use to get this study stopped." Summer had grudgingly agreed; it'd be stupid to get caught trespassing.

Summer flicked through another couple of photos. If she wasn't allowed to enter the property, she'd done the next best thing. She'd pushed her long telephoto lens through a hole in the fence and taken snapshots of everything within her field of focus.

"The place was pretty much deserted. Paige told me all the construction workers and other staff would've gone home for the night. They'd built no living quarters yet," she explained as they both leaned in closer to the screen.

"What about security?" Mårten queried.

"They probably had someone stationed at the front gate; I don't know. But the large fence and all the scary authoritative signs threatening prosecution would stop most people from attempting to enter." Summer lifted her shoulders in a shrug as she continued to scroll through the photos. Mårten's proximity was doing strange things to her concentration. Her attention now on the slight bump of his shoulder against hers. Her entire focus whittled down to that one point of contact as she anticipated his next touch, and her upper arm became a quivering mess.

"Wait." Mårten leaned in sharply, jostling her arm and brushing her hand as he tried to get closer. "Go back," he demanded.

Summer pushed the arrow to show the previous photo. It was a close-up of a large machinery shed, behind which sat the power plant still under construction. The rest of the area was taken up with a series of round towers of various sizes nestled together, a couple of squat buildings surrounded by scaffolding, and a tall metal structure that reared up to the sky at least five stories high, plus a whole heap other smaller equipment and outbuildings that Summer couldn't identify.

"I thought you said the place was deserted," Mårten said, eyes fixed on the screen.

"Paige seemed to think it should be," Summer reiterated. "And I didn't see..." She trailed off.

"So what is that, then?" Mårten lifted a finger and pointed at a small blob on the monitor. "Can you enlarge it?" They both angled in closer, so that their heads were almost touching. "It looks like someone is climbing that structure," he said with a frown.

He was right; that blob was a man scaling the scaffolding.

"Yeah," she replied slowly. "But that could be an employee; maybe he was working late. Doing some last-minute repairs." She shrugged.

"I don't know." Mårten tapped his finger thoughtfully against the screen. "Keep scrolling," he commanded.

Summer did as she was told, wondering what Mårten was looking for as she peered at each new photo. She barely remembered taking these images and wasn't even sure why she'd done so. She'd been clicking almost randomly, with Paige standing beside her getting more impatient by the second. They were wasting precious time; the sun would disappear soon, and they needed to find a proper campsite.

"Stop," Mårten said again. What had he found now, she wondered, as she followed the tip of his finger? The photo was dark and blurry—the light had been fading rapidly—but she could just make out the shape of the nose of a small, white van poking out from the other side of the machinery shed. "Does that look like an official mine site vehicle to you?"

"I don't know," she answered again, but she was staring now as she moved to the next photo. This one was a close-up of the shed, and she could see at least half of the white van now. There were no obvious markings. Nothing to show it belonged to the mine. But if she zoomed in, she could just make out the number plate. "I guess we can get the company to confirm if this van was there on official business," she said, only part of her concentrating on what she was saying. The rest of her was absorbed by the delicious feeling of Mårten pressed up against her. By the magnetic pull of his warm, solid body.

"Mmm," Mårten was as unmoving as a statue beside her, focused on the screen. How could he sit so still? He must not be feeling the same electrical charge that she was, because all she wanted to do was turn her head and draw the slightly musky, slightly citrusy smell of Mårten deep into her lungs. God, if she tilted her chin just an inch, her lips would graze the dark stubble on his cheek. How long had it been since she'd been this up close and personal with a man? Her heartbeat doubled at the thought of what it'd feel like to let her mouth explore the contours of those strong cheekbones.

Blast, blast, double blast.

She multiplied her efforts to concentrate, edging away from him to create some much-needed space where she could breathe once again.

As she advanced through more photos, she realized she must've been moving along the fence, as the angles of the buildings changed. Paige had been chivvying her onward, and now some images had a blurry chain-link fence obscuring them. Ten or twelve photos on, they finally got to an image showing the other side of the machinery shed with the power plant in the background, with the figure of the man almost to the top of the tall structure. And there was the complete, clear picture of the entire van.

With a second person standing at the back of the vehicle.

There were two people at the mine site. This person had been obscured by the shed, and it wasn't until Summer had taken a photo from this angle that he'd become visible.

The next photo jumped to a fire glowing with a dark forest as the backdrop; their campsite for the night. Blast, that must've been her last photo of the mine site.

"Go back," Mårten said, at the same time as Summer hit the reverse button to return to the previous image. She didn't need to be asked; she zoomed right in on the figure next to the van. It was a man, she could see his face now. And he was staring straight down her lens. Summer shivered, as if a cold gust of wind had blown over her skin. Whoever this man was, it appeared he'd seen her and Paige on the other side of the fence. And it seemed he didn't like the fact that he'd been spotted. What were these men up to? Why were they on the site? Were they authorized to be there? Or were they doing something clandestine?

She turned to look at Mårten as he sat back with a grunt of surprise.

"That's...unexpected," she whispered.

"Did you know these guys were in these photos when you took them?"

"No. I think by this time Paige was rushing me along, and I was just taking random snaps, not really looking down the viewfinder." She racked her memory to see if she could find any hint that she'd knowingly taken photos of the guys. "I'm sure it was a coincidence. I was clicking away as I walked, trying to keep up with Paige."

"Well, he saw you. And he didn't look happy that you

were taking photos."

Summer couldn't help but agree.

"Do you think Paige saw these men?" Mårten asked.

"I'm not sure," Summer mused. "I was using a telephoto lens and zooming right in on the buildings. They might not have even been conspicuous to the naked eye. I mean, I didn't even know they were there until I looked at the photos."

"Hmm. I reckon if we enhance the photo and get the registration of the van, I'll ask Jacob to run it, see who it belongs to. It'll be much quicker than waiting for the mining company to get back to us," he qualified when Summer cast him a curious glance.

"I don't mean to be crass, and I don't want to get too excited because this is a long shot, but this could be the clue we've been looking for that links this guy to the man who ransacked your apartment. Could he have been searching for the SD card with the photo you took of him? Is that why he stole your camera?"

Summer considered him. Mårten might be right. The thief had escaped down the stairs with the camera she'd used on the field trip. But how would he have known? Was it mere coincidence he'd stolen that exact item? Or had he known what he was looking for?

A mounting heaviness in the pit of her stomach had alarm bells jangling in her head. If Mårten were right, then this photo made it even more real. She and Paige had seen something they weren't supposed to—or rather, she had seen something and dragged an unsuspecting Paige into it—and now they were both paying the price. Did someone abduct Paige thinking she had knowledge of these photos? But Paige was innocent. And she could be in real danger. *Summer* could be in real danger. She fisted her hands into the bedclothes, fighting the growing panic clenching her insides into a tight ball.

"Then maybe he came back for your computer afterward," Mårten mused, not registering that Summer was no longer listening. "He got the camera, but he's smart enough to realize you would've already copied the photos across. And you had your computer with you that night. Am I right?" Mårten finally turned to her, his lips tilted upward in a question mark. He must've seen the distress evident on her face, however, because he immediately said, "Oh, shit, I'm sorry. I didn't mean to upset you. I was thinking out loud. It's a bad habit of mine."

"No, no, you didn't," she proclaimed, cursing the stupid tears that were forming against her will in the corners of her eyes. "It's just that… if Paige has been abducted, and that guy came to my house because of a photo I took, then this is all my fault. If I hadn't been so nosy…"

"That is utterly ridiculous," Mårten said with a snort. Then after a momentary hesitation, he added, "I could be on the wrong track. I've been known to get a little carried away sometimes, just ask Jacob." Mårten was trying to backtrack to placate her. "Why don't we wait and see if Jacob turns up anything before we—I—jump to conclusions?"

For once she didn't feel like arguing, and so she nodded, lowering her head as she tried to regain her composure. She was surprised when she felt the heavy weight of his arm drape around her shoulders.

"Come on. You need to believe that none of this is your fault. You are the victim; trust me on that." His masculine body was so substantial next to hers. Her skin tingled with awareness, her tears drying in an instant as something more carnal took their place.

"Summer, look at me."

She didn't want to lift her head, but the low command in his voice pulsed right through her until she had no choice. She found herself staring into his silver eyes.

"Repeat after me: I am the victim here."

She opened her mouth to do as he asked, but it was suddenly so dry she could form no words. His face was mere inches from hers. The heat from his arm burned a brand into her neck. She should pull away, disentangle his arm from around her shoulders, sit back on the bed and pretend this was just the act of a simple friend comforting another friend. But those otherworldly gray eyes held her immobile, as if a laser beam had attached itself to her soul, and she couldn't move if she'd wanted to. They were face to face in the muted light of the bedroom, and she could think of nothing to say, nothing to do, except... The need to kiss him hummed through her like a surging wave. His gaze slipped to her mouth, and she knew he wanted to kiss her too.

His hand came up to cup her face, and he lowered his head so that his lips landed on hers, hot and firm. Needy, but not overbearing, giving her the leeway to end this if that's what she wanted. But she didn't want to. The blood pounded in her ears as she slipped her tongue inside his mouth and tangled it with his. Heat and desire surged through her. This man was everything. The kiss—this first kiss—was everything she'd thought it would be. And more. So much more.

Then, without warning, he drew back, and she was left panting for breath. She could see his chest rising and falling in time with hers. What had just happened? Why was he stopping?

"I shouldn't have done that. I'm sorry," he said, and got off the bed.

CHAPTER EIGHT

"I shouldn't have done that. I'm sorry," he said, and got off the bed.

He was a jerk. What had he been thinking? But she'd been staring at him with those dark, soulful eyes like pools of liquid sable, and he'd wanted to dive right in. The last thing he should do was take advantage of her, especially when she was feeling vulnerable and scared. It was unprofessional as well as reprehensible. Before this, when he'd wanted to kiss her, he'd been able to control himself. Just. But this time something had slipped and overridden that restraint. She'd been so close, she was disrupting all his defenses, drawing him in with a siren call so strong he was unable to ignore it.

That was it. It was her proximity that'd caused his lapse in judgment. He was stupid to have sat so close to her on the bed. All he needed was to keep his distance, and everything would be fine. He'd be able to maintain his equilibrium if he just stayed away from her.

Mårten still had his back to Summer, a part of him not wanting to turn around to see the hurt in her eyes. Hurt that he knew he'd put there by being a jerk and letting his urges get the better of him. Then he'd been a double jerk by leaping off the bed as if she'd burned him. He'd rejected her, and they both knew it. But he had plenty of good reasons if he could only make her understand.

Steeling himself, he turned to face the bed. "Look, Summer," he started. "I'm a police officer. I make it a rule not to—"

She cut him off. "It's fine, Mårten," she replied, voice tinged with ice. "I get it. I'm sorry it happened too."

Okay. It looked as if she didn't want to hear his reasons. Which was fair enough. Part of him wished he could take his words back. How could he regret something as primal and hot as that kiss? But that would do neither of them any good. He needed to leave this room for both their sakes. He opened the door and stalked out into the passage, almost letting out a shout of alarm when a dark figure emerged from the kitchen in front of him. Jesus Christ, it was only Jacob.

Not allowing his shock to show, Mårten walked toward his friend as if nothing was wrong; as if he hadn't just appeared from Summer's bedroom in the wee hours of the morning. "I have a favor to ask of you," he said, ignoring the look of open surprise on Jacob's face. Mårten wasn't about to account for himself. They'd known each other long enough for Jacob to know not to probe, and he wouldn't be offended when Mårten proffered no explanation. But Jacob was also very good at not letting things go. He'd bide his time, survey the situation, and launch an attack when Mårten was least expecting it.

"Okay," Jacob replied, slowly taking a seat at the kitchen table as Mårten did the same.

But before Mårten could open his mouth to elaborate, Summer appeared in the doorway looking all rumpled and cute and stealing his breath from his lungs. Was it just his imagination, or were her lips slightly swollen? Swollen from his kisses? *Shit*. Mårten dipped his head, not wanting to meet her gaze.

"Have you told him yet?" she demanded.

Mårten's stomach twisted and flipped over, and he kept his gaze lowered, not wishing to meet Jacob's eye now either. It took him a few seconds to realize she'd meant the photos and not their illicit kiss. Shit, he needed to get his head back in the game.

Because Mårten hadn't proffered an answer, Jacob leaned forward and asked, "Told me what?"

"No. Yes… I was about to," Mårten replied with a sigh, lifting his chin; he couldn't avoid her now, she was right there, and Jacob was looking at them both with growing incredulity. He locked his gaze with Summer's, caught in her powerful tractor beam of silent recriminations and hurt feelings, reminding him just how much of a jerk he was.

If only he couldn't still feel the echo of her lips upon his, he might be able to act half normal. But as it was, he could barely stop himself from standing and taking Summer in his arms, to apologize for being an ass, to tell her how much he wanted to kiss her again, to protect her from all that was to come. None of which he could do, so he just sat there like a dumbass, staring at her.

"Told me what?" Jacob repeated a little louder this time when neither of them answered, a frown drawing deep lines across his forehead.

"Anyone want some hot chocolate?" Nikki shuffled sleepily into the room to stand beside Summer, stifling a yawn. Then she seemed to catch the vibe and stopped. "Or do we need something stronger? Shall I break out the whisky? What's going on here?"

Great, now everyone was awake and asking questions. Mårten gave a resigned sigh. Perhaps it was for the best; at least they wouldn't have to tell their story more than once now. He just hoped Nikki wasn't as adept at picking up the awkward vibe between himself and Summer as Jacob had been. Because she wouldn't let it drop like Jacob had. She'd want to know in minute detail what'd just passed between him and Summer. And there was no way he was going to mention how he'd given in to temptation and kissed the woman he was supposed to be protecting. Yeah, he knew Jacob would say that technically, Summer wasn't his problem; she was the Seattle Police Force's problem. But now that this thief had attacked a second time, Mårten was determined to keep her safe, whether she was in his jurisdiction or not. The police here were doing a piss-poor job as far as he was concerned, and no one else seemed to take her plight seriously. Yet, anyway. Maybe after tonight, they would.

"No need for whisky," Summer said, breaking the impasse. "Hot chocolate would be nice." She moved to grab four mugs out of the cupboard. "I'll help." Nikki gave her a curious glance but turned to fill the kettle, saying nothing.

"So," Jacob said impatiently as the two women busied themselves at the countertop. "What's going on?"

Mårten schooled his features into what he hoped was his normal implacable mask before he answered. "We may have found a clue," he said. "Can you pull some strings and run a license plate for us? Or get Miller to do it?"

Jacob sat up straighter. "Possibly," he hedged. "But I'd need to know why first."

"Summer discovered a photo that might be important," Mårten replied, then filled them in on his and Summer's unexpected find of the image of the two men who were acting mighty suspicious on the mine site.

Nikki said nothing, merely made an interested humming sound and looked to Jacob for his response.

But Jacob pursed his lips for many seconds before he said, "That sounds like a long shot."

"I agree." Mårten steepled his fingers on the table, saying not a word more, waiting as silence descended and everyone turned to stare at Jacob. The ball was in his court now.

Jacob rolled his eyes. "Fine. It's a little early in the morning, but I guess it can't hurt to give it a go. What's the vehicle registration number?"

Mårten gave it to him, along with a description of the white van.

"As long as you don't get in any trouble," Summer added, her forehead crinkling with lines of tension as she watched Jacob like a hawk.

Jacob didn't answer. Instead, he kept his face shuttered, pulled out his phone and tapped out a number, then disappeared down the hallway.

"He wouldn't do it if it were going to cause problems," Nikki assured Summer. But Mårten and Nikki both knew that wasn't strictly true. Mårten was usually the stickler for the rules, and Jacob was usually the one who bent them. Mårten had known that when he'd put forward his request. He hoped he wasn't asking too much of his friend and that Jacob wouldn't be risking his career.

Jacob returned to the room ten minutes later, his lips pursed in thought.

"Well, that was interesting," he said, taking a sip of his cool chocolate and then grimacing with distaste. Without a word, Nikki took the cup and warmed it up in the microwave. "I think I may have just stirred up a hornet's nest." He let his gaze rest on Summer. "Or rather, *you* have just stirred up a hornet's nest."

"What? Why?" She leaned forward, her long hair draping across the table as she fixed Jacob with her astute gaze, momentarily distracting Mårten with images of running his fingers through those silky lengths. Jacob's next words pulled him back to reality.

"The guy on night shift agreed to run the plates for me after I mentioned I work with Agent Miller. I didn't want to wake her unless I had to this early in the morning, but it seems her reputation precedes her, and that was enough for my colleague," Jacob began. "He got an immediate hit on the car, and that's when things got interesting. He wanted details about where someone had spotted this van and my reasons for asking." Jacob waved a hand in the air to forestall questions. "I won't go into specifics; this stuff isn't highly classified; it's more that it's available on a need-to-know basis within the FBI, and he wasn't sure why I needed to know. Turns out that the registration for this vehicle belongs to a man connected to a known eco-terrorist group. A man who's on top of our Most Wanted Terrorist list."

Mårten sat back in his chair at the unexpected news.

"Oh, wow," Summer breathed, eyes going wide. "I mean, of course I've heard the term *eco-terrorist*, especially as I work with lots of environmental groups, but aren't they just toothless tigers? They're not real terrorists, are they? They're not dangerous? So why would he be on a Most Wanted list?" Summer continued.

Jacob considered Summer for many long seconds, perhaps wondering how much to reveal. "I guess you could say that most of the time you're correct. At the heart of it, these eco-terrorist groups all want to save the environment, similar to any other band of greenies," he said evenly. "But they're not the same as the protesters who wave placards and chant for peace. They can be far more aggressive, even resorting to violence. They use economic sabotage and guerrilla warfare to stop what they see as so-called exploitation. So yes, in some cases they may be just as bad as the real terrorists." Jacob's voice was now low and serious.

Summer looked a little stunned by Jacob's revelations, so Mårten took up the line of inquiry. "What exactly is this eco-terrorist group doing that's stirred up a hornet's nest in the FBI then?" Much like Summer, he'd heard the term bandied about, but had no personal experience with them on the job. A frisson of ice slid down his spine. Summer might not realize these groups could be dangerous, but the look on Jacob's face told Mårten these guys might be trouble.

"The FBI has been keeping tabs on this particular group," Jacob said. "They call themselves Earth In Crisis, or EIC, and have been linked to arson attacks on at least three industry sites and as many as six private houses of company CEOs."

Mårten let out a low whistle. This faction was indeed badass if they were resorting to attacking ordinary citizens. That was usually a no-go zone for these groups, as it took away their sympathy vote in the eyes of the rest of the population.

Jacob continued, "I know most of this because every agent is required to memorize the top twenty people on our wanted lists."

Which was much the same as in the Swedish police, Mårten thought, as he listened to Jacob go on.

"We believe there are at least three EIC members, possibly more. They're a splinter group from another well-known eco-terrorist group, called ELF, or Earth Liberation Front, but EIC specifically targets large mining companies who they believe are making exorbitant profits by pillaging pristine natural environments."

Aha, at last here was the link they were looking for. Mårten sat forward again. "Have they made any threats to this gold company at Yellowstone?"

"No, not exactly," Jacob replied. "But the EIC has had a worrying escalation in its offensives of late. Like I said, they've taken to targeting individuals, such as company CEOs. A few months ago, the husband of an employee was badly injured in a fire caused by their arson attack while trying to rescue his two children. Unfortunately, one child died from smoke inhalation."

Nikki gasped, halting in the task of retrieving Jacob's hot chocolate from the microwave to stare at her boyfriend with a terrified gape.

Summer also caught her breath and covered her mouth. "Oh no," she whispered.

Mårten enfolded her other hand with his, offering his comfort, forgetting all of his recently sworn promises not to touch her again. This was a bad omen. If EIC were prepared to maim civilians and kill innocent children—even if it was accidental—to get their message across, well then... The notion didn't bear finishing. This group was not mucking about; they meant business.

"I thought eco-terrorists operated with a set of rules," Nikki cut in indignantly, her face pale with shock as she returned to sit at the table. "I've encountered a few groups throughout my career, when I've traveled to areas of ocean most under threat by human practices, and some of them can be overzealous, I agree. But I always believed one of their hard-wired commandments was not to injure animals, people, or the environment in their quest for justice."

"It is," Jacob agreed quietly. "Under normal circumstances. But this group is different. Their leader, Tyrone King, has developed extremist views. It all seems to stem from when the Trump administration opened up federal land to be used for mining leases again a few years back. A lot of federal land includes national parks and watershed areas, and if mines are allowed to go ahead—which it seems likely they will be—the quality of the water we drink and the survival of the forests and animals may be at risk. Tyrone has been extremely outspoken about these new rules, as have many other eco-terrorist groups. But Tyrone remains the most vocal and most persistent, becoming almost manic in his tirades. Which is why the FBI has been monitoring him. But six months ago he went underground, and we haven't been able to track him since. Which is also when the arson attacks started. We think Tyrone might be one of the men in that photo you described."

"So how can you be positive that this Tyrone and his EIC are the ones carrying out the strikes?" Mårten queried, his hand still protectively covering Summer's.

"We can't. Not for sure," Jacob replied, accepting his now-hot cup of cocoa from Nikki with a grimace. "But when the FBI suspects something, or someone, it's for a good reason. They also believe he's been planning another attack. Something big. And you may have stepped right into the middle of it." Jacob leveled his gaze at Summer now as he continued. "I know this is a lot to take in. And all of this is conjecture at the moment. My colleague said he would get back to me as soon as he confirms a few things. And I'll need to bring Miller in on this after all. But I think it's prudent that you continue to stay here under our protection until we find out more."

Summer looked confused, then dubious, then rebellious. "But that could take days. Or weeks, even. I can't ask you to do that for me."

Mårten still had his hand over hers, and he tightened his grip slightly. "Summer, don't be silly, you need to do this for your own safety," he urged.

As if noticing for the first time that he was touching her, she yanked her hand out from beneath his, a little crease forming between her brows. He was beginning to understand that wrinkle meant her stubborn streak was about to kick in, and he pulled his chair forward so that their knees made contact and she was now trapped between him and the table, unable to move with the wall at her back.

"Jacob knows what he's talking about. You need to listen to him." Mårten wasn't going to plead with her, not in front of Jacob and Nikki, but he could feel the urgency simmering inside him. She didn't trust him right now, not after the way he'd rejected her. Hell, the fact she was shooting daggers at him with her eyes, she probably hated his guts. But he was prepared to weather her dislike, embrace it even, if only she'd hear him out. "Please promise me you'll stay here, at least for the next few days." Mårten needed her to give him this assurance. With his imminent departure back to Sweden looming, he needed to make sure she was going to be in safe hands. And Jacob was the only person he truly trusted in this city, in this whole damned country, even, to do the job.

He watched several emotions swim across the dark pools of her eyes as she studied him.

"Are you okay with this?" Summer asked, looking at Nikki now. "I mean, this is your house. What if this madman finds out I'm here and targets me here? You could be in danger." Underneath the table, where only Mårten could see, Summer was scrubbing her thumb across the palm of her other hand over and over. It was the same habit he'd noticed back at her apartment. Now he could see it was a mannerism brought on by stress.

She sat in her chair scowling at him as she waited for Nikki's reply. This time, it was Nikki's turn to lay her hand over Summer's, only now she didn't pull away. "My priority is to see you safe, Summer. And of course if you need to stay here, then you're more than welcome. I understand the risks, but I also trust Jacob with my life. He won't allow any harm to come to me. Or to you. If you'll let him."

Jacob nodded earnestly in Summer's direction, then draped an arm around Nikki's shoulders, tucking her under his shoulder in a comforting move that was also slightly possessive. Mårten was struck by a sudden jolt of yearning as he watched Jacob show his complete support for his woman. What would it be like to have someone to care about as deeply as Jacob did? Someone who cared equally about him in return.

Summer lowered her gaze, humbled by Nikki's compassion. And by Jacob's determined offer to protect her. At last she said quietly, "I'm not saying no. But I need to go for a run. I need to clear my head and think about all this, if that's okay?" She pushed her empty mug away and went to stand.

"Of course," Nikki replied. She and Jacob stood as one, concern etched on both their faces. Jacob flicked Mårten an almost imperceptible glance, letting him know they were both thinking the same thing.

Mårten didn't stand, however, knowing that he was still blocking Summer in at the table. He checked the window. It was barely light outside. He agreed with Jacob's silent communication. "I'll come with you." It wasn't a question. He was going to be her shadow, whether she liked it or not. She could hate him as much as she wanted, but he wasn't letting her out of this house alone.

Summer studied him for a long time, heavy lashes fringing her narrowed eyes, and it was all he could do to stop himself from being drawn in to her, to drown in those pools of emotion.

"Provided you can keep up with me then, police inspector," she said with a derisive snort, snapping him out of his reverie.

"I'll go and change," he replied, pushing his chair back and moving out of her way. "Don't go anywhere without me," he commanded over his shoulder.

"I wouldn't dream of it," she replied, saccharine sweet. But that tone didn't fool him. He knew what she had in mind. She was going to push him as hard as she could, to punish him, and he was going to have to run as if his life depended on it to keep up with her. Which was ironic, because maybe it did.

CHAPTER NINE

Mårten's breathing was labored as he pounded up the hill behind Summer. Jesus Christ, this girl could run. Mårten was fit, but not nearly as fit as her, it seemed. Even his police training didn't come close to covering conditions for triathlons. The only good thing about the past half hour of pure torture was the view of her gorgeous ass encased in black lycra shorts as she ran in front of him. And the way her long ponytail flicked jauntily down her back as she moved was also doing strange things to his insides.

He knew she was going to punish him for pulling away from that kiss, and she was succeeding. He might even have to call a halt soon, before he passed out. He was no judge of how well Summer might be doing in the triathlon world, but if this run—and it could be called nothing less, there was no jogging going on here—was anything to go by, Summer must be very competitive.

They crested the slight incline, and Lake Washington came back into view. They'd been following the shoreline off and on, as Summer snaked her way through the suburbs, Mårten trusting she knew where she was going because he would not admit he was completely lost. The sun was just coming up, with a delicate mist rising off the calm water and the sky tinged a pale pink above. A grassy verge led down from the path to the edge of the water, bordered by pretty shrubs and even a flush of summer flowers. It was quite beautiful, and it reminded him of the lake near his hometown where he sometimes went hiking whenever he had a day off. Seattle wasn't a terrible place to live, he decided.

Mårten was just about to call out and ask Summer to stop —ostensibly to admire the view—when she slowed so that he nearly ran into the back of her and had to pull up short.

"I thought we should pause before you keeled over and died," she said tartly, flicking him a haughty look over her shoulder. Even while he was trying to hide just how much he was struggling to breathe, an urge to kiss that smart mouth of hers overtook him. But she took off at a light jog toward the water's edge, and he followed, his retort stuck in his throat as he gasped for breath.

She stopped, studying the view unfolding before them, and he took a moment to appreciate her shape outlined against the luminous water. Long legs, the jut of her hips and then a dainty waist that he longed to wrap his hands around so he could pull her to him. She was tall and athletic, muscular and strong. Everything that he appreciated in a woman. No wonder he was so drawn to her. But it was her feisty temperament, and the fact there was clearly lots going on inside that quick mind of hers, that intrigued him as much as her body.

She turned to stare at him as he stepped alongside her. A hint of perspiration and a slight rosy glow around her cheeks were the only suggestions that she'd run five miles at a breakneck pace. While Mårten was sweating heavily and his chest burned from the unusual, arduous exertion. He knew his face was as red as a beetroot, but he stood up taller, pretending he was fine. The thought that he now had to run at least five miles back to Nikki's again was pushed to the dark recesses of his mind. He was here to keep Summer safe. And if she wanted to run ten miles, twenty even, then he'd just have to keep up. His muscles were going to scream at him tomorrow, but that was a price he was happy to pay. Maybe he should take up running when he got home. Just to increase his cardiovascular fitness. That was all; no other reason.

"So, you compete in triathlons then?" He asked when he finally had his breathing under control. They'd already touched on this subject, but perhaps it was an opportunity to find out more. Triathletes were a special kind of person. From the little he knew, it took dedication, lots of time, and sheer unwavering grit to be any good. And he wanted to know if she was any good.

Her gaze remained fixed on the view, and he wondered if she was going to answer. At last, she said. "Yes. I like to keep busy when I'm not working. And owning my own photography business, I can usually schedule my jobs around my training timetable."

That made sense. "And you've been doing this for a while?"

She nodded slowly, but the stubborn turn of her lip told him she was considering not answering. Then she let out a sigh of capitulation. "I started when I first moved to Seattle about six years ago. My friend, Serena, got me into it. She was born in Namibia and was lucky enough to be relocated here as a refugee when she was young. She got into the modeling business and started doing triathlons as a way to stay fit and trim. But now she's shifted to the other side of the camera, and she takes the photos instead of posing for them. She gave up triathlons a few years ago to concentrate on her photography, which was good for me, because she's one of the best runners I've ever known and I could never beat her. But I could always catch her in the swim leg," she added with a wry twist to her lips.

This was the most Summer had revealed since he'd met her, and it was fascinating finding out more about her life. Mårten kept his gaze directed forward like hers, not wanting to break this fragile truce. She might not have forgiven him, but at least she was talking.

"It becomes a bit addictive, you know," she added thoughtfully.

He wasn't sure he agreed with that. To him, exercise was merely a means to an end. He couldn't say that he enjoyed the endless hours of sweating. And if they ever brought out a pill that meant you never had to work out again, he might well take it.

"You must train most days then?" He said, not letting on to his true thoughts.

She looked at him for the first time since they had stopped, then quickly averted her gaze. "Yes, most days. I swim twice a week, run at least twice a week, and train on my bicycle at least twice a week."

That left scant opportunity for rest and relaxation, he decided, and he looked at her with renewed respect. "It sounds like you're quite competitive."

"I guess so. There's a big event coming up in the last week of June in Pontevedra, Spain. If I do well there, then I'll qualify to join the US team to go to the World Championships. I've just moved up to the 30 to 35 age group, but the competition is still fierce and..." Summer stopped, then grimaced and shot him a look from beneath lowered brows, clearly wishing she hadn't given away that information. Mårten had already guessed she was in her late twenties and was a little surprised to hear she was at least thirty. That made him only four years her senior. An age gap like that was nothing; why, he'd dated women way younger than him before. Wait...what? Why was he even thinking this? He wasn't about to date Summer, so the difference in their ages was irrelevant.

"The end of June is only a couple of weeks away," Mårten commented, pushing thoughts about dating out of his head.

"Yes," she agreed. "That's why it's so important I don't lose any of my training momentum."

"I can imagine," he replied. "Do you often travel to events?" He'd never considered when or how these kinds of things were organized; it was interesting. Plus, he was enjoying talking to Summer. Her guard had dropped now that she was discussing something she was passionate about. It made her light up, made even more attractive, if that was possible.

"Yes, I'm often overseas at least two or three times annually. Sometimes I can work a job into the destination if I'm lucky. The meets are always at a different location every year. Last year—"

The sound of Mårten's phone ringing cut her off. He had half a mind to ignore it so he could continue this discussion. But when he saw it was Jacob, he decided to take it. He could have a new lead from his FBI sources.

"Mårten, get back here, now." Jacob didn't even wait for Mårten to say hello. His tone was tight and gruff, immediately putting him on edge.

"Why, what—"

"Someone tried to set fire to Nikki's house. We're okay. Nikki's very shaken up. But the guy got away." Jacob cut him off again before he had a chance to frame a sensible question.

Holy shit. Mårten couldn't keep the fear off his face, and as Summer read his features she reared back, shock widening her eyes.

"What's happened? God, please don't tell me Nikki or Jacob have been hurt," she said, both hands coming up to cover her mouth.

"We're on our way," Mårten said into the receiver, ushering Summer up the hill as he spoke. "We should be there in ten minutes. We'll catch an Uber home." This wasn't the time to be running, and for once he had no disagreement from Summer as she turned and went obediently in the direction he was pushing her.

"Tell me what's happened," she pleaded over her shoulder as she jogged up the hill in front of him.

Mårten looked up from tapping his details into the ride-share app. He couldn't keep this from her; it was too big. "Someone attacked Nikki's house. Both Jacob and Nikki are fine, though."

She shook her head, stopping dead and then taking two steps away from him. "Oh God," she moaned. "This is because of me, isn't it? I was afraid this would happen."

He laid a hand on her shoulder, forcing her to look into his eyes. He could feel the agitation thrumming through her, like she was ready to bolt at a moment's notice.

"We don't know that yet," he said, keeping his voice calm and neutral. He didn't need her any more spooked than she already was. "The main thing is Jacob and Nikki are fine. Let's just wait and see what the FBI decides when we get back. This could be completely coincidental," he soothed as he returned to punching buttons on his phone. But inside, his guts roiled with a tornado of emotions.

Because he knew his words were hollow. This attack was definitely connected to Summer. There was no doubt in his mind.

CHAPTER TEN

Summer sat at the kitchen table staring wretchedly into her cold coffee, the fingers of her right hand resting lightly on the cross around her neck. She never took this necklace off; it was her last link to Marco, and she often felt he was with her when she touched it. Maybe he had been protecting Nikki and Jacob when she couldn't. Summer knew it was a stupid superstition, but she sometimes wondered if his spirit was still around, kept close by this gold chain.

She could hear Jacob and Nikki talking to the forensics guys out in the yard. Summer didn't even want to think about the blacked doorway and the few remaining stumps of the front porch. And the back door was nearly as bad. The attacker had firebombed both entrances to make sure whoever was in the house would find it almost impossible to get out. At least the slew of firefighters had left twenty minutes ago, confident any risk of a flareup was now gone, taking with them their muddy footprints and loud voices.

Summer was so lost in her own thoughts she didn't hear Nikki coming down the corridor until she burst into the kitchen, and Summer stood in a rush, guilt twisting her insides. Nikki's pretty face was drawn into lines of tension, her long hair falling out of the hasty bun she'd tied it up into earlier this morning.

"I'm so sorry," Summer said hurriedly. "Your beautiful house." Tears pricked at the back of her eyelids. This was all her fault. If she hadn't taken refuge here, Nikki's place would never have been targeted. "I don't know what to say. If there's anything I can do, if I can help in any way. I want to pay for all the damages," she added with a lift to her chin.

Nikki said nothing for a few seconds, but her face softened as she looked at Summer. "Don't be silly," she replied. "That's what insurance is for." As she came closer, Summer noticed a smudge of charcoal over Nikki's left eye, and the guilt twisted sharply once more in her belly. This poor woman had had to flee her burning house, breaking the window in her bedroom to get out. And now her charming cottage was scarred and blackened, and yet she was the one showing Summer compassion.

"I already told you, we got out okay, and thanks to Jacob and my wonderful neighbors, the damage is minimal," Nikki added.

Summer had previously heard Nikki and Jacob's account of their escape. They had gone back to bed after Mårten and Summer left for their run, ostensibly to grab an hour more sleep. But it was clear the loved-up couple hadn't been sleeping when, fifteen minutes later, Jacob heard something suspicious and got up to find smoke pouring through the front door. He'd broken the bedroom window and gotten them both out unharmed, raising the alarm as he did so. Then he'd turned the garden hose on the flames at the entrance, while some of Nikki's neighbors helped her do the same at the rear, which saved the house from complete destruction.

Summer's heart clenched as she remembered Nikki's face, white as a sheet when they'd first arrived back. She'd been terrified, almost swaying on her feet. The only thing keeping her upright was Jacob's solid presence beside her as firefighters and police swarmed all over the house. She had recovered quickly, however, soon yelling at a firefighter to stop trampling all over her beloved azalea bushes and telling the police officers to please ask *her* first if they needed anything moved. But that didn't make her raw emotions at the time any less valid.

"But. Oh, God… it could have been so much worse," Summer groaned. "What if you'd been asleep and hadn't heard the fire start? What if—" Summer daren't finish her sentence. What if they'd been burned? Or died of smoke inhalation like that poor child Jacob and told her about. Her shame was so strong that she doubled over as pain sliced through her stomach.

"I know you want to blame yourself, but you shouldn't." Nikki bent down so she was level with Summer's face, the other woman's blue eyes intense and fixed on hers. "Like I said before, I know what it's like to need a place of sanctuary, and I was happy to let you stay here. Stop letting the guilt crush you. You need to have your head screwed on right if you're gonna outfox this fucker, and overwhelming guilt will not help you." Nikki's use of the curse word made Summer straighten up; in the short time she'd known Nikki, she'd never heard her swear. "If you're going to feel anything, you should feel angry at whoever did this. Get mad," Nikki continued, slapping her closed fist into the palm of her other hand. "You need to fight, Summer, not give in. Otherwise, he will win."

Summer considered the other woman as they stood almost nose to nose in the middle of the kitchen. Nikki's compassion was going to be her undoing. Summer didn't think she could be so forgiving if the tables were turned and it was her house that'd been partially destroyed. But perhaps she was right. She had to stop feeling sorry for herself and start standing up for herself. If not for her own safety, then for the safety of those around her.

"Okay?" Nikki asked, narrowing her eyes at Summer, hands on hips.

"Okay," Summer replied slowly.

"Good." With that, Nikki gave Summer a quick, hard embrace, then let her go. "I think the cops are finishing up, and the insurance assessor will be here soon. It's not as bad as it looks," Nikki finished kindly as she busied herself tidying the kitchen.

"That's true," Jacob said, entering the room, Mårten close behind him. "A good carpenter will have it fixed in a few days. There was no major damage to the roof or any of the walls. We put it out before that could happen."

"Yes, that's correct," Mårten added, his eyes anchored on Summer's as if trying to gauge her mood. "The destruction is minimal; it can be repaired, and then the house will look like new."

She'd forgotten in all her panic over Jacob and Nikki's safety just how good Mårten looked in a pair of running shorts. She'd been shocked to see how muscled and tanned his legs had been, and she'd barely been able to force herself to look away from those powerful thighs when he'd emerged from his room earlier this morning. And that tight black T-shirt, which did nothing to hide the hard walls of his stomach, tapering off to a narrow waist, as well as how it stretched so tightly over bulging biceps. Oh God. And now seeing him again, she was hit with a second wave of that same smack of lust right in the groin as her gaze traveled up and down his torso of its own accord. Blast, she was in trouble. He was too sexy for his own good. Too sexy for her own good.

She'd also forgotten that she was supposed to be mad at him. He'd kissed her this morning, and then rejected her, as if that kiss had been the worst mistake of his life. As anger seemed to be the easier path to choose, she raised eyebrows at him defiantly. He wasn't getting away that easily. She had a long memory, and just because he was being all solicitous and sexy now, didn't make everything okay again.

But before she could come up with an appropriate retort, Jacob said, "Everyone take a seat. We need to figure out what our next steps are, and I can bring you up to speed on what Miller and I have discussed."

Jacob's FBI partner, Agent Claire Miller, had arrived at Nikki's house seconds after she and Mårten had returned, looking way too cool, collected, and professional for that early in the morning. Her first act had been to make sure Jacob and Nikki were both okay, and Summer could see the genuine care and concern she had for her new colleague and his girlfriend. But after a few moments' perusal of the burned sections of the house, the lines of unease had cleared from her brow and she'd taken Jacob aside for a tête-à-tête, then left again soon after.

"Miller is back at HQ right now, to talk to our boss and organize a few things." Jacob's gaze zeroed in on Summer. "Things that will affect you, Summer," he added.

"I already know what my next step is," she muttered half under her breath as she took a seat. "I need to get out of here. So this can't happen again." When Summer looked up, three pairs of eyes were all staring at her in disbelief.

Jacob was the first to break the heavy silence. "I agree." His reply caught her by surprise.

"Oh, good, I—"

"Miller thinks you should go into witness protection. She's talking to the boss about taking you to a safe house this morning." Jacob said, his face deadpan.

"What? No." This was the last thing Summer had expected.

Jacob held up a hand to stop her protestations. "Miller and

I agree this is the same MO as the other arson attacks the FBI have been investigating. In all the previous blazes, the perp set fire to both the front and rear entries to prevent the occupants from escaping. This has Tyrone King's stamp all over it. We've confirmed by your description that the guy you saw in your stairwell wasn't actually Tyrone, which means he's brought someone else in to do his dirty work. Whether it's just to scare you into submission, to get you to hand over those photos, or worse, we're not sure yet. But either way, you're in extreme danger."

Summer faltered, knowing that by *worse*, Jacob meant Tyrone wanted her dead. "Yeah, I get all that..." she said eventually, once she got past the idea someone wanted to murder her. The last thing she desired was to go into witness protection, however.

"I'm not sure that you do," Mårten said, banging his hand down on the table hard so that she flinched in her chair, and turned to face him in surprise. "I've felt all along that this guy was dangerous, and I'm glad someone is finally taking your plight seriously. I'm sad that it took Nikki's house to be firebombed for people to understand." He sent Nikki a brief glance of solidarity. "But this is a life-and-death situation. I'm going back to Sweden in two days, so I won't be around to cover your pretty ass anymore. Don't forget, there is already a woman who's gone missing, and if she's linked to this case..." Mårten let his words trail off.

Of course, Summer hadn't forgotten about Paige. She wanted the ranger found as much as anyone, and it sent shivers of ice down her spine thinking that her friend could've been abducted, maybe being held prisoner, or... Summer daren't even think of other alternatives. But that didn't mean the same thing was going to happen to her.

"I can't go into witness protection," Summer ground out from between gritted teeth, glaring at him like this was all his fault. Which she knew it wasn't. But she was already angry at him; he was a convenient target, and it felt good to let some of that anger boil to the surface. To use it to drive away the fear. Because the idea of going into witness protection was scaring her even more than the idea that some maniac might be after her. The concept of someone else dictating her every move, of her being stuck in a house under lock and key being watched twenty-four hours a day, not being able to control anything in her life scared the shit out of her. Her heart was fluttering like a bird in a cage at the mere notion. She needed to shut this suggestion down right now. But they'd scoff at her claim she would be like an animal trapped in a zoo; they just wouldn't understand that autonomy over her life was how she managed to stay sane. So she needed a plan B.

"I'm not letting some asshole disrupt my life. Besides, I've already handed the photos over to the FBI. I shouldn't be a threat to him anymore, should I?" she said with more forcefulness than she felt. She was grasping at straws, but she had to start her argument somewhere.

"Perhaps not, but we require more time to figure this out," Jacob said in that most annoying know-it-all tone. "We need you in a secure place until we can be sure about a whole lot of things."

"No." Summer wasn't having this, so she took a different tack. "I have a world championship meet in two weeks, and I don't plan on missing it. And if I'm to do well at that meet, I need to continue my training schedule. Which I'm pretty sure I won't be able to do if I'm hidden away in a safe house for weeks on end. I don't think you understand how important this is to me." Yes, this was good, she decided; she could use this as her defense, and the theory gelled more decisively in her mind. She'd told them all about it just this morning. It should be fresh in everyone's minds, and hopefully she had put enough passion into her speech that they believed this was the only reason she was defying them.

Mårten stared at her as if she'd morphed into a brainless idiot. "You can't honestly tell me that some stupid triathlon event is more important than your own safety?" There was sheer exasperation in his voice now.

"I'm sure we can arrange something for you." Jacob jumped in. "A way for you to continue your training," he said with a smile that was supposed to be convincing. But she wasn't fooled.

It was Summer's turn to bang her hand on the table. This time she directed her anger at Jacob, her emotions in full flight now, and she rode that wave to drive home her point. "How? How are you going to arrange it? Does this safe house have a fully equipped gym? Are you going to let me out of this place long enough to swim laps at the local pool at five a.m.? Are your agents going to take me to a nearby running track, so I can do sprints, or follow me on my ten-mile runs?" She glared at him bitterly as he sat back in his chair, shrugging one shoulder ruefully.

"I'm not positive about all of that," he admitted with a wry twist to his lips. "But surely—"

"Surely nothing," Summer spat back. "I need to do all that and more to make sure I'm in peak condition for this trial." She knew they were all trying to help her, but she felt hemmed in, like a set of prison bars was closing in on her.

"You might just have to miss this stup—this meet," Mårten added.

Summer pursed her lips and narrowed her eyes at him. "What did you say? Were you about to call this a *stupid meet*?" Summer could barely credit her ears. He'd been about to denigrate one of the major passions in her life.

But then why would Mårten think anything else? He was a complete stranger, and there was no way he could understand how important this was to her. And now that she was on this train, she was starting to believe her own rhetoric. It was a good excuse not to go into witness protection, but everything she was saying was also true. Most people who didn't run triathlons could never understand the deep competitive urge driving her on. The personal challenge she set herself every time she ran, to do better, finish faster, get her technique just right so that each stroke in the swim leg was perfect and effortless. There was a sense of accomplishment like no other when she finished a race. Not many individuals could finish a full triathlon. It was an adrenaline high few other people knew. A part of her enjoyed being among that elite number.

She also hadn't told the complete truth when she explained to Mårten that she started triathlons to stay fit. This was something she'd barely admitted to herself, but six years ago she'd been looking for a means to rid herself of her demons. And running until she was so physically exhausted that she could scarcely suck in a breath, let alone think beyond taking the next step, had helped her push that terrible night when Marco had died into the recesses of her mind. When she was running, or swimming, or riding, she was no longer haunted by the harrowing images. Her senses drifted free, almost as if it were her own personal form of meditation. It was a way to give her memories a break. Slowly, the nightmares had receded, and she had begun to find her equilibrium again. She never wanted to stop running. Because if she did, a tiny part of her was afraid those nightmares would come back with a vengeance.

She let none of that show on her face, however, just allowed the anger to boil over. "What I do is not *stupid*," she spat, getting to her feet.

"I didn't mean it like that," he retorted, also standing so that now they were arguing nose-to-nose over the table. "Don't twist this around to suit your own truth. This is not about stopping you from doing what you love. This is about keeping you alive! How can you be so stubborn that you cannot see that?" Mårten's face was turning an interesting shade of red, and a part of Summer was intrigued as to why he seemed to care so much. But she wasn't about to let him win, and so she started talking over the top of him, until they were both shouting at each other like truculent children.

"Why don't you take her to Sweden with you?" Nikki said so quietly that Summer almost didn't catch her words. She turned to stare in Nikki's direction, letting her argument trail off. Mårten continued to count off on his fingers all the reasons she needed to listen to Jacob and himself, unaware of what Nikki had said.

"What are you suggesting?" Jacob asked, raising a curious eyebrow, as Mårten kept on blustering, talking over the top of him as well. But now all of Summer's attention was on Nikki, ignoring the annoying Swedish cop who was a major pain in her ass.

"I mean, think about it," Nikki continued, her voice remaining quiet.

At last, Mårten stopped speaking, one finger still poised in the air, a scowl darkening his features. "What did you say?" he growled.

"We can probably assume this Tyrone King person doesn't have a clue who Mårten is or where he's from. So, it's the perfect hiding place. You'll be out of the country, but you can continue to train as much as you like. It's summer in Sweden at the moment, and the weather should be ideal."

Was this woman mental? That was possibly a worse idea than going into witness protection? Summer opened her mouth to retort, wracking her mind for reasons she couldn't go. There was no chance she was going to spend the next two weeks in close quarters with Mårten. He was too... She was too... Nope, it just wouldn't work. Nikki thought she was helping Summer, giving her a way out, but little did she know she was pushing her right into the lion's den.

"What if Tyrone works it out? What if he follows me to Sweden? Then I'd be putting Mårten in direct danger as well," she countered with a defiant lift to her chin.

Mårten remained frozen, his finger still raised is if to make his next point, but his face became thoughtful, which worried Summer. He tilted his head to the side and considered her over his hovering hand.

"That could be an option," he said into the ensuing silence.

"What? No! I'm not going to Sweden. I'm staying right here, and I'm going to continue my life, and not let some asshole scare me off."

Mårten ignored her, turning to Jacob to say, "Do you want to run it past your superiors?"

"Don't you dare talk about me as if I'm not here. I refuse to go, and that's the end of it." How could this all have turned so quickly? She was losing control again. Spontaneity had never been her strong suit, and her body trembled at the thought of her life being governed by someone else. By Inspector Mårten Viskten, no less.

Summer pushed her chair so she could back away from the table; she'd been smart enough not to sit in the corner this time. She stormed down the hallway and slammed the door to her bedroom behind her. She would not continue this conversation. Not when all three of them were staring at her as if it was already a done deal. She was going to pack her things and get out of here. End of story.

Summer had few belongings with her, and so she'd almost finished stuffing clothes and toiletries into her backpack when there was a light tap on the bedroom door. "Summer, can I come in?" It was Nikki, and Summer's shoulders sagged. Blast that woman.

"Yes," Summer said begrudgingly; this was her house after

all, she couldn't very well keep her out. But it was also her fault she was in this mess. Summer didn't turn around as Nikki entered and closed the door behind her, then came to hover beside the bed.

"I'm sorry; I didn't realize I'd cause such a problem. Your training is so important to you, and this seemed like the obvious answer. I was only trying to help," she said, craning her neck to catch Summer's eye.

"I know you were. Thank you anyway," Summer conceded with a sigh, continuing to push things into her bag, not wanting to face the other woman. But how could she stay mad at Nikki? Of course, she'd only suggested it because her heart was in the right place; she couldn't have known what was going on in Summer's head. Especially when Summer wasn't even sure why she was so adamant she shouldn't go. All she knew was that spending two weeks in close proximity with Mårten would be dangerous. Dangerous to all her well-constructed rules and regulations. He was a threat to her self-control.

"So what's going on? Help me understand." Nikki opened her palms beseechingly. "What's the real reason you don't want to go? Is there something happening between you and Mårten? I know you seem to rub each other the wrong way? But do you hate him that much that you can't spend two weeks with him?"

Summer stopped packing, sat on the end of the bed and pouted. How could Nikki so quickly delve to the core of the matter? Summer liked to think she kept all her thoughts and feelings well hidden, but Nikki could see right through her. She couldn't very well tell Nikki it was because she liked Mårten too much that she couldn't go. How could she explain her jumbled feelings?

"I don't hate him," she replied finally. "It's just that..." Summer sighed, wondering how she could put this.

"Oh, I see," Nikki said with a sly grin. "You don't hate him. It's actually the complete opposite."

"No. I wouldn't go that far," Summer protested.

"When was the last time you dated?" Nikki asked, plonking herself on the bed next to Summer.

"What?" She'd only known Nikki for a few days, how could this woman already be so determined to ask her such intimate things?

"Well, if you don't hate him, then there's clearly a lot of conflicting emotions going on, and I wondered why you didn't have a boyfriend. I am right; you don't have a boyfriend, do you?"

"No, I don't." Summer sat up straighter, on the defense now. Why was that any of Nikki's concern? Who and when she went out with was her business alone.

"So, if you aren't seeing anyone right now, I was wondering when you last dated? You know, when did you last have sex?"

Summer turned to gape at Nikki. Has she just asked her how long it had been since she'd slept with another man?

"Just because you're not looking for a long-term relationship doesn't mean you can't have sex," Nikki continued.

"What?" The word came out kind of like a screech, as Summer's hands flew up in utter surprise. Summer had had this same conversation with Bianca on more than one occasion, but she barely knew Nikki, so how could she possibly expect her to confide in her? "I don't... I haven't," Summer stumbled over her words. Even if she could remember the last time she'd taken a man to her bed, she wasn't about to reveal that to Nikki.

"Because I think that is what you're afraid of. That you and Mårten might end up having sex," Nikki stated, giving a satisfied nod of her head. "Is that such a bad thing?"

Summer looked at Nikki, incredulous. Words failed her. Only Bianca would have been this forthright with Summer. Everyone else was afraid of hurting her feelings. Trent might not-so-subtly hint that Summer needed to find love, even suggesting he could set her up with someone nice, but he would always back down if she got angry enough. And Serena would often point out good-looking men when they were on a girl's night out, gently pushing Summer in their direction, but then she'd shake her head sadly when Summer would find some invisible flaw; a reason she couldn't talk to the man. All her friends understood innately that Summer had been scarred badly by love gone wrong, and so while they wanted her to experience love again, they didn't push too hard. Bianca was the only one who knew the true reason. She was also the only one who was blunt, telling her that everyone needed someone special, and that to live without intimacy was a form of basic survival, but not of true happiness.

"He obviously likes you. And you like him, even if you don't want to accept it. Aren't you tired of sleeping alone?" Nikki's words interrupted Summer's thoughts.

Surprisingly, the answer was yes. Yes, she was tired of sleeping alone. But she wasn't about to admit that. Because sex led to dating, and dating led to commitment, and commitment led to falling in love. And when she fell in love, it ended in tragedy. So there was no point in even trying. It was much safer to stay single. Then you wouldn't get hurt. Much easier to never let yourself get hurt in the first place.

Summer knew Bianca would tell her she couldn't change what'd happened in the past. Nothing would bring Marco back. And she would be right. But there was one thing Summer could do to protect her heart. And that was to be sure not to make the same mistake again.

But Nikki wasn't Bianca, and Summer didn't know how

she was going to convince her new friend—because that's what she was fast becoming, a friend—without revealing the truth. She let out a sigh containing all her frustration and confusion. Nikki covered Summer's hands with hers in a soothing gesture, and Summer was surprised to find she'd been rubbing the scar on her palm again; she'd been so agitated she hadn't even felt the pain.

"Okay," Nikki said. "I'm sorry. There's something going on here, and you're not prepared to let me in on the details, and I'm fine with that. I get it; we hardly know each other. I shouldn't have pried into your private life." Nikki gave a rueful smile. "Jacob is always telling me I have a tendency to butt in where I'm not wanted."

Summer felt a sudden jab of self-reproach. Nikki was only trying to help. "And I have a tendency to be a closed book," she replied.

"I shouldn't have shot off my mouth and told you to sleep with Mårten," Nikki continued apologetically. "I got a bit sidetracked on that point." She twisted her plump lips together in a childish pout. Nikki had amazing lips. She was just as pretty on the outside as she was on the inside, which made it almost impossible not to like her. "But that doesn't mean my idea was a bad one," Nikki continued. "I know Mårten. He's a man of honor. He's tough and dependable. And even though I'm sure he fancies you…" Nikki raised a hand as Summer went to open her mouth to protest. "He wouldn't touch you if you didn't want to be touched. And I know he will protect you, no matter what."

Summer hung her head, staring at her runners, considering Nikki's words.

"I'm also supposed to be a bridesmaid at my friend's wedding. The ceremony is three weeks away, just after I get back from the triathlon event. What am I going to tell Josie? There're all sorts of bridesmaidy things I'm expected to do for her before then," Summer added miserably. Summer had almost forgotten about Josie and Mark's wedding in all the ensuing chaos. But it was one more reason that leaving Seattle wasn't a good idea.

"Hmm, it's not ideal if you have to leave her in the lurch," Nikki acknowledged. "Is she the sort of person who'd understand that you've got mitigating circumstances? Or is she a Bridezilla who'll never speak to you again if you abandon her?"

Summer had to smile. "Josie is far from a Bridezilla. But her mother is another kettle of fish," she said with a chuckle. "No, you're right, Josie would be mortified if she found out I was being chased by a maniac and disregarded my safety just to be at her beck and call."

"So, she'd want you to go to Sweden too?" Nikki asked.

"Mmm hmm," Summer conceded with a nod of her head.

"And you'll be back in time to attend the wedding," Nikki persisted. "If it's after the triathlon, then they'll surely have all this sorted by then, and have this Tyrone fellow in custody." She scrutinized Summer with her sharp, blue gaze.

"I've never been to Sweden," Summer said with a sigh, knowing when she'd been beaten. "I've heard it's beautiful in the summer. And it would be a good place to train," she admitted.

"Does that mean you'll go?" Nikki's face was so eager, Summer had to give a rueful smile. "I guess, as long as Mårten is still okay with it. Anything has to be better than being cooped up in a safe house with a twenty-four-hour guard watching my every move."

"Oh, good." Nikki bounced off the bed, clapping her hands. "Let's tell Mårten, then."

"Hmm," Summer narrowed her eyes at the door. As far as she was concerned, this was the lesser of two evils. That was all.

CHAPTER ELEVEN

Mårten pushed open the front door of his house, suddenly self-conscious. While his cottage might still require some work on the outside, Mårten had always thought of it as quaint and traditional. But now, seeing it through Summer's eyes, he admitted it could more rightly be called in need of a good coat of paint. At least he'd just about finished the renovations on the inside.

He'd bought the hundred-year-old cottage on the outskirts of Luleå five years ago, charmed by the fact the owners had kept the wooden exterior painted in classic Swedish dark red, as well as the rambling forest surrounding the house on all sides giving him space and privacy. The cabin had been cheap because of its poor condition, but he'd been slowly doing it up ever since.

"Welcome to my home," he said a little awkwardly, unsure what she would think. He hadn't thought it through properly when he'd invited to stay. His place was a little cramped; big enough for him, but perhaps not big enough for the both of them.

"Oh, wow!" Summer exclaimed as she followed him into the mudroom. "This is…cuter than I expected."

By the tone of her voice, she sounded pleasantly surprised,

so he took *cute* as a compliment as he kicked off his shoes and indicated that she do the same. The mudroom led straight into the small kitchen cum living room. He'd knocked out one wall to make the place more open-plan and livable, and installed large sliding doors at the rear of the house to let in more light. A quick perusal told him that at least he'd left the house tidy. Which was a minor miracle, because who would've thought he'd return to Sweden with a beautiful but headstrong woman in tow.

"This is gorgeous," she breathed, doing a twirl so she could take everything in. A ridiculous little fizz of pride at her words echoed in his chest. But then, why shouldn't he be proud of how the kitchen had turned out, considering the state of the place when he'd first moved in? He'd ripped out the original kitchen cabinets, which were rotted and falling apart, and installed brand new cupboards himself, painting them a pale green to offset the natural timber countertops, adding in modern appliances and a large farmhouse sink. Then he'd taken his mother's advice when she'd come up to visit after he'd bought the house, and painted the wooden walls cream to make it feel bigger. At least his mother could see the potential of the cottage. Her visit had been bittersweet. She'd been a little sad that he'd settled up here so far away from Stockholm, but happy to see her youngest son putting down some roots at last.

"This will be your room," he said, leading her to a doorway off the main living area. The cottage comprised only two bedrooms. The guest bedroom was downstairs, while his master suite took up the whole attic space upstairs. "There's only one bathroom," he added almost apologetically, pointing to the door next to hers. Which meant they'd have to share, he thought with an uncharacteristic surge of heat. One more reason this was a bad idea. Sharing a bathroom with Summer might just try his self-restraint to the limit.

"I'll get our bags," he said, needing to get out into the fresh air, leaving her to take a better look around.

The Uber driver had helped him unload the bags, but they'd left them on the front porch while he'd led her inside to give her a tour. As well as her bag of clothes, Summer had also brought her bicycle in a specially designed bag; she took it with her to all her triathlon meets and was used to the logistics of traveling with it. He wasn't sure where that was going to go in his small house, but he guessed he was going to have to find a spot somewhere.

Mårten leaned against the porch railing and drew in a deep, cleansing breath. This was one thing he'd missed while he'd been in America; the pure sweetness of Swedish air in the summer. There was nothing else like it. The faint waft of the birch leaves as they were warmed by the sun, the untainted verdant smell of the tall, green grass, waving in the soft breeze. It evoked memories of summer holidays spent as a child, when his mother had brought them north, away from the city, to the visit the crystal clean lakes and forests, and he and his brother Eric, would spend hours splashing in the cold water and then dozing in the sun to get tanned on the small, rocky beaches.

A thump came from inside, pulling him out of his reverie, and reminding him of his guest. Had he done the right thing by bringing her here? The same question had rolled around in his head for the entire twelve-hour flight from Seattle to Stockholm. Not that he didn't have faith in the FBI—and Jacob—to protect her. But she was point-blank refusing to go into witness protection, and it seemed the only way he could ensure her safety at the time. But perhaps he should have pushed her harder to stay. Now that he'd analyzed his proposal to Summer, he was wondering if it was the stupidest thing he'd ever contemplated. Not for the reason that most people would assume—that he had now made himself a direct target for the eco-terrorist, Tyrone. No, it was way worse than that. Now he was going to have to endure the next two weeks of her sleeping in his house.

He'd already proved that he couldn't resist her when he'd given in to temptation and allowed himself the luxury of that kiss on the bed in Seattle. Afterward, he'd decided the only tactic to stop it from happening again was to put space between him and her. And then what had he gone and done? Invited her back to his house on the pretext of keeping an eye on her. Where they would share the same bathroom, eat their breakfast at the same kitchen island, drink coffee on the same couch in the small living room. He'd have to watch her comb out her long, silky hair in the mornings, and she'd most likely wear those tight little shorts, especially if she was going running. And that brief tank top that revealed her bare, toned midriff. It would be sheer torture.

He groaned and pushed his forehead hard against the wooden post, relishing the pain as the rough texture bit into his skin. He was an idiot.

But he was also a grown man, and he would find a way to fight this attraction, no matter if it killed him. She trusted him to keep safe, and that was what he planned to do. He would not think about her sleeping only meters away from him, or about how much he might want to crawl into bed with her, and kiss those soft lips again, just to make sure he hadn't dreamed that fiery animal magnetism from their first time. He hadn't imagined the way she'd responded, however, as if she'd come alive at his touch and wanted to devour him. The mere memory of it was doing weird things to his insides. And his dick.

"Are you coming back inside?" The sound of her voice made him jump.

"Yep, yep," he replied, swiveling on his heel and quickly bending to pick up a bag in each hand, swinging his duffel in front of his body, ostensibly so he could fit through the door, but in reality hoping to hide his straining erection. Jesus Christ, he couldn't even go five minutes with her in his house without getting turned on. How was he ever going to get through two whole weeks? "I'll bring your bike in later," he told her.

"The guest room is lovely," she gushed, as he carried her bag—she must pack light, because it was smaller than his, which surprised him, most women always took more than they needed—and laid it on the luggage rack next to the compact wardrobe in the corner. There had only been space to fit a king-single bed along one wall, and a small reading chair, with the cupboard occupying the rest of the room.

Ebba had helped him pick out the color scheme, with more cream paint, a simple white duvet and pillowslips, accented with a taupe throw-rug and cushions. A jute mat covered the wooden floorboards, with a few pretty Swedish landscapes hung on the walls.

Ebba had a knack for interior decorating—like most women did, he assumed. It was just a pity she also had a knack for subtle manipulation. Thank God he'd found out before it was too late that Ebba had been so desperate to get pregnant, she'd gone off the contraceptive pill without telling him eight months after they first started dating. Mårten would've been trapped like a rabbit in a snare. He would have married Ebba if she'd announced she was going to have his baby, and she knew it. But that was no way for a marriage to start; Mårten would've resented her forever. He'd been wary of relationships after that, only having two very short, but unsatisfying encounters with women he'd met on a dating app. For the past six months, he'd been celibate, but if he was truthful with himself, he hadn't missed having a woman by his side. Had he missed the sex? Yes, definitely. But companionship, not so much. Mårten enjoyed the bachelor lifestyle and had no real urge to change.

Which was one more reason to stay well away from Summer. Not only was he sexually attracted to her, which was raising all kinds of red flags, but he also found her mind appealing in ways no other woman had done. He was already invested in her story; who wouldn't be after finding out that a simple break and enter had morphed into something much more sinister and now she was the target of an eco-terrorist? The protector within him was desperate to keep her safe, but another part of him was also desperate to delve deeper into that dark well of emotions simmering just below the surface. There was a sad past there; he could tell.

Which was no business of his, he reminded himself, shaking his head to clear it of the lame thoughts.

"Thank you," he replied, squeezing past her to get through the doorway. "Just let me know if there's anything you need. I'm going to make a coffee and some toast. Are you hungry?" There wasn't a lot of food in the house; he'd left it pretty much empty when he'd gone on holiday, and he'd need to make a trip to the local supermarket this afternoon if they were going to eat anything decent for dinner.

"Yes, please, that would be lovely." He'd noticed that Summer had eaten nothing on the flight, and while he didn't blame her—airline food could be abominable—she must be starving by now. While it was mid-afternoon here, it was still only early morning back in Seattle, so his stomach was confused, not knowing what it wanted to eat. He guessed she was probably the same.

She settled on a stool on the far side of the kitchen island and watched as he busied himself taking bread out of the freezer and popping four slices into the toaster. Then he turned on the coffee machine, filling it with water and ground beans. All the while, her eyes followed his every move. It was a little disquieting, but also…homely somehow.

"Does your family live close by?" Her question surprised him.

"Not really. My mother, Nora, lives in Stockholm, as do my brother, Eric, and his family," he replied, placing the butter and jam on the island bench. "It's only a seven-hour train ride to see them, or a couple of hours on a plane."

"So, you moved away when you became a cop?"

"Yeah, I did my training in Umeå, a town a few hours drive south of here. I was offered a position here as a newly minted cop, and I guess I stayed."

"What about your father? You didn't mention him."

"He died just before I was born. Crashed his car into a frozen lake in Norway. That's one reason my mother moved us to Sweden." Not that Mårten didn't like to talk about his dad; it was just that he had no memories of him, so there was nothing to talk about. Eric had been two when their father, Anders, had died, and even he admitted he couldn't remember him. It was only through photos and Nora's stories of how she'd fallen in love at first sight with the American architect that Mårten knew him at all.

"Oh, I'm sorry." Summer's face crumpled. "That must be hard."

"Not really. I grew up in a family with a single mother— she never remarried or even dated until we were old enough to move out—and so I knew nothing different." Which was all true. The part he didn't tell most people was that money was always tight. His mother had moved them to Stockholm to take her dream job at a holistic healing clinic, but the salary was barely enough to get them through. Even though both he and Eric got jobs as soon as they were old enough, it was still a struggle. Now, however, both he and Eric earned good wages, and his mother had taken the plunge after they'd left home and started her own holistic healing business, which was doing well.

"I guess." Summer shrugged delicately, and his eyes were drawn to the smooth roundness of her shoulders, bare beneath her dark blue tank. She'd traveled in an oversized hoodie and leggings on the plane, but as soon as they'd stepped out into the Swedish sunshine, she'd removed the sweater with a sigh of delight and he hadn't been able to look away from how the tight tank and leggings hugged her curves, showing off her sculpted body.

Quick, think of something else. He was about to open mouth to inquire about her family when she changed the subject, asking, "What is this?" She picked up the jar and tipped it so she could examine the orange contents more closely.

"It's cloudberry jam. This one is homemade." He didn't hide his grin of delight. "It's a northern delicacy. The cloudberries grow wild in the forest. Only the locals know where they grow, and their picking spots are kept a tightly held secret, often passed down within the family. If you're very lucky, someone will share a jar or two with you when they make a batch."

"Do you have your own clandestine cache?" she asked, tipping her head to the side coyly.

"This was a present," he admitted. "I help one of the elderly residents down the road sometimes. Chop her wood, shovel her driveway in the winter, that kind of thing."

"And she repays you with jam." Summer's sardonic smile turned thoughtful. "That's nice of you. I like that idea. A community doing things for each other. It's good."

Mårten shrugged. That was just how it was here; Summer was a city girl, not used to the way people took care of each other in small towns. When he looked up from where he'd been placing clean plates on the countertop, he found her dark eyes riveted on him, her chin resting in her palm.

"The hardened cop has a softer side," she said, almost to

herself.

"What?"

"Never mind." She waved a hand in front of her face. "Hurry up, I'm desperate to try this jam."

Right at that moment, the toaster popped, and he juggled two pieces onto her plate, then did the same to his. He came around, took the stool next to hers and watched her sideways as she slathered butter and then cloudberry jam on her toast. She took an enormous bite, and he couldn't help himself, he had to turn and observe her expressive face as she tasted one of his favorite things in the whole wide world. First, she closed her eyes, long dark lashes laying on her tawny cheeks. Then she pursed her lips, but continued to chew slowly, rolling the food around in her mouth. At last she swallowed, the tip of her tongue coming out to lick the crumbs off her lips, and her eyes flew open as a broad smile spread across her face.

He was so fixated on her tongue as it disappeared, leaving her plump lips succulent and pink, that he almost forgot to breathe, catching himself just-in-time to force his gaze upward to meet hers. God almighty, that'd been about the sexiest thing he'd ever seen.

"It's delicious," she declared.

"I'm glad you like it," he replied, hoping she couldn't hear the slight hoarseness in his voice.

She went back to eating as he buttered his toast, shifting uncomfortably on the stool to ease the bulge in his pants. This was the second time in half an hour he'd reacted to her presence. It was as if he was hyper-aware of her, and every little thing she did turned him on.

He needed to get laid; it'd been too long. Just not with Summer. Right now, give him ten minutes alone in the bedroom and he'd have himself sorted. He should have thought of that earlier, while they'd been back in Seattle, even. Maybe he wouldn't be so focused on her every move then.

He returned to the topic of her family, just to give himself something to take his mind off his edginess. "Jacob texted earlier and confirmed they now have an agent watching each of your family's houses." That'd been part of the deal. Summer had been worried that if Tyrone knew who she was, he might target her family to get back at her. In a private conversation, Jacob had admitted to Mårten he thought the risk was low, but his boss had agreed to give the family protection, at least for the next few days. Summer could have peace of mind on that count.

"Mmm, thank you," she mumbled through a piece of toast. "I got a message from Jasmine earlier telling me she felt like she was living in a spy novel, because there is now a dark sedan parked the other side of the road to her house, and a sinister-looking man who follows her everywhere," she went on, swallowing her mouthful. "I hate scaring her and the rest of my family. And I hate not being able to tell them what's really going on." She screwed up her pretty nose in disgust. "Surely, this is all a storm in a teacup. I've handed over the photos; it's too late, the FBI know everything. What more can he want from me now?" Summer grimaced, her lustrous mouth turning down at the corners. "Anyway, I texted Jasmine back it wouldn't be for long, and I'll explain the whole situation soon."

He had to disagree. Tyrone didn't necessarily know she'd found the incriminating photo, let alone given it to the cops. And even if he did, his violence seemed to be escalating alarmingly. He may want her dead as retribution. Which was why her family was being guarded. Tyrone was a wild card; no one could predict what he'd do next.

"You told me your family was from Mexico, and they moved to live in San Jose?" He'd heard the bare basics of her background, that she had three sisters all of who still lived in San Jose to be near their parents, but he'd like to know more.

"Yes," she replied, then gave her last piece of toast a longing look before she replaced it on her plate so she could keep talking. "My dad is very smart. He landed a job in Silicon Valley, and he moved the family from Mexico to San Jose before I was born. We're among the lucky ones. My sisters and I are so fortunate to have great lives here, free and financially secure in this country. My dad gave us that opportunity, and we're all terribly grateful to him. But we left others behind. Both my parent's families still live in Chilpancingo, and things are not good there. Lots of drug cartels, gang violence, corruption, that kind of thing," she explained. "My dad has been trying to get his brother and wife and two kids into America for as long as I can remember, but without luck." There was definite sadness in her voice.

"Oh, I didn't know."

"It's okay. Few people who live outside Mexico do." She shrugged one shoulder nonchalantly, but he could tell she was trying to make less of the situation. It seemed like a heavy burden the family had to shoulder; they were the lucky ones who made it, but in doing so they'd left loved ones behind. He guessed it was the same story all over the world for refugees and immigrants alike. Everyone wanted a better life, but at what cost?

"And so what made you move to Seattle?"

"Oh, ah, I always wanted to study photography." Summer's gaze slid to the window above the sink, and he wondered why his question had made her uncomfortable.

"Don't they have good universities in California?" He knew of Stanford and Berkley, some of the best institutes in America, just to name a few. They ran photography courses there, didn't they?

"Oh, yes, sure. But Seattle University offers small class

sizes and great mentorship programs," she said, dipping her head to give her toast another longing glance but not offering any more information.

"Hmm." Seattle was a long way from San Jose. The rest of her family seemed close-knit. She'd just admitted that she and her sisters owed a lot to her father, and all the rest of them had stayed. So why had she been the only one to leave? Had she been running away from something? Maybe there was some kind of rift between her and her parents. Or was it something else?

Mårten had also moved away from his family to take up a new career, so she wasn't alone in her decision. But he was good at reading people, and he'd picked up that Summer had some trauma that she was hiding from her past. She'd left her family behind. But what about a boyfriend? Had she left him behind as well? Or was there no one special to keep her in San Jose? She'd been very clear that she had no current lover. She was a gorgeous woman, so men should be clamoring to ask her out. Did she just choose not to date? Or was she scared of commitment, a little like him?

"And you never wanted to move back, even after you finished your degree?" He continued to probe.

"I thought about it," she confessed. "I mean, I miss my family, and I'll definitely visit as soon as all this is over. My mom would never forgive me if I didn't go and explain to her face-to-face why I brought the family into danger." Summer pursed her lips into an anxious moue, but her face soon morphed to become wistful. "Lily is getting married next year, so I'll go home for that, of course. And Jasmine, my eldest sister, is pregnant with her second baby. My mom is always nagging me about how much I'm missing out, asking why I chose to live in that cold, miserable city so far away and on my own. And maybe I am. Maybe I am missing out." She turned to face him, and for a split second, he could see real, raw emotions etched onto her face, until she blinked and the look was gone.

"Mom thinks that the only route to being truly happy is to get married, settle down and have kids." She gave a soft, derisive snort. "But that's just not in my future, so it's easier to stay away, then I don't have to listen to the nagging." Summer lifted her chin. "I'm happy living alone; it's easier that way."

He wondered at her use of the word *alone*. When he'd first met her, she had seemed terribly lonely. She'd just suffered a major trauma and admitted she had friends, but hadn't wanted to bother any of them, like she didn't think she was important in their lives. She preferred to sort out her own problems. Summer was a strong lady, but she was also a bit of a control freak. And she didn't like to cede that control to anyone—he'd found that out the hard way when she'd stubbornly refused his help on the night of the break in— almost as if she let go of the reins for even a second, something bad was going to happen. If she truly wanted to remain alone, then he found that a little sad. A woman like her had a lot to offer.

But then who was he to talk? He'd just admitted he was happy being a bachelor, at least for the near future. He hadn't given the distant future much thought. Marriage and kids were words that meant little to him right now. His mother would say it was just because he hadn't met the right woman yet. But to never get married. Never have kids. That felt…like it might be a big mistake, like he might regret the choice later on. But it seemed Summer had made that intentional decision and was sticking to it.

He'd been so engrossed in their conversation, he wasn't aware they were now sitting facing each other on their stools, knees touching. She was rubbing her thumb across her palm again in that habitual little movement, and in an instinctive action, Mårten reached over and grabbed her hand.

"Why do you do that?" he asked, turning her hand in his so that her palm faced upward.

Summer blinked up at him as if frozen by his touch.

For one heartbeat.

Then two.

Then she snatched her hand back, but not before he saw the old scar running the diagonal length of her palm.

"It's just a bad habit," she said, not meeting his gaze.

"That's a nasty scar," he said gently. There could be lots of reasons she had an old scar on her hand. But his experience on the force made the worst kinds of scenarios circle in his head. Domestic violence was rampant everywhere. It looked like a defensive wound. Had a lover attacked her? Or a family member perhaps? Was that why she'd moved away?

Whatever the reason, it could be a clue as to why Summer was so determined to remain alone.

"Summer?" He reached out and tilted her chin until she was looking at him, and it was only then he realized he was leaning in close, his body angled toward her as he searched her face. Her caramel skin had paled, her dark eyes widening at his touch. His eyes drifted to her lips without his consent.

Oh God, he wanted to kiss her. Again. Wanted to gather her into his chest and comfort her. Wrap his arms around her, draw her mouth to his and use his body to shield her as well as console. She was a lost soul in need of rescuing. But this feeling was more than wanting to rescue her soul. His body was singing with desire. Nothing good would come of his kissing this woman. It wasn't a smart move. There was nothing simple or easy about Summer, and so he shouldn't start something he couldn't finish. But he was so painfully aware of her, it was as if she had invaded every brain cell, every muscle and bone in his body. Unconsciously, he leaned further forward.

She was the one to break the spell when she got off her stool and practically ran to her bedroom, shutting the door behind her.

Fuck. He was a complete idiot.

CHAPTER TWELVE

Summer swished her hand through the tall grass as she followed Mårten down the small trail between the houses, enjoying the tickle on her palm. It was already after seven at night, but the sun still had no intention of setting. The soft evening light gave the surrounding birch trees an ethereal look, and Summer breathed in deep. It was hard to imagine this stunning place meters deep in snow for six months of the year, as Mårten had described. It was warm enough to wear shorts and a tank top, and Summer relished the heat on her skin.

Nikki had been right; summer in Sweden was beautiful. The season was her namesake; her mother had thought it so American to name her first child born in the country in June with a modern, trendy name. Sometimes Summer wished for a normal name like her two older sisters. Jasmine and Lily had both fared well because they'd been born in Mexico. Herself and younger sister, Riviera—who was named after a Country Club in LA because her father had been asked to play a round of golf there by one of the company's rich clients, and never stopped talking about it since—had been products of their new life in America.

"Here we are," Mårten called over his shoulder as they

emerged from the forest trail onto a road. They were on their way to the neighborhood supermarket to stock up on food. Mårten had promised to cook her some of the local salmon, freshly caught in a nearby stream and sold at this little gourmet shop within walking distance from his cottage.

Summer had hoped to do a run this afternoon, just a short one to stretch her legs and shake the hours of travel from her bones. But then Mårten had made her some toast, and they got talking. The subjects had been touchy ones, and she'd opened up to him more than she wanted. The conversation had left her a tad mortified that she'd revealed more than she intended, as well as a little depressed, and confused as to why telling Mårten that she was going to remain single felt like some kind of failure. He hadn't condemned her. Well, not in so many words. But she was sure she saw pity flicker through those ice-blue eyes, and that made her mad. Not so much mad at him, but mad at herself. None of these feelings were conducive to running. Even though she was here to train, and she rarely, if ever, let her emotions rule how she trained, she'd decided that sometimes you had to listen to your body.

And then there was the other elephant in the room. She'd been sure he was about to kiss her. How dare he try that again after his callous rejection last time? And how dare her traitorous body want him too. She'd been overcome with humiliation, and this time it was she who'd done the running away. Spending the next hour lying on her cute bed in her even cuter bedroom, staring at the ceiling, mulling over her life choices. Nikki's comment that *'she should just sleep with Mårten, and what was the problem with having sex for sex's sake?'* kept playing over and over in her head. Until Mårten had suggested a walk to get something to eat and she grudgingly agreed.

She had reached no conclusion as to how she was going to

handle living in close quarters with him for the next two weeks. But being outside in the gentle air with tiny songbirds flittering from tree to tree above her had lightened her mood immensely, and now she was feeling almost like herself again. Maybe this trip might be good for her. Get her out of her normal routine; out of her rut. If the truth be known, a tiny part of her that she barely acknowledged had been considering giving up on triathlons. Sometimes it all seemed a little pointless. Why was she killing herself just to win a race, then returning home to start training anew? It was like each win wasn't enough anymore. At times she thought the only reason she ran, and swam, and bicycled was to keep those damn nightmares at bay. But she would not think about Marco today, not with all this soothing nature around her.

Red-painted wooden cottages, much like Mårten's, lined the road, along with a couple of pale yellow and pale green ones scattered amongst the trees. Summer almost laughed. How many times had she seen these little historical places in tourist brochures or glossy magazines and thought they were quaint but not where people still lived. Now that she was here, however, she could see they really existed, that the Swedes took their traditions seriously and most folks out here would rather maintain a hundred-year-old building than knock it down and build a modern monstrosity.

Mårten stopped outside a small doorway at the beginning of a row of shops. The window was full of mouthwatering treats, from fresh fruit and vegetables to jars of pickled fish, boxes of crackers, jellies and pâtés, dried salamis and tubes of what looked like cheese spread. Weird, but wonderful.

"I'll get the salmon and salad ingredients." Mårten handed her a small shopping basket. "Why don't you take a look around, see if anything else takes your fancy?" She watched as he headed straight to the fresh food section, trying hard not to notice those muscular thighs bend and flex beneath the hem of his shorts as he walked. Forcing herself to pivot, she wandered the other way, perusing the shelves, gawping at all the strange items, mostly in Swedish so she couldn't decipher them. There was a deli counter that not only sold cold meat cuts—most of which she'd never heard of before—and so many cheeses she lost count, but also a selection of pre-cooked meals. There was fish stew with aioli, beef bourguignon with mashed potatoes, shrimp salad, and the famous meatballs with gravy and red sauce. Her mouth began to water and her stomach rumbled, reminding her she'd only eaten two pieces of toast today.

By the time she made it back to the checkout where Mårten stood waiting, her basket was nearly full. "Wow, you must be hungry," he said, his eyes lighting up at the sight of her. Nope, it wasn't her he was smiling at, it was the sight of all that yummy food, she told herself.

"I thought I'd try a few of your delicacies," she quipped, even though she had no idea what most of the food in her basket was.

"Hmm. I'd go easy on the salted cod roe paste if I were you." He picked up the blue tube that Summer had grabbed from the shelf because it looked interesting. "It's a bit of an acquired taste."

"I know that," she said, grabbing the tube back, even though she didn't. And though she wasn't a huge fan of salted fish or caviar, she was determined to broaden her horizons, and she was damn well going to try every single thing in her basket, just to show him.

Mårten insisted on paying for everything, much to her chagrin. She was a single, independent woman, she didn't need a man buying her food. But she didn't want to cause a scene at the checkout either.

They exited the shop, laden down with paper bags, and Summer was trying to work out a nice way to tell Mårten that she would pay for our own food in future, when his phone rang. He juggled the bags, trying to pry his cell from his back pocket, until Summer took half his load so that he had a hand free. They continued to meander as Mårten talked, Summer pretending she wasn't listening. It sounded like he was talking to Jacob, and a half-frown descended his brow the longer he talked.

"That was Jacob," he said, taking back his shopping bags after he ended the call.

"Yes, and?" She glanced up and squinted at Mårten through the setting sun's rays, watching as his stubble-clad jaw worked as if he was trying to decide how much to tell her. The golden light set off the planes of his face, highlighting his long, straight nose and sensitive mouth. Why did he have to be so blasted good-looking? It was distracting. She forced her gaze onto the gravel road so she could concentrate on what he was saying.

"As you know, along with throwing everything they have at trying to find Tyrone King, Jacob and Miller's team have also been searching for clues to Paige's disappearance," Mårten began.

"Yes." Summer tried to keep the impatience out of her tone.

"Well, they've discovered something a little unsettling about Paige." He cast her a quick glance, then returned his gaze to the front as they continued to stroll toward the house. "Her phone and handbag are still missing—we assume they were taken along with her—but the fiancé handed over her private computer to the feds. And while they found her work and personal email accounts, they also found a third email account that the fiancé knew nothing about. It contained some interesting emails that the IT specialists are still going through."

Summer stopped walking. Where was he going with this?

Mårten stopped too, and she glanced up into his face. "It looks like she may have been opposed to the gold mine at Yellowstone going ahead. Like genuinely opposed to it. She was mad. Mad enough to say some outrageous things."

Summer turned this information over in her head. "So what?" She squinted up at him. "Surely that's not such a revelation. She's a ranger who cares about the land she's supposed to be protecting. Of course, she's not happy about the mine."

Mårten's frown told her he remained unconvinced. What was he hinting at? Were the FBI trying to suggest a correlation between Paige and the terrorist organization?

"Was Tyrone mentioned in any of the emails? Or his little EIC group?" she demanded.

"No."

"So what are you saying? Who was she sending these emails to?"

"We're not sure yet. They were encrypted."

Summer blew out a breath and juggled the bags to her other hand. What did that even mean, they were encrypted? There had to be some logical explanation. But until the FBI found that explanation, she needed to nip this conspiracy theory—because it seemed that was what Martin was alluding to—in the bud.

"You can't possibly consider that Paige had anything to do with Tyrone King. Paige didn't just disappear of her own accord. She would never be that cruel. Not to her partner, or to her work colleagues. She loves her job. Love's what she does. She knows she's making a difference by helping to save the national parks."

"I agree; you're probably right," Mårten replied, walking forward once more. "But Jacob sounded pretty...convinced there was something else going on," he added with a shrug. She slotted in beside him, matching her step with his. Then he halted again, put his bags on the ground and drew in a breath, waiting till she stopped as well and looked up at him. "But you need to know, Summer, that it's not unheard of for someone as passionate as Paige to get frustrated and feel like no one is listening, like no one was doing enough." He spoke softly, not wanting to upset her, but it was too late; she was more than upset. He was acting as if she were some naïve fool who thought everyone was beyond reproach. She was far from naïve, but she knew deep in her bones Paige wouldn't do something as morally reprehensible as reaching out to EIC —or any eco-terrorist group—to make her point.

She was careful to keep her temper under control; Mårten was only repeating what he'd heard, and she shouldn't shoot the messenger. But he needed to understand she wasn't having any of it. "So, you think she took things into her own hands? Joined a Neo-Nazi violent group instead? No, nope," Summer stated emphatically. "I don't believe it."

"Okay." He picked up his bags and continued walking, apparently not wanting to take this conversation any further. Which was fine with her.

Summer followed meditatively in Mårten's wake, trying to make sense of this new information. In some ways, Summer also sympathized with Tyrone and his cronies; she was just as desperate for the slated gold mine at Yellowstone Park not to go ahead. As was Paige; she and the ranger had discussed the possible consequences at length while on the trip. Summer was an environmentalist at heart; it was the main reason she'd accepted the Yellowstone job, as well as most of her other projects. So she could help save an endangered species. It made her wonder how anyone could want to ruin something of such pristine natural value. It was pure, despicable greed, nothing less. But she couldn't sympathize with Tyrone's methods. Fear and violence weren't the solution to the problem. And the poor little boy dying because of a fire Tyrone had started was utterly reprehensible. How could that group live with themselves now?

A thought struck her. "But my family are all still safe?" she asked, hurrying to catch him up.

"Yes, of course," Mårten said. "Jacob confirmed it again."

"Oh, good." She returned to her rumination with relief, but still had reached no conclusion by the time they made it back to the house. She helped Mårten put away the food robotically. Deciding to drop the subject for now, she leaned on the island bench to watch him. "Can I help with dinner?" she asked as he put the salmon on a plate and heated a skillet on the stove.

"You could chop the dill, if you like. I'm going to make a quick sauce to go with the fish."

"Cool." Summer found a knife and a wooden board. She enjoyed cooking, but living alone, she often ate simply, and couldn't be bothered fixing a complicated meal just for herself.

"I've ordered a bike rack for you, like the one you had at home, so you can train inside. It should be delivered tomorrow."

"Oh, thank you." She was taken aback; she needed to train, but was wary of riding on these unfamiliar roads after Mårten had told her it rained a lot in summer. But she hadn't mentioned her fears to him; he was already doing enough. Being able to exercise inside whenever she wanted would be a luxury. This was very sweet of him. Although where she was going to set up her bike in this small cottage was a bit of a puzzle.

They settled into a comfortable silence while she chopped herbs and he got the fish sizzling. Without being asked, she started on the salad ingredients, chopping fire-engine red tomatoes, and slicing juicy green cucumbers. She felt more relaxed than she had in days. It was almost intimate, and

Summer found herself enjoying Mårten's silent company. Enjoying his gorgeous country-style kitchen, with its pale colors and glowing wooden countertops. He passed her the red onion to chop and gave an approving nod at the salad bowl that was filling with vegetables. It was effortless. Much too effortless. But for once, Summer didn't question it.

They took their meals out onto the front porch, sitting at the little wicker table and chairs and watching the birds coming in to roost as they ate. Her heart did a little double-kick at the beauty and the serenity. Blast. It would be so easy to fall in love with Mårten's house. With this lifestyle.

* * *

"I'm just heading out for a ride," Summer called up the stairs. It was only six a.m., but she'd been awake for hours, her body-clock struggling to come to terms with the time difference. Mid-summer this far north in Sweden meant the sun never really went down; it just skimmed beneath the horizon, and so it was already light.

"Wait," she heard a sleepy voice call down from Mårten's attic bedroom. Two seconds later, he appeared at the top of the stairs, wearing only sweatpants, his hair all tousled, and… Oh… My… Mårten was spectacular shirtless. Better than she had imagined.

"I'll come with you."

"No… No, you won't," she stuttered, trying and failing to avert her gaze. Holy hell, she needed to get out of here now before her gaze drifted back and got stuck on those ridged abs, those solid pectoral muscles.

Quick, think. Mårten had an old mountain bike he kept in a small shed at the back. It seemed most Swedish people owned at least one bike.

"There's no way you'll keep up with me on that… thing." She pointed vaguely in the direction of the shed. "And I'm not waiting for you."

Mårten descended the stairs, running a hand through his hair and looking perturbed. And very, very sexy. "But…" he started.

"No." She held up her hand to ward off any more complaints, taking a step backward to keep the distance between them. "I'm here to train. You agreed I should be safe here, that no one knows where I am. So leave me to do my thing, please. I don't need a babysitter. Anyway, don't you have a job to go to?"

"Yes," he admitted, but the tiny frown lines between his eyebrows told her he wasn't happy with the situation. "How about we compromise? Will you let me put a tracking app on your phone? That way if anything goes wrong at least I'll know where you are."

Summer considered him for many long moments. It did kind of make sense. She was in a foreign country, and even with Google Maps, she could possibly get lost. Or get a flat tire. And if that would keep him happy, and get her out of the house quicker, she'd concede, just this once.

"Okay," she agreed, handing over her phone, trying not to let her fingers skim over his. But her move backfired spectacularly, and instead of not touching him, their hands collided, fumbling together, and she almost dropped her phone. The shot of energy that fizzed up her arm from his touch sent shockwaves through the rest of her body, and she gave a squeak of surprise.

Mårten's sleepy gaze sharpened, his ice-blue irises becoming intense, almost molten. It seemed as if he'd felt it too; his eyes raked up and down her body, cataloguing every dip and curve. A tingle started low in her belly at his perusal, spreading quickly, so she felt as if she were melting inside. She resisted the urge to cross her arms over her breasts, instead returning his probing gaze with what she hoped was a cool one of her own. Why would he look at her like that after he'd rejected her so bluntly? It made little sense.

"You should be careful going out like that. You'll have every guy in every car driving past crashing into the nearest tree," he said finally.

"Huh?" Summer didn't understand. Had he just paid her a compliment?

"All I'm saying is that you look very…distracting in that outfit."

It was just lycra; a one-piece suit that helped streamline her body. Summer wore it every time she rode and never thought twice about it.

"Um…" She wasn't sure how to respond and stood mutely while Mårten lowered his gaze to tap away at her phone. It was all so blasted confusing. She waited, trying not to inspect the way the muscles in his strong shoulders sloped upward where they joined his neck. Or the way each muscle in the top of his arms was clearly defined, as if he'd been carved from marble. A glowing, tanned, alive sort of marble. God, did he do like two-hundred push-ups every day to look like that?

"Here you go." He said at last, regaining some of his professional cop tone. "I can see you wherever you are now. You can also see me." He stepped in closer and bent his head over her phone to show her how it worked. "If you tap here…" Her eyes followed his finger on the screen, but her mind was somewhere else completely.

Oh, blast. He smelled so good. Musky and manly, with a hint of the aftershave he must've used yesterday still lingering on his skin. Summer tried not to breathe.

"Thanks, got it," she said, snatching the phone from his hand. She'd already assembled her bike and left it on the front porch. Now she practically ran with it down the front steps, vaulted on, still strapping on her helmet, and took off in a random direction. She hadn't even programmed a route into her phone. All she knew was that she needed to get out of there.

"Text me when you get home," Mårten called out, but she was already bumping her way down the gravel driveway.

Mårten had warned her that the roads would be in bad condition here in Karlsvik; it was a small outer suburb of Luleå where the locals had a fondness for the country feel and the council had little money to spend, so it remained rustic and a tad run-down. She needed to concentrate on navigating the potholes and gravel, and at one stage let out a growl of frustration when she nearly tipped over sideways trying to ride around a fallen branch.

At last she stopped on the roadside and pulled out her phone. Mårten had mentioned a few routes that'd give her the distance she needed along some more well-maintained roads. Swedish drivers were extremely bicycle aware, unlike most ignorant, inattentive, and downright rude American drivers, so she should be safe on most of the roads here.

But instead of studying the map on her phone, she stared off into the middle distance, her thoughts turned inwards.

Matin's throwaway comment, insinuating that she looked hot in her riding gear, had made her feel sexy for the first time in forever. Yes, she knew other men looked at her, and a detached part of her understood they liked what they saw. But their glances and whistles had been like water off a duck's back; she hadn't taken any of them seriously.

When was the last time she'd thought of herself as a desirable woman? She honestly couldn't remember. What she could remember, however, was just how firm and touchable Mårten's abs had looked this morning. It made her squirm even thinking about running her fingers over his skin. What would his reaction be if she worked up the courage to go through with her fantasy? If she touched him? Would his eyes go molten again? Would he step up and tug her into his arms, hold her against that rippling chest and stare deep into her eyes? Then her stupid mind went even further, wondering what he'd look like naked.

Summer shook her head. Blasted Nikki, she wished that woman had never planted the idea of her and Mårten together. But now, the idea of sex with him wouldn't leave her head. She could think of nothing else. Not even Jacob's revelation about Paige's encrypted emails could distract her this morning.

"Blast!" Summer flung her leg over her bicycle seat and took off as if the hounds of hell were after her. If riding until she was so exhausted could help rid her of her nightmares, then surely it would help banish these crazy longings as well.

CHAPTER THIRTEEN

The water was a touch too warm for Summer's liking. She'd only done twenty laps, with another twenty yet to swim, and she already felt like she was going to overheat. Still, this indoor pool was her only option; it was the sole one within riding distance of Mårten's house. At least it was sparkling clean, and there was a gym right next door where she would lift some weights after her laps.

She reached the end of the pool, somersaulted into a turn, and kicked off to start another lap. She was in the rhythm now, in her groove, and she quite enjoyed the weightless feeling of gliding through the soft, clear water, her arms slicing like knives through butter, her legs kicking strongly, her breathing regular and smooth. Stroke, stroke, breathe. Stroke, stroke, breathe. It was akin to meditation. But it was doing little to rid her of all these insidious thoughts of Mårten.

She'd been in Sweden for six days now, and she felt like she might be going insane.

They'd settled into a sort of routine, an almost domestic, homey routine. He was easy to live with; she'd give him that much. Apart from the grilling he gave her as to where she'd been and what she'd been up to all day when he came home from work—as if he were some kind of cop or something—Mårten was laid-back about most things. He was a skilled cook, coming up with nutritious and tasty dishes most nights. She always helped him in the kitchen; she hated anybody waiting upon her. And she was a pretty good cook herself.

When he asked what she wanted to eat, she'd requested healthy, high-protein meals, with lots of vegetables, and he'd come through every night. She'd need to start carb-loading three to four days before the race, but right now she was enjoying all the fresh, tasty ingredients, often stopping off at the little gourmet grocer to pick up a few things after a ride.

But it was more than just the cooking. Mårten also kept his house tidy. She couldn't vouch for his bedroom as it was the one place she hadn't yet been invited, even though the devil on her shoulder had her halfway up the stairs more than once while Mårten was at work before she stopped herself. The man deserved to be afforded the same privacy she would've wanted for herself. He was even good with his hands. Look at the beautiful kitchen he'd built all by himself, and the way he had restored his little cottage.

He even did the neighborly thing and helped the old lady down the road, for God's sake. Summer knew he was far from perfect, but right now it was difficult to find a flaw in the man. As long as she ignored the fact he'd got all growly and overprotective back in Seattle, as if he had some kind of right to tell her what to do because he was a cop and she was a woman in distress. And maybe he was a little OCD about some things. But then, wasn't she the same?

They'd chat over their meal, sitting on the front porch, slapping away the annoying tiny gnats and listening to the songbirds searching for their last morsel before retiring to bed. She learned a lot about him during those evenings. He was compassionate and caring, with a very strong moral compass. It was almost like he didn't want to see the bad side of anyone, which was an interesting trait for a police officer, and made Summer wonder how he coped with seeing the darker aspect of humanity on a daily basis.

The problem was she was beginning to like Mårten. Really like him. It wasn't just physical lust anymore. She liked that he was a closet romantic; she could tell by the books on his bookshelf. And they weren't just fifty shades of gray; there were a couple of Nicholas Sparks novels, and she'd even spotted Outlander lying open on the coffee table when they'd first arrived home, which he'd quickly removed. They might well have been left by an old girlfriend, but Mårten had mentioned in passing that he'd never actually lived with anyone before. Which was a shock in itself, but it explained the masculine feel to his cottage. While it'd been sensitively renovated, it was lacking those small, almost insignificant touches that only a woman could bring.

Summer finished her laps, got out and showered off the chlorine. It was still early, and she had the whole day to fill before Mårten came home. If only she could stop that stupid little desperate flutter of her heart every time she thought about cooking with Mårten in his kitchen tonight. Bumping elbows with him as she chopped vegetables. Watching the quirky way the corner of his mouth lifted as he concentrated on stirring a sauce on the stove.

Oh, blast! This would never do. More distraction was called for. And the gym next door would do nicely.

An hour and a half later, Summer stumbled out of the door to where her bicycle was locked to a special rack; she loved how the bike-centric lifestyle here in Sweden made everything so easy for someone like her who relied on her bicycle. Her legs wobbled a little as she lifted her bike from the rack, and she cursed silently. She'd overdone it with the weights today in an effort to rid Mårten from her system. Which was stupid; the last thing she needed was to injure herself a week out from a major race.

Looking up as she put on her helmet, her fingers stalled at the buckle as something caught her eye.

A woman was getting into a car on the edge of the parking lot. She had short, dark hair and was a little on the plump side. She looked very much like Paige. But that couldn't be right. The FBI was still looking for her missing friend on another continent. Summer must've been seeing things. Her too-hard workout was making her hallucinate. It was a trick of the shadows cast by the flickering birch leaves in the sunshine, that was all. There were plenty of women out there who resembled Paige, and it was wishful thinking on Summer's part. She wanted Paige to be alive. Wanted her to be rescued from this savage abductor so she could be reunited with her fiancé and then they could put Tyrone in jail forever.

The FBI was learning more about Tyrone King as they dug deeper into his past. His upbringing had been anything but stereotypical, as he'd been born in Pennsylvania, when his Black father had married a white dairy farmer's daughter, not a common occurrence in that state. But it seemed he'd left Pennsylvania as an impressionable teenager after his father had committed suicide when the bank repossessed the dairy farm.

The story was terribly sad, but the real tragedy of Tyrone's life emerged when Jacob told Mårten the reason the family believed they'd lost the farm was because a large gas company had drilled fracking wells on the outskirts of the farm and it'd poisoned their water, and in turn all their animals. Tyrone's hatred of mining companies was now making sense, not that she condoned his actions. His story was that of a tragic villain with a painful past. But surely someone as astute and dynamic as Paige wouldn't be drawn in by that narrative of heartbreak and woe. Would she?

Summer stared thoughtfully after the car as it completed a U-turn and sped off down the narrow country road and she lifted her leg over the bike seat and pedaled slowly back to Mårten's.

CHAPTER FOURTEEN

"That was yummy." Summer leaned back in her chair and patted her stomach with relish. "If you keep feeding me like this, I'm going to be like a whale wallowing through the water, not a honed athlete in the prime of her life," she joked.

"You could never look like a whale." Mårten replied. "As a matter of fact, you look great," he added.

Where the hell had that come from? It was supposed to be a joke, but it'd come out wrong. He glanced accusingly at his wine. This was his third glass. Normally, he had one beer with dinner, and that was it. But he'd bought this red as it went exceedingly well with the reindeer steak he'd planned for dinner, or so the bottle shop attendant had told him.

Problem was, Summer did look great. Fantastic even. Relaxed and casual as they sat on the front porch in the evening sunshine in a pair of jean shorts and a tank top that again showed off her gleaming golden-brown skin, and long, toned legs. Black hair left long to cascade down her back.

She was staring at him with a confused look on her face. She'd also consumed three glasses, and her stare was a tad glassy-eyed. They'd both had more alcohol than they should've. Summer said she didn't drink this close to a competition, but when he told her it'd bring out the flavors of the dish and made puppy-dog eyes at her, she'd relented.

She continued to stare at him, and he continued to be unable to withdraw his gaze, ensnared as he was by the dark pools of her irises, all huge and tempting. If there hadn't been a table between their two chairs, Mårten may have leaned across and touched his lips to hers. Shit. Not good.

"I think we should go for a walk." He stood, and Summer leaned backward in surprise. "It's a beautiful evening, and we could walk off some of this food." They needed to get out of here; it was becoming dangerous. She was becoming dangerous, this casual chatting, as if they were friends. Because he was finding it harder and harder to resist her. Yes, a walk was a great idea. It'd put some distance between him and Summer, help him get rid of some of that pent-up energy coursing around his body.

With a loud clatter of plates, Mårten cleared the small table and took everything inside. "Are you coming?" He didn't wait for her answer as he banged through the fly screen door.

Three minutes later, Mårten was striding out, leading the way through the undergrowth around his house to a hidden walking trail that circled the outskirts of the suburb only the locals knew about. It wound between the birch trees, the white bark of their trunks glowing in the orange light of sunset, and led through open patches where you could often pick smultron, a small native strawberry. But Mårten barely noticed any of it; he was intent on only one thing. Getting his libido under control.

"Slow down. I can't enjoy the scenery if you're gonna pretend this is some kind of race." Summer was only half joking as she jogged to catch up with him.

With a force of effort, he slowed his pace, listening as Summer exclaimed over a red-capped woodpecker tapping madly against the side of a tree, or a rare red squirrel darting across in front of them. After a few more minutes, the peace of the forest worked its magic, and he drew in a deep, calming breath. That was better. He needed to remember next time he got horny around Summer that a good dose of nature would set him straight again. Yeah, right, as if that was gonna work.

The path meandered through a little dell, with a ring of trees around a clearing of green grass and wildflowers. The setting sun filtered through the leaves, and it was very pretty.

"Did you tell Jacob about the woman I saw in the parking lot at the gym?" Summer's question took him by surprise; he thought she was going to keep waxing lyrical about the forest, and he wondered why the sudden change in topic.

He stopped and casually leaned against the trunk of a tree facing her. "Yes, I did."

"And what did he say?"

"That they would follow it up."

Summer gave a loud snort. "That's their standard line for everything, isn't it?" She'd picked a long grass stem and was shredding it between her fingers.

Mårten couldn't disagree; the FBI didn't give away any information they didn't need to. But he wasn't worried either, as there was no way the woman getting into that car this morning could have been Paige. This Tyrone guy wasn't one to muck around. He had an agenda, and it seemed like nothing and no one was going to get in his way. Including one nosy ranger. Both he and Jacob agreed Paige had been missing too long now. It was unlikely that she was still alive. Not that he would ever admit that to Summer.

"You think she's dead, don't you? That's why you're not in the least bit worried I might've seen her today."

He looked up sharply. Oh, shit. Perhaps his poker face was no longer as good as he thought. Either that, or she was extremely good at reading him. He straightened against the tree as she began pacing through the long grass in front of him.

"Well, do you?"

Now he was in a pickle. "You know Jacob's team is doing everything in its power to find her. We're still hopeful we can locate—"

"Don't give me that police rhetoric bullshit," she interrupted. "Answer the question."

He held up his hands in surrender, and she gave another sort of derision. "Typical. You'll never tell me the truth because you think you're protecting me. Well, you're not."

Mårten was at a loss. He couldn't very well tell her he believed that at best they'd find Paige's body buried in a shallow grave somewhere near where she went missing. And at worst they might not find her at all, because she'd been dismembered and disposed of down a deep dark hole in the middle of nowhere. Both scenarios were possible; he'd seen it all in his years as a cop. But Summer didn't need to know the awful truth.

"She could still be alive," he said carefully. "If it is in fact Tyrone who abducted her—and we don't even know that for sure—then perhaps he's holding her hostage, to use her as a bargaining chip if we get too close. He might be trying to flee the country." This was one of the many theories put forward by Jacob's team. They had to consider every scenario.

"Do you think so?" There was a note of entreaty in Summer's voice that hadn't been there before, her face scrunching up in concern. "God, I hope that's true. Because I really need her not to be dead."

"Of course you do," Mårten replied. "I know you must be scared for your friend. And it must be alarming thinking he might be after you too."

"No, that's not it." When she looked up, there was a steely glint in her eye as her hair swung in an angry arc across the shoulders.

Surely she wasn't still blaming herself? He thought they'd already resolved this on the night back at Jacob's. It wasn't Summer's fault. She needed to remember that she was the victim here. Perhaps he should've picked this up sooner; he was trained to see when a person was suffering from survivor's guilt. But Summer had seemed so together, so strong. And he'd spent all of his energy convincing this stubborn woman that she was in danger and needed to take her plight seriously. So when she'd agreed to come to Sweden with him, he'd thought it was only her physical safety he needed to look after. Now he wondered if he'd been wrong.

"Well, okay, yes, I guess some of it is fear," she admitted. "But I've been thinking a lot about Paige's secret email address. It's been bugging me ever since you mentioned it."

Oh, that caught him by surprise. "That's probably nothing." The emails had seemed like a dead-end. Apart from her mentioning the gold mining company at Yellowstone and how it had the capacity to destroy a large part of the park if it went ahead, the IT guys could find else nothing incriminating in the banal communications, which seemed to be mostly about the weather. If there was an underlying message, the specialists hadn't cracked it yet. The only other suspicious thing about the email trail was that the receiver had since closed their account, and IT was struggling to track down the individual who'd owned it. Mården took a step toward her, arm outstretched is if to give her shoulder a gentle pat

"No." She held up a hand to ward him off. "Let me talk. I didn't want to believe it at first. All I could think was, if I hadn't taken those blasted photos, then she'd still be eating dinner with her fiancé, and driving to work every day, to do a job she absolutely loved. Not missing, presumed dead." There was a hitch in her voice as she said the word *dead*. "But then I got to thinking, dredging up memories from our field trip. And I started to remember little things that I'd ignored at the time, or passed off as Paige just being overly passionate about her job and saving Yellowstone."

"Okay," he said. "Like what, for instance?"

"Just a few odd things she said to me when we were chatting by the campfire at night. She was very anti-Trump, and very anti all of his policies, including any notion that mining companies should be allowed anywhere near a National Park. Which on its own isn't so strange, because she is a ranger whose first duty is to care for the environment."

"Yeah," Mårten drawled, distracted by her long, slender fingers as they darted through the air; she liked to talk with her hands when she got animated about a subject. But she was right; none of that specifically pointed the finger at Paige.

"But there were other things," she continued. "Like when we were approaching the fence surrounding the mine site, she tried to lead me away, to distract me, saying there was nothing interesting to photograph, and we should check out this great little creek that would be teaming with frogs we could photograph instead. But I wouldn't listen; I was intrigued by what might be hiding behind the big tall fences."

"Hmm."

"Then she rushed me past the buildings, saying we needed to make camp before it got dark. But now that I think about it, there was still enough light left. We'd made camp later in the evening before. There was no need to rush."

"Do you think she knew Tyrone was there?" he asked, his cop brain kicking into high gear. This might explain a few things. It might explain how Tyrone got into the locked mine site. Paige would know the country well; so she could've shown him a way to sneak in, so that he didn't have to go past the guard at the front gate.

"I don't know," she replied miserably. "I really hope not. But then, the next day she asked a few questions about the photographs I'd taken, wanting to look at them. She said something like the mining company would be outraged if they found out we were taking unsanctioned photos. She wasn't happy when I said we didn't have time to go through them all right then as we needed to get back to the ranger HQ that morning, so I didn't miss my ride back to the airport, but I promised I'd send her a file with all the photos when I got home, and I wouldn't publish anything until I'd spoken to her."

"And did you? Send her the photos, I mean?"

"No, I completely forgot." Summer gave a noncommittal shrug. "I never thought twice about it. I sent the relevant photos and videos of the black-footed ferret to the lead person on the project, and I cc'd Paige in. All the other images were irrelevant to the project, but I always keep all my photos. Maybe she got that email and thought that was all I had."

"Not sure about that," Mårten mused. "But if she was in league with the eco-terrorists, it'd make sense how Tyrone knew you were the photographer. How he knew your name and where you lived. And when you didn't forward the photos like you promised, maybe he took the matter into his own hands."

"Exactly." Summer nodded, her pretty eyes glittering in the sunshine. "But doesn't that just make me look like a complete fool?" Summer stopped pacing and tilted her head. "Here I am worried about Paige, thinking she might even be dead, and maybe she's been playing me all along."

"You're anything but a fool," Mårten murmured.

"Yeah, well, even if I'm no fool, then perhaps I'm being a complete bitch. I mean, how could I think such terrible things about my friend? I'm jumping to conclusions and being just as distrustful and cold-hearted as the rest of you. I'm trying to justify something that just isn't true, and I hate myself for doubting her."

"Summer, you're not an idiot. And you're also not being disloyal to her by telling me this." He stepped forward and put a hand on each of her shoulders, wanting to offer comfort. But as soon as he took hold of her, he caught a trace of the lavender-scented shampoo she'd used in the shower this afternoon. Then his mind imagined her in the shower—in his shower—and it made him forget why he was offering her comfort. Made him want to run his hands down her graceful shoulders instead, wrap around her slender waist and then run them over her supple buttocks. Pull her into him…

"But it can't be both ways." Her voice dragged him back to the present. "Either she betrayed me, or I'm betraying her, and whichever way lies the truth, it still stinks. I just want her to be safe. So part of me doesn't even care which one it is." She tipped her head back to stare at the sky, then closed her eyes.

Oh, shit, was she going to cry?

"Blast, I made a promise I would not break down in front of you again," she mumbled, eyes still closed.

A shaft of guilt hit his stomach so hard he nearly doubled over. She'd made that promise to herself because last time she'd cried in front of him and he'd tried to comfort her, they'd ended up kissing and then he'd panicked and pushed her away like some teenage idiot. He would not reject her again.

"I hate it when you cry," he said softly.

"Then I'll stop." But the tears continued to stream down her face, and so he pulled her to him, resting her face against his chest. Her breath hitched, and his heart clenched painfully. Now he really was going to have to hunt down this Tyrone King and take him apart piece by piece. Just to make sure she remained safe. And to stop her from ever crying again.

"Thank you," she whispered, looking up at him.

Using a thumb, he wiped away her tears. "For what?"

"Looking out for me. Letting me live in your house so I can keep training. You didn't need to do any of this."

Those eyes. So dark and fascinating. Without thinking, he lowered his mouth to hers. As if surrendering, she went soft and malleable against his chest. Nope, this time he wasn't going to reject her. It was too much to ask of a man. Not to be taken in by this vulnerable, beautiful woman. Not to need her. Not to want her. Professionalism be damned. Ethics be damned.

He turned them both so that her back was against the tree. This time he kissed her until the blood pounded so hard in his head, he couldn't think straight. It was some kind of miracle she was even letting him touch her, but he was going to take it, regardless. His whole body throbbed, his cock aching to be released. He needed to claim her, to make her his. This woman who pretended she was made of steel, but who was so, so soft-hearted underneath. This woman who gave him a hard-on every time he thought about her. But there was more to it than that. He was also getting a clearer picture of who she was as a person, and he liked her more and more.

His hands slipped up and under her tank top to find her breasts covered by a slip of silk. He dropped his mouth to her collarbone, then lifted her top over her head in one swift move, his lips finding the lacy edge of her bra and pushing it down to reveal a pink, pert nipple.

Her fingers were at his belt, even as she whispered hoarsely against the top of his head, "Won't somebody see us?"

"Hardly anyone uses this trail," he groaned against her skin, which was as soft as velvet. It wasn't strictly true, but Swedish people were renowned for minding their own business, and even if anyone happened by, Mårten couldn't care less if they saw anything. He had eyes only for Summer. Together, they slid his jeans over his hips, setting his throbbing cock free at last, even as she yanked his T-shirt over his head, her eyes going wide at the sight of him. Naked in the forest. Standing there for her to see.

He picked her up in his arms, dropped to his knees and laid her gently on the flattened grass at the base of the tree. Now it felt as if they were in their own little cocoon, a nest of soft, fragrant grass, that would hide them from any prying eyes. He dropped a kiss on her belly, snaking his mouth up to the mound of her breasts beneath the fabric of her bra, and she arched up to meet him.

He began to undo the button of her shorts when a thought hit him. Were they really going to do this? Have sex in the middle of the forest? Perhaps he was being too presumptuous.

"Is this okay?" He asked.

Her answer was to drag his mouth down to meet hers, a low groan escaping between her lips as he tasted her, sucked at the corner of her mouth, a moan echoing in his own chest at the sweetness of it all.

"I'm tired of playing it safe," she said. "I'm tired of always having to be in control. I want this."

If she wanted to lose control, he was quite happy to help her achieve her goal. He craved to watch Summer finally give in and surrender to her desires. That would be a sight to see. With her eyes fixed on him, she arched her back and reached behind, and it took him a moment to understand what she was doing. Until her bra slipped sideways, revealing those glorious breasts, painted golden by the setting sun's rays. He couldn't help himself, he took one nipple in his mouth, and she uttered his name on a moan.

He wasn't sure how it happened, but they were soon both naked, her shorts and panties cast off with the rest of her clothes. And now he was free to look his fill; she was even better than he'd imagined. Her hand came to rest on his chest, small fingers entwining in the hairs curling from his pecs.

"I like this," she purred. "I've never had sex outside before, but with you... I like it," she repeated. "And I like you." Her hand curled as she dug her nails lightly into his skin, sending ripples of heat flashing through him, heading straight for his cock. Then her hand drifted lower, exploring, experimenting, making it obvious what else she liked. What else she wanted.

One thing he would not leave to chance, however, was a condom. Safe sex was still important. He fumbled with his discarded jeans, searching for his wallet and the protection he always kept in there. Summer lifted her head to see what he was doing, strands of her dark hair falling across the face. She looked oddly artless and trusting in that moment, and his heart swelled with... What? He didn't want to dissect that emotion right now.

He covered himself with the condom and levered up onto his elbows to hover above her. Slowly, he slid into her, intent on giving her pleasure. He wanted her to enjoy this. But she bucked her hips against his and whimpered his name, and the idea of slow went out of his head. Sweat beaded on his skin as he thrust, going deeper, harder. And she answered each of his surges with a tilt of her hips, her head thrown back into the grass in abandon.

Right at this moment, Summer belonged to him alone. It was just the two of them; no one else existed in the world. He felt like she'd hollowed out his soul.

Afterward, they lay in the grass panting as if they'd just run a marathon. He was completely wrung out, his brain numb as the flood of endorphins coursed through him. A single thought flitted across his comatose mind, and it scared the living hell out of him. Once wasn't going to be enough. Not with this woman.

CHAPTER FIFTEEN

The digital readout on her cycling computer flashed up at thirty-eight kilometers, three-hundred meters—four-hundred meters—five-hundred. Just over a kilometer to go and she'd be finished her workout. Upbeat music pounded through her earbuds. Her heart rate monitor said she was cruising at around a hundred-and-thirty bpm, and her legs felt pretty good. If she'd been competing in a proper race, then she'd be getting ready to transition to a ten km run after this, and right now she was feeling great; ten kilometers would be no problem at all. She didn't want to jinx herself, but she knew she was pretty much ready. Her lead-up to the triathlon in a week's time was going well, even taking in the triple traumas of the shock of her apartment break-in, Paige being reported missing, and having to go into hiding in a foreign country.

Mostly, it was thanks to Mårten.

He'd been so sweet ordering this bicycle stand so she could train indoors if she needed to. This was the first time she'd used it, as until today the weather had been perfect. A summer thunderstorm had washed over the sky this morning, however, and Summer had decided not to chance the roads, texting Mårten at work to tell him her plans so he wouldn't worry. He would see that her phone was still at his house and guess what she was doing, but she wanted to put his mind at rest. She owed him that much.

Especially after last night.

Last night.

What a revelation.

She'd never had sex outdoors before, and the experience had been noteworthy. But this had also been next level, more than just the added titillation of doing it where they could be discovered any second. Sex between her and Mårten had been inevitable, with her being able to think of nothing else most of the week. But the explosiveness, the absolute compulsive neediness, had caught her completely by surprise. The first touch of his lips on hers had ignited a fire inside so hot she felt like she'd turned to liquid lava. She'd been so greedy for him, she almost felt ashamed of the way she'd practically ripped his clothes in her eagerness to rid him of them. And then she'd called out his name as his tongue painted his desire all over her body. The way she couldn't stop staring at his cock, as if it were a thing of beauty. Which it was.

Just thinking of the way he'd brought her to orgasm so easily, so fast and hard, had her lady parts tingling with desire all over again.

It'd been a long time since she'd slept with a man. But that was no excuse for her sheer wantonness. For her impulse to hand over all control. That wasn't like her at all. The part of her that needed those rules was aghast at what she'd done. But there was another part, a growing voice in her head that was more than a little satisfied. Like the cat who'd got the cream.

She glanced down and saw her pace had dropped dramatically. Blast. Now, thoughts of Mårten were interfering with her training. She needed to stop thinking about him. She figured that by giving in to temptation, she would've washed him out of her system. But instead, she found herself wanting him even more. If she got the chance, she knew she'd do it again. Once wasn't enough.

Wait... What was that noise? Summer pulled an earbud out, cutting off the music, and turned to face the front door, legs still pumping the pedals. Someone was knocking loudly. She glanced at the digital readout. Forty-nine and a half kilometers. She couldn't stop now. A couple more minutes, that's all she needed.

"Who is it?" she yelled.

"PostNord," a disembodied voice called from the porch. "I have a parcel for Mårten Viskten. It needs a signature."

"Blast!" Summer glanced at her clock once more. "Can you just wait two more minutes?" she pleaded.

"I can take the parcel back to the depot, if you like. But someone will have to come and collect it from there." The voice had become impatient.

"No, no. I'm coming," Summer huffed. Perhaps if she jumped off the bicycle and left the pedals going around, she might get back in time to start pedaling again before it stopped completely and the digital clock ended her session.

It was hot in the house; the rain making everything humid but not really cooling it down. Summer had sweat beading on her forehead and running between her breasts and down her back, the one-piece Lycra suit doing nothing to keep her cool today. She knew she'd look a sight to whoever was standing out there, but right now she didn't care.

Unlocking the deadbolt, she yanked the door open, ready to snatch the parcel and scrawl a signature, when she stopped in surprise, her mind scrambling to catch up with what her eyes were seeing.

"Paige! Oh my God, it's so good to see you. I thought you were—"

Paige rushed forward, pushing Summer inside. Summer

backpedaled through the mudroom and stumbled into the kitchen island, hitting her back hard and emitting a yell of pain. But before she could recover, another figure charged through the door. A man she didn't recognize grabbed her by the arm, and she screamed in fear.

"Do it. Do it fucking now," the man yelled at Paige, while Summer struggled to get free.

Then something was covering her face, a cloth over her mouth and nose. It was sweet smelling and pungent, and Summer tried not to breathe, clamping her mouth shut, still fighting the man, but he had hold of both her arms, pulling them behind her so that her shoulders felt like they were being torn from their sockets. Her lungs were bursting; she needed air. Her mind screamed at her that this was all wrong; she needed to fight, needed to get the cloth away from her face. But she couldn't move, couldn't twist away from the man, and the urge to draw in a breath became too much. When she finally opened her mouth to gasp in essential air, Summer knew it was a mistake. Her vision went dark around the edges, and she felt her legs give way beneath her. Then there was nothing.

*　*　*

Summer groaned and rolled over. Her head throbbed as if she'd been hit with a sledgehammer, and she wanted to open her eyes, but they felt like they were glued shut. Something was terribly wrong. For a second, she couldn't think what. She was lying down, but she wasn't in bed, because the ground was cool and gritty beneath her bare legs. It was this revelation that finally forced her eyes to open to narrow slits.

Everything was dark. Where was she? What'd happened?

Summer tried to sit up, but her head swirled; she was dangerously dizzy, and she had to lie down again, careful not to move as she shut her eyes. Once the dizziness had passed, she cracked open one eye and then the other, letting them adjust to the dim light. Now she could see slivers of light crisscrossing the space. She was inside a small wooden shed, and the sunlight was filtering in through the gaps between the planks. The shed was empty. There was no furniture, not even a bench, and no windows either. Or if there were, they'd been boarded up. It was warm in here with no ventilation. The air oppressive. Summer noted that she was still wearing her one-piece Lycra suit and her cycling shoes.

Much more hesitantly this time, Summer levered herself up onto her elbow. Her head still pounded, but if she moved slowly, at least she didn't get dizzy. It was all coming back to her now. Paige had been standing on the front porch when she'd answered the door. Alive and well. And in Sweden. And probably in cahoots with the eco-terrorists, if her abduction was any clue. Just like Mårten had been afraid of.

How long had she been unconscious? It was light outside, but that didn't mean a lot. It could be well after dinnertime, and the sun would still be up. Or it could be the middle of the day; she might've only been out for a few hours. Surely, Mårten must know she was missing by now? He'd already be out looking for her, wouldn't he?

Shit. Her phone was sitting on the kitchen table where she'd left it while she was training. Mårten would think she was still safe at home. He wouldn't know what'd happened until he got home from work. And that might be too late for her. The idea that she was in some serious trouble caused a hard ball of fear to form in her chest. Tears prickled at the back of eyelids. How could she have been so stupid? Mårten had warned her to always check the door before she opened it. To always be aware of her surroundings. But she'd been lulled into a false sense of security during her stay in Sweden.

This was no time to give in to her fear, however. Mårten would expect more from her. She expected more from her. And if he wasn't coming, then she'd need to rescue herself.

Sitting up gingerly, she leaned her back against the wall, careful not to make any sharp movements with her head. What did Paige want with her? Summer wracked her memory banks. She was sure that the man who'd been with Paige wasn't Tyrone King. She hadn't had a good look at him before he'd taken her prisoner, but the fact he wasn't Black, added to the photo Jacob had shown her of Tyrone, gave her all the clues she needed to know it wasn't him. And it wasn't the guy who'd broken into her apartment either; she'd remember his face anywhere. So who was he? At least she wasn't tied up and was free to move around. Did that mean her captors were too stupid or too lazy to bother? Or were they so certain she wouldn't escape that it didn't matter? The second option had a sliver of alarm slicing down her spine.

Where the hell was she? That was the first question that needed to be answered.

She crawled about on her hands and knees, exploring the small space with her fingers, not yet confident enough that she wouldn't get dizzy and fall on her face if she were to stand. The wooden slats were old and splintery, but also thick and sturdy, built to withstand the severe winters of northern Sweden. The shed was about two meters wide by four or five meters long. After she had brushed through more than one thick, sticky spiderweb, she gave up with a shudder. She didn't know what types of spiders they had in Sweden, but she had a bit of a phobia of those eight-legged marauders. And as far as she could tell, none of the boards were loose, and there was no door she could find. Maybe she could kick her way out of here? But that wasn't an option until head stopped swirling.

Loud footsteps crunching on the gravel outside interrupted her musing. But before Summer could do much more than turn to face the sound, one of the shorter sides of the shed slid open, grinding and squeaking along rusty tracks. Ah-ha, that's why she couldn't find the door; the entire wall was a door.

Summer blinked in the brightness of the afternoon sun. Paige stood silhouetted in the doorway. And outside, just beyond the opening, Summer could make out fields of long grass and wildflowers, with a Nordic forest of pine and conifer trees running along the left of the field. Summer tensed. If she could push Paige out of the way, she could be out of here like a shot, to freedom.

"I wouldn't try to run if I were you. We're in the middle of nowhere. You'd be lost without a trace. No one would find you for weeks or even months," Paige said as if she'd read her mind. Was that why they hadn't bothered to tie her up? And the way Summer was feeling, she might trip and fall flat on her face before she got more than three steps outside the building. So, running wasn't an option just yet.

But Summer remained tense, ready for anything.

She got to her knees and then instantly regretted the move, her hand reaching for her forehead where it felt like someone was again pounding away with a hammer inside her skull. Nope, she wasn't going anywhere right now.

"Still a bit groggy?" Paige came further into the shed, so that now Summer could see her features properly. "Sorry about that. It wasn't my choice to drug you." Her voice held no menace. In fact, she sounded decidedly convivial, as if they'd just picked up their friendship where they'd left off. Summer studied the other woman for a few moments. She didn't look much different from the last time Summer had seen her. Dressed in casual civilian clothes instead of her USFWS uniform, she was plump and curvy, with an endearing smile, and could easily pass as an American tourist, all rosy cheeks and enthusiasm. Although this time her short bob had been allowed to grow out and was now a mousy brown color rather than rich dark auburn. And now, as Summer looked closer, Paige's once happy, smiling mouth was bracketed by lines of tension; her brown eyes shuttered and defensive.

"What do you want with me?" Summer growled, not at all taken in by Paige's friendly act.

"Not much. As long as you do as you're told, we won't hurt you, and you'll be free to go in a few days."

"What?" That didn't sound right. Why would someone abduct her, then let her go again?

Paige came to stand in front of Summer, leaning down to hand her something. Summer shied away reflexively. "It's just a bottle of water." Paige sounded almost wounded at Summer's reaction. "You must be thirsty. Nathan said you'd have a dry mouth for a day or so."

Summer ignored the bottle Paige dropped on the bare earth beside her, even though she could probably swallow all that water in one long, satisfying gulp. "Who's Nathan?" Was that the guy who'd held her down while Paige had shoved the rag over her mouth?

"He's…a friend."

Summer gave a loud snort. "Friend my ass. He's a collaborator in whatever crime you're committing here. Why did you kidnap me, Paige? Are you working with Tyrone King? Are you one of these eco-terrorists now?"

Paige looked taken aback at Summer's fierce tone. Then she narrowed her eyes and got down on her haunches so she was level with Summer.

"Tyrone is an amazing man with an amazing vision. He's doing what other people won't. He's putting a stop to all this greedy consumerism. He's making them see they can't keep destroying the Earth. There will be nothing left if they do." The tense lines around Paige's mouth softened as she spoke, her eyes going a little dreamy.

"Oh my God, you've completely fallen for his bullshit."

Summer could barely believe it.

"It's not bullshit, Summer. We're doing everything humanly possible to get the word across, but people just aren't listening. They only care about themselves. You know all these research trips and feasibility studies aren't worth the paper they're written on. The mining companies are doing exactly as they please, and Trump is going to let them. Nobody cares anymore. But Tyrone is making them give a damn. He's making them sit up and take notice."

"Yes, but at what cost, Paige? You can't condone his violent acts of arson? A little boy died in one of those fires. Tyrone killed him."

Paige scowled, her eyes sliding away for a few seconds. "Of course I don't condone that poor little boy's death. I'm not an animal. And neither is Tyrone. He was sick with guilt after that."

"Not enough to stop what he was doing," Summer spat.

The problem was, Summer did understand some of Paige's frustration. Sometimes it didn't matter how many feasibility assessments or environmental impact studies were done. Even if they all came to the same conclusion that the new mine site would be catastrophic and more development would be detrimental to the environment, the government tended to ignore them if the outcome wasn't in their interests. Summer was aware of just how devastating it could be when you spent months or even years working on a project to save a piece of land or an endangered species, only to have your work disregarded by the powers that be. She'd been involved in more than one of these projects herself.

"Look, I get it, Summer. I get why you're disgusted with his tactics. I was too at the beginning. But after listening to him, he makes sense. We need to prioritize what remains of our pristine ecosystems before there's nothing left. If we keep destroying the planet, then humans will perish in the end along with all the other animals. Sacrificing one life to save the rest of us…well, maybe that's just what needs to be done."

"No, it's *not* right," Summer emphasized the word. "If you're prepared to kill for your cause, then you're wrong, Paige. What you're doing is wrong." How could the other woman not see this? Paige and seemed so rational when they'd worked together. Optimistic that their field trip would help save the black-footed ferret. Extremely passionate about her job, knowing that she was helping to safeguard the unique environment of Yellowstone National Park. There'd been no sign of any underlying doubt. No sign she was about to betray her own morality. Summer wondered how long Paige had known Tyrone. How long had he been pumping her full of his poison?

"It was regrettable," Paige admitted. "But Tyrone has promised it will never happen again."

"And you believe him?"

"Yes."

It almost felt like Paige was trying to recruit her. Did she think that with enough time, she might convince Summer to join the cause? The idea was laughable.

But then again…perhaps if Summer pretended to go along with it, would she be able to escape when the time was right? Maybe she should stop arguing with Paige and start agreeing with her instead.

Summer said nothing, merely glared at Paige.

The other woman stood with a sigh. "I know you don't believe me, but I am sorry you had to go through this."

Summer shifted on the dirt. If she were going to make a break for it, now was the time. Paige was clearly too trusting. But where was this other guy, Nathan? Was there another house or building nearby she couldn't see? Or was he waiting just outside with a gun in his hand? Waiting to shoot her if she made a run for it? Her head throbbed at that moment, reminding her she wasn't physically able. There were too many unknowns. So Summer stayed where she was, kneeling on the ground, watching Paige retreat through the door.

"I'll be back with some food in an hour," Paige promised. She turned and hesitated in the doorway. "I don't expect you to see it our way immediately. I certainly didn't. But you should think about what I said." She slid the entryway shut, and Summer was in darkness once again.

She reached for the bottle and swallowed it in two gulps, wishing Paige had brought two. Maybe when she came back with the food, she'd bring more water. And maybe when she came back, Summer might soften her stance against Tyrone. At least on the outside where Paige could see it. If she thought she was sympathetic to their cause, they might give her more freedom. Or even release her alive. Because at the moment, Summer didn't believe Paige's claim that they were going to let her go.

CHAPTER SIXTEEN

Mårten glanced at the clock on the wall in the squad room. It was just after three. He couldn't find the enthusiasm he needed to complete the paperwork for the break-and-enter down on Länggatan Road. The wealthy resident hadn't been present at the time, but the intruder must've known about her impressive collection of diamond jewelry, because they'd targeted the safe without touching anything else in the house.

All Mårten could think about was Summer. Maybe he should head home early this afternoon. There wasn't much going on at work anyway. It'd been a slow couple of days, apart from the break-in, and the paperwork Mårten still needed to catch up on from before he left to go on holiday to do. The Chief had been riding his ass all week to get it done. Chief Inspector Rydberg was still unhappy about Jacob's defecting to America. And even though it wasn't Mårten's fault, it seemed because he'd been his police partner for so long, that Rydberg was taking his dissatisfaction at losing one of his best cops out on Mårten as the next closest thing.

Mårten put down his pen. Yes, he'd go home early, surprise Summer, Rydberg be damned. Maybe they could take a picnic out to Mörö Beach, where he could show her some of the archipelago. It was a bit of a drive, but it shouldn't be too crowded. Or maybe they could find somewhere more secluded and have a replay of last night.

At the mere thought of the previous evening, his cock sprang to attention. Mårten quickly wiped away the image of Summer lying in the long grass, head thrown back in abandon, as he moved inside her. Shit, the last thing he needed was to get a hard-on at work. He slid his gaze sideways toward the desk that Aurora sat at on his left. She had her head down, a set of headphones on, as she wrote out yet another report on the jewelry heist. Thank the Lord she was so fixated on her task, she hadn't even noticed him daydreaming, let alone working himself into a later.

He returned to his paperwork until his libido had subsided. But he wasn't really concentrating. All he wanted was to get home. Summer was a distraction from his work, but not necessarily an unwanted one. Mårten had spent the last few years working long hours and weekends, building his career, his focus on his job, to the detriment of his personal life. Perhaps it wasn't such a bad thing if he took a step back for a few days. Summer was only here for one more week, so maybe he should make the most of it.

"Hey, Aurora," he said as he pushed his pile of paperwork to the side.

"Yeah, boss." She lifted her head, pulling her headphones to the side, and looked at him with her intense gaze, reminding him of an eager puppy, straining to be allowed off the leash.

"I'm taking off for the day."

"Oh. Okay."

He had to hide his smirk at her crestfallen expression; she'd been hoping he was about to tell her they had a new job to attend. Had he ever been this keen when he'd been a rookie? He couldn't remember. She readjusted her headphones with a sigh and went back to stabbing impatiently at the ream of forms on her desk.

His phone vibrated in his pocket just as he stood to slide his chair away from the table. It was Jacob. Mårten grabbed his bag and headed for the door, answering with a cheery, "What's up?"

But he got the opposite of a pleasant reply from Jacob, whose tone was somber. "We think Tyrone King might be in Sweden," he said without preamble.

"What?" Mårten stopped dead in the middle of the hallway.

"We got a hit from one of his aliases late yesterday. It looks like he boarded a flight to Stockholm two days ago."

Shit. This wasn't good. "And you're just telling me this now?" Mårten was on the move again. He needed to get his car. Needed to check on Summer. He took the stairs to the underground car park two at a time.

"Sorry." Jacob sounded grim. "This guy has a lot of aliases. It's taken us a while to track them all down. It was Miller who found it. She only came across it this morning, and when we cross-referenced it…" Mårten could imagine Jacob's face, his mouth tight with contrition. This wasn't his fault. Or Miller's. Not exactly. But it was still a giant stuff-up. There could be only one reason he was coming to Sweden.

"What identity is he traveling under?"

"Amir Kingadams. We think it's his middle name, along with an addition to his last name."

Simple yet effective, Mårten thought. He made it to the parking lot and ran to his car.

"We've got agents checking cameras at both airports to confirm, but I wanted you to know as soon as possible," Jacob continued.

"Thanks. Keep me updated. I'm on my way home now." Mårten ended the call, and as he jumped into his vehicle, he tapped his phone to pull up the app and check on Summer's location. It showed that she was still at his house, and he let out a gust of relieved air.

Once he was on the road, he tried to call Summer, but it rang out and then went to voicemail. He tried again with the same outcome. This time, he left a message telling her not to leave the house and that he was on his way home. She could be in the shower, or taking a nap. He wasn't worried. Yet.

Fourteen minutes later, he pulled into his gravel driveway. The house looked quiet and serene. But when he pushed the front door open, his stomach lurched. Summer's bicycle rested on its stand in the middle of the room, but there was no sign of her. Only his head moved as he took in the rest of the space. A mug was smashed on the kitchen floor. Signs of a struggle? Everything else seemed normal, nothing else broken or out of place, but Mårten's guts were churning with alarm. Summer wasn't the type of person to leave broken crockery lying on the floor.

"Summer," he called out, but he was already striding toward her bedroom. Without knocking, he pushed open the door. It was empty. Then he went to the bathroom. The door was ajar, and he already knew what he'd find before he got there. More silence. Then he saw Summer's phone on the kitchen table. She wouldn't go anywhere without her phone. And now he had no way of tracking her.

"Shit, shit, shit." He had his cell out of his pocket even as he darted up the stairs to his bedroom, although he knew she wouldn't be there.

"She's gone. She's fucking gone," he shouted into the phone. Part of him wanted to punch the wall, wanted to scream at Jacob. If the FBI had done its job, this would never have happened. He wouldn't have left her alone if he'd known Tyrone was in the country.

"Shit." Jacob didn't ask what Mårten was talking about or even if he was certain. He knew there was only one person

Mårten cared about this much to make him swear like that, and that his ex-partner would've already conducted a thorough search of the house. Mårten didn't panic about nothing. "Have you called it in yet?"

"No." Mårten's breath was coming in short, sharp pants. He needed to regain control of his emotions. He was no good to her if he was a physical and emotional wreck. "Fuck, what if he's killed her?" The words were out of his mouth before he could stop them. Before he could govern the thought. A pain so sharp it was as if someone had sliced him with a knife shot through his chest. He couldn't think anymore. If Summer was dead…

"Mårten." Jacob's voice was just as sharp as the imaginary knife stabbing straight through Mårten's heart. "Get on the phone and call in backup. Now!" There was an edge to Jacob's tone Mårten had never heard before. "Then call me back."

The urgency in Jacob's voice cut through the stupor clouding Mårten's brain. "Yep. Yep. Will do," he replied. He was standing on his front porch with no idea how he had got there. Staring out into the surrounding forest, still hoping to see her miraculously walk out of the trees in one piece. She could be anywhere by now. It was his fault she was missing. He hadn't done enough to protect her.

CHAPTER SEVENTEEN

By Summer's calculation, it was over two hours before Paige returned, because even though food was the last thing on her mind, her stomach was rumbling loudly. Summer had spent the time sitting on the ground, massaging her temples to try and rid herself of this terrible headache so that she could think clearly. And now she was feeling much better. Feeling like she could even take on Paige. Tackle her to the ground and make a run for it. If that were an option.

When Summer heard footsteps on the gravel, she got onto her hands and knees, ready to pounce, to tackle, to run, to hide. It was only then she felt the pain in her palm and realized she'd been obsessively rubbing at her hand again. She just hoped it wasn't bleeding, but didn't have time to stop and look.

But the idea of escaping was put to rest when Paige slid the door aside and a male figure loomed close behind her. It seemed Paige had brought backup this time, and Summer unclenched her hands. She needed to reassess the situation. The man was wearing khaki cargo pants and a loose black T-shirt with a Greenpeace logo on the front. He wasn't much taller than the ranger; he could almost be called weedy. But Summer didn't underestimate his strength; she already knew firsthand how he'd been able to hold her down so easily when they'd taken her hostage back at the house. There must be a lot of wiry muscle beneath all that clothing hanging off his skinny frame. He reminded her of many of the male triathletes she competed with, who were often almost gaunt looking, but underneath resided a strength and stamina that had to be seen to be believed.

The one difference between this man and the triathletes she was used to, however, was the large knife sheathed at his waist. It gave him a subtle air of menace. And it gave Summer more than a second's pause.

"I brought you some food," Paige said, moving forward so she could place a tray on the ground in front of Summer and blocking her view of the man. Glancing down, Summer made out a plate full of bread and cheese and cold cuts. And thank the Lord, two more bottles of water. Quickly assessing her options, Summer decided to play the subdued captive for now, with a large side helping of grateful. It seemed her best option with two of them standing in the doorway. Let them think she was defeated and slightly indebted to them; they might drop their guard that way.

"Thank you," she replied meekly. "I am very thirsty, just like you said I would be." She smiled up at the Paige, completely ignoring the man behind her, as if he didn't matter. As if his knife didn't scare her. Taking up one bottle, she didn't have to pretend to gulp at the cool water. "Oh, thank you," she said as she finished it.

"This is Nathan," Paige said by way of introduction, watching as Summer picked up a piece of bread and cheese; she may as well keep up her strength, who knew when she might get an opportunity to escape.

"She doesn't need to know my name," Nathan snarled, glaring at Paige's back. "Just give her the food and let's get out of here." His words gave Summer her first insight into the personality of the man and the dynamics between them.

This guy was a completely different kettle of fish. While Paige had been solicitous and almost friendly, he was menacing and cold. And clearly the alpha male of the group. Was this part of some pre-ordained game? Were they playing good cop, bad cop? Or was Paige really that gullible? If this guy was involved with the EIC group, as Summer suspected, then he might also be the other man Summer had photographed at the mine site. It was highly probable. The last thing she wanted was to be caught studying Nathan, to alert him to the fact that she knew who he was.

So, completely ignoring him, Summer again addressed Paige. "This is delicious. Thank you."

"No problem," Paige replied brightly. "Like I said, we're not animals." She rolled her eyes in Nathan's direction to show that at least *she* wasn't an animal, but kept talking. "You don't need to be afraid of us, we're not going to hurt you."

Nathan made a noise of contempt but continued to stand behind Paige, a silhouette in the doorway, legs akimbo and arms crossed, making no effort to hide the fact he was guarding the door.

Summer made a show of taking a bite, chewing and then swallowing, before asking her next question. "That's good to hear. It makes me feel a little less…worried." Using the word *worried* was a conscious act. It made it sound like Summer wasn't terrified out of her wits, so terrified it was all she could do to force the food down her dry throat. She was downplaying her emotions on purpose, to put them at ease. She tried to phrase her next question casually, with a hint of pleading, as if appealing to Paige's compassionate nature. "Would it be possible to use a bathroom?" She looked around the tiny shed, eyes wide with concern. "Because I really need to go, and…well…," she gestured with her hand at the solid dirt floor.

"Oh." Paige looked uncomfortable and half turned to stare at Nathan. "Maybe we could—"

"No," Nathan interrupted. "You can even go in the corner over there, or you can hold it. But you ain't getting out of here. Got it?" he said, a knowing sneer on his face. "Hurry up and finish," he growled. "Or I'll just tip your food onto the ground."

"Oh." Summer quailed away from him, the fear on her face, only half pretense. "Okay." She rallied a little and managed to lift her chin. "So how long do you expect me to go in the corner? I mean, will it be days? Weeks? Because that's pretty disgusting." Summer screwed up her face, this time not having to fake her disgust. This shed would get warm in the middle of the day, and to be locked in the small space with her own excrement was not a pleasant thought.

"Oh no, it won't be weeks," Paige replied hurriedly. "We're just keeping you here until—"

"Shut up. Shut the fuck up woman." Nathan stepped in front of Paige with a feral snarl on his face. "Can you just keep your fucking mouth shut for once? I can't fucking believe that Tyrone thought you'd be any good at this. You're a fucking nightmare."

Paige took a step away from her snarling colleague. "I'm sorry," she stuttered as if only now realizing her mistake. "I wasn't going to tell her. I wasn't."

"Well, it sounded like you were." He took another step toward her, getting right up in her face. Summer's gaze caught on the knife at his belt. He hadn't drawn it yet, but if he did, Paige might be in a lot of trouble. And so might she. "You haven't got a clue about any of this. You left her unbound and without a gag, for fuck's sake. What if she'd escaped? Stop trying to be her friend. This is fucking serious, Paige. You could put this whole plan in jeopardy with your stupidity. We're not here to play nice. We're here to do a job.

Remember?"

"Yes, I know," she replied meekly. This wasn't the Paige Summer remembered. Why was she deferring to this man? This Paige had lost her self-confidence, was no longer the bold, tough ranger Summer had met two months ago. She'd obviously joined the group because she believed in Tyrone's righteous claims. But perhaps the reality of what she was doing had finally sunk in. And perhaps this Nathan wasn't so much to her liking; his moral code seemed very different from hers. Summer wondered if Nathan had threatened her with violence. Or perhaps had even been physically violent with her. Nathan's hand came to rest on the hilt of his knife, and Summer suddenly had her answer. This man was certainly capable of intimidation, and she had no doubt he could use that weapon if need be.

Summer watched the growing tension between the two with wary interest.

Paige lifted her chin and said, "I just thought she might see things from our point of view. Then we could…you know…"

"Fuck! Are you trying to tell me you want to convert her?" Nathan's hand came up away from his knife, flying toward Paige's throat, almost as if he wanted to strangle her, and she flinched away from him.

"I'm calling Tyrone. I've had enough of your bullshit. I told him not to saddle me with you, that I could do this on my own." Nathan withdrew a phone from a pocket in his cargo pants, spittle flying from his mouth.

"No, don't." Paige was pleading now, still cowering away from him. "I'll listen to everything you say from now on. I promise. I'll even tie her up."

Summer quailed at that. She didn't want to be tied up, it would make everything harder, including any escape she might plan.

"Yeah, you'll do everything I tell you." Nathan grabbed her

arm, turning her to face him. "Because I'm gonna tell you to fuck off. You can go back to bloody America. Tyrone can look after you. I'm done with you."

Summer almost felt sorry for the other woman. But not sorry enough to intervene. The arguing pair were now paying her no attention. They were facing the door, and Tyrone was talking rapidly into his phone. And most importantly, his hands were nowhere near his knife. Summer slowly got to her feet and braced her legs as if she were a sprinter about to take off from the starting blocks. If she could knock the pair to the ground, it'd give her precious seconds to escape. It wasn't much of a plan, but it was the only one she had. And she wasn't sticking around to find out what Nathan had in store for her, especially if Paige left.

Summer hit Nathan so hard he went down like a ton of bricks, and she heard the thud as his head smashed into the side of the door. She struck the pair of them at such an angle that Nathan fell on top of Paige, pinning her underneath him. Paige screamed, trying to push his heavy weight off her. But out of the corner of her eye, Summer could see Nathan was as floppy as a rag doll. Hopefully, she'd knocked him unconscious.

Summer leaped over the prostrate pair and ducked through the doorway, ready to sprint away to freedom. But something small and black lying on the gravel out front stopped in her tracks.

It was Nathan's phone.

She must've knocked it out his hand when she hit him and it'd gone flying. Bending down, she scooped it up, pushing it down the front of her Lycra suit.

Then, without waiting to stop and get her bearings, Summer took off, running straight into the field a grass she seen through the doorway. It was thigh-high, which slowed her down a little, but it'd also slow down anyone who might follow her. She was an athlete. This was the one thing she knew how to do. The cycling shoes weren't helping, but at least she wasn't barefoot. And she kept going, legs pumping, chest heaving, running for her life.

There was a roar of rage from behind, and Summer knew without looking that Nathan must've regained consciousness. The roar of rage became words flung at her back. "Come back here you bitch. If you don't stop right now, when I catch you I'm going to cut you."

She had a good couple of hundred meters head start on him, and she was faster than him, so she just kept running. All she had to do was to stay on her feet and not trip over, so she focused on lifting her legs high, making sure there were no hidden logs or boulders that might put an end to her escape run, the thought of Nathan wielding that large knife pumping extra adrenaline around her body. Had she been stupid to take such a risk? But there was no turning back now, she had to keep going.

Risking a quick glance backward, she determined it was only Nathan who was running after her. Paige stood in the doorway next to the shed, shading her eyes and watching Nathan chase her. Paige's strength was in her stamina, her ability to climb up steep inclines like a mountain goat, and just keep going forever. Her short legs would never keep up, and she obviously knew it. Nathan, however, was the opposite. He could well have been a runner too, the way he was pumping his arms and legs, still screaming obscenities at her.

He kept up with her for longer than she expected; she'd been right about that wiry physique. But a couple of hundred meters later, Nathan gave up. Yelling curses as he put his hands to his knees to suck in air. Summer kept springing like a gazelle through the field. Thankfully, it was huge, at least two kilometers long. But she didn't celebrate; she wasn't safe yet and needed to get out of sight soon. Try and find her bearings, and see if she could get out of this godforsaken place.

Changing direction, she angled toward the edge of the pine forest. Had Paige been correct when she told Summer they were so isolated she could keep walking for several weeks and still not strike civilization? She bloody hoped not.

The hard, cold metal the cell phone pressed against the skin of her breast where she'd shoved it down into her sports bra. It was the one thing that gave her hope. And if Nathan had been talking on it, that meant there was reception out here. Which also gave her hope that perhaps Paige had been bluffing about where they were.

It was dark and cool in amongst the tall tree trunks, after the heat and openness of running through the field. Her heart was pounding out of her chest, her breathing coming in great gasps. She stopped and turned around to make sure no one was following, needing to catch her breath, to take stock of where she was, what to do next.

She could just make out the field and the shed where she'd been held captive through the tangle of tree trunks. Positioning herself behind one of the larger pine trees, the bark rough and sticky with resin beneath her palm, she peered back the way she'd come. The shed was now just a speck partially hidden but the long, swaying grass. There was no sign of movement. Neither Paige nor Nathan was visible. Where have they gone? Surely Nathan wouldn't have given up already? Summer thought she could make out more buildings behind the shed, but they were a long distance away and she couldn't tell if they were a house, or just more sheds. Had her abductors retreated to one of the other buildings? Were they on some kind of farm? The extensive field she'd just run through could perhaps once have been pasture for an animal. Cows maybe? And it'd been left to be taken over by wildflowers. The shed had certainly been old, and probably unused for a long time. An abandoned farm perhaps?

Now that she'd recovered some of her breath, she turned and continued walking quickly into the forest, having to clamber over fallen tree trunks and fight her way through thick underbrush. There was no path that Summer could find. She retrieved the phone and studied it while she kept walking at a steady pace, careful not to lose her footing and making a fair bit of noise as she pushed aside branches and kicked through the thick leaf litter covering the ground. It was a cheap Sony model she wasn't familiar with. Probably a burner phone, if she had to guess. Nathan's call to Tyrone must've ended when she knocked the phone flying. It was a wonder he hadn't called back, but then again, perhaps this wasn't the first time Nathan had called to complain about Paige.

The only person she wanted to talk to the moment was Mårten, but she couldn't remember his cell number.

"Blast," she muttered under her breath. Why hadn't she memorized his number. Bloody technology that stored everything for you so you didn't have to think any more. Mårten had made her memorize the Swedish emergency number, however. Would they be able to patch her through directly to Mårten? There was only one way to find out. She dialed 112 and waited. The operator answered in Swedish. Shit!

"Can you speak English?" she shouted into the phone.

"Of course," came back the measured reply, the operator switching seamlessly into perfect English. "What is the manner of your emergency?"

"My name is Summer Perez. I need to speak to Police Inspector Mårten Viskten." God, she hoped she'd pronounced that correctly. "He works at the Luleå police headquarters. I'm a visiting American, and I'm under his protection. Two people have abducted me. I'm not sure where I am, but Mårten will be able to find me." God, she hoped those words were true.

"Please hold the line." The phone went silent, and Summer fervently wished that the woman on the other end of the line believed her and was now trying to track down Mårten. She knew her story might sound far-fetched, and that the operator could just as easily put her on hold and left her hanging. Summer continued to pick her way through the forest with the phone pressed to her ear. It was clear this forest was old, untouched for many decades, with long strands of lichen hanging from the branches, bright green moss growing on the trunks, and much dead wood and fallen trunks littering the ground.

Finally, there was a voice at the end of the phone. "I'm transferring you now." There were a couple of clicks and then silence.

"Hello," she said hesitantly.

"Hello." The voice was deep, rich and oh so familiar, and she almost danced a little jig of joy.

"Mårten, thank God. It's me," she yelled, not sure how long the connection would last, suddenly scared that she wouldn't be able to get her message across. "They took me." She had no time for niceties. "I escaped and stole one of their phones. But I don't know where I am. Can you trace this phone?" she asked urgently.

There was a second's hesitation before Mårten's explosive reply nearly had her holding the phone away from her ear. "Jesus Christ, Summer. I've been so worried." Then he seemed to collect himself; she could almost imagine his handsome face going from expressive to impassive as his cop brain kicked in. "If I were at work, then yes, I could track you. But I'm at home right now." This time his tone was less agitated, more commanding, even as her heart sank at the news. She'd been counting on him tracing her. "Can you tell me if you can see anything distinctive, anything out of the ordinary nearby? A large building or a road sign. Something that might help me figure out where you are?"

"No." Summer stopped walking and turned in a large circle. "I was being held in a small shed. I might've been on an abandoned farm, but I'm not really sure. Now all I can see are just lots of trees and the open field I ran through to escape. There's nothing. It all looks the same." She began to panic all over again. How was Mårten ever going to find her? She could be anywhere within a two-hundred-mile radius, secreted in the forest where no one would find her. Paige had been right; there was no escape from this isolated place.

"Hang on. What's that noise?" Mårten's voice was sharp and urgent.

For a second, Summer didn't know what he was talking about. She'd been so fixated on the sound of his voice she barely heard anything around her. Then she looked up, spotting a shape in the sky through the tangle of branches. "Yes, I see something. It's a big white bird, lots of them, actually. They're circling overhead." She squinted through the trees, looking in the direction that the birds were flying. There was a sparkle, like sunshine glinting off water. "I can just see a lake in the distance. It looks like they might be heading there."

"Good, that's good," Mårten said. "They sound like they could be a whooping swan. The bird has quite a distinctive call, and they often have nesting sites on inland lakes around Luleå. I need you to head toward the lake. I'll—"

The phone went flying as Summer was knocked to the ground, the air leaving her lungs in a loud whoosh.

"You fucking bitch. You're going to die for that." She felt the cold bite of a knife blade against her throat and she froze.

"Now you're going to do exactly as I say, or you'll die, and no one will find your body. Do you understand?" The blade was so tight against her neck, Summer dare not move her head to nod in agreement.

"Yes," she whispered.

Nathan removed the knife and dragged her to her feet. "Walk, bitch," he commanded, and she did as she was told. Had Mårten got enough information from her phone call to find her? She might not live long enough to find out the answer.

CHAPTER EIGHTEEN

Mårten was driving like a maniac, but he didn't care. He was in his personal vehicle, which had no lights or sirens, and he was weaving through the traffic and speeding up the motorway as if the devil was on his tail. Which he very well could be.

His phone buzzed in its cradle on the dashboard, and Mårten stabbed a finger on the answer button. It was Jacob. "I reckon I might have a clue," Mårten said without waiting for Jacob's greeting. "I'm heading over to check it out now."

"Where? Are you alone?"

"I'm driving toward a lake called Långnästjärn, about half an hour out of town. And yes, I'm alone. Rydberg didn't think my lead was strong enough to follow up." Mårten couldn't hide his scathing tone. "He's still got a forensic team at my place, as well as people canvassing the area to see if anyone saw anything. And he's tasked Aurora and Tuckberg with looking into CCTV footage. But it's all happening too slowly, Jacob."

It'd been five hours since Mårten had returned home to find Summer missing. Rydberg had been quick to set up a crime scene and a search area; Mårten couldn't fault him on that. And Tuckberg was good at his job; if there was anything to find on any of the cameras, he or Aurora would find it. But it'd take time. And time was Mårten's worst enemy. He couldn't just stand around and do nothing.

"I realize you're anxious." Jacob's tone was soft. "But you shouldn't go without backup."

"I had no choice," Mårten barked. "You should understand that, of all people." Mårten was referring to the way Jacob had dropped everything when Nikki had been in trouble, going against explicit orders and boarding a plane to America just to protect her.

"Yeah, yeah, I get it," Jacob sighed. "So, does this have something to do with Summer's phone call? Where did you get your intel? Why does Rydberg think it's not worth sending a team?"

Mårten had phoned Jacob soon after Summer had been cut-off mid-sentence. Of course he'd tried to get her back. He'd rung and re-rung that number, desperate to hear her voice. What'd happened to her? Had she just run out of reception? Or had something more sinister befallen her? He'd never felt so helpless in his life.

The phone she was calling from turned out to be a burner, so there was no way anyone at HQ could pinpoint its location. It was so frustrating that he was practically yelling when Jacob answered. Jacob had calmed him down, telling him it was a good thing she'd called; at least they knew she was still alive. He then told Mårten that he was jumping on the next plane to Stockholm; he thought he could be of more help on the ground in Sweden. Mårten didn't ask if he had the FBI's permission, because Jacob often did things whether or not he had permission, and Mårten wouldn't have been able to stop him anyway. A tiny part of Mårten was also relieved; having his friend and ex-partner here to help in the search would make him feel a little easier.

"It was something you said that got me thinking," Mårten

replied. "About how your use of local knowledge, local geography, local connections might be beneficial in the search, which was why you wanted to come." Mårten heard an intake of breath on the other end of the phone, as if Jacob was about to comment, but he didn't wait for his answer. "I called your friend, Petar, over in Jokkmokk. I asked if he could use his Sámi connections to pinpoint a particular spot from the hints Summer gave me." Those few precious moments he'd talked to Summer on the phone kept replaying in his mind over and over. He desperately hoped he was right.

"Okay," Jacob replied slowly. "And Petar came back with a possibility?" There was no censure in Jacob's tone. And while Mårten hoped he hadn't stretched the friendship too far by contacting Petar without first consulting Jacob, he knew his ex-partner would've done the same thing.

Mårten had met Petar once or twice, had even stayed at his house when they'd spent a weekend out hunting moose and then got too drunk to drive home. Mårten also knew that although Petar wasn't a police officer, he'd be discreet. He knew not to talk about anything Jacob or Mårten discussed with him about a case. So, while Petar had sounded surprised to hear Mårten on the other end of the phone, he'd quickly agreed to help.

"Yes. I told him about the whooping swans flying overhead, and that she was somewhere near a small lake, perhaps even being held on an old abandoned farm. He'd said to leave it with him for a bit, and he'd ring around some people who might know something. He got back to me an hour ago with the name of this Lake Långnästjärn. Supposedly it's one of the main areas where the swans have a nesting site outside of Luleå."

"Pardon the pun, but are you sure he didn't send you on a wild goose chase?" Jacob asked. "There could be plenty of whooping swan nesting sites nearby."

"Yes, I know." Mårten was almost stumbling over his words as his excitement grew. "But he also said that a rumor has been passing around the Sámi grapevine of someone squatting on the old Nilsson farm, which has been empty for over a decade. Of lights shining in windows late at night and of a car parked at the back of the house over the past few days. The report came from one of your reindeer herders, who's been camping near the lake for the last week with his small herd."

Mårten almost held his breath as he waited for Jacob's answer. If he didn't think there was merit in the information, Mårten would start second-guessing himself.

"Right," Jacob said, taking time to digest the news. Because of his Sámi heritage, Jacob would know even better than Mårten that many of the native Laplanders still lived a semi-nomadic lifestyle. They'd been given free rein to graze their reindeer without restriction across state-owned as well as privately owned land. And their social network was extra-strong to keep the nomadic community linked.

Rydberg had scoffed at the idea Mårten would put faith in the rumor mill of the native people. That he was grasping at straws, jumping at shadows, wanting to find clues where there were none. Like most Swedish city-born people, he had a distinct lack of understanding of the Sámi's culture and how fiercely protective they were of their heritage. But through spending time with Jacob and his family, Mårten had come to value their close connection with the country. They understood the rivers and the lakes, the mountains and the grasslands better than anybody else. And they would see small nuances where the metropolitan cops might not.

He desperately hoped Jacob would read between the lines and agree with his choice to take matters into his own hands.

"It's a bit of a stretch," Jacob mused. "But I can see why

you want to follow it up. I probably would too," he added.

Mårten let out a relieved breath. He would've gone anyway, even if Jacob had said it was a bad idea, but now he had renewed faith.

"But I still think you should talk Rydberg into sending someone out with you," Jacob continued.

Aurora would've jumped at the chance to come with him if he'd asked. But he didn't want to stick around for the extra twenty minutes it'd take for her to arrive at his cottage, so he'd gone by himself. "If I find anything, I'll call it in," Mårten hedged. They both knew that wasn't an ideal situation, as help would be half an hour or more away. And they both knew he wouldn't wait for backup before he went in. Especially if Summer was in trouble.

"Just promise you won't do anything stupid," Jacob said with a sigh.

Mårten ignored him, saying instead, "Tell me you've got some good news. You called me, remember?" The FBI had access to resources that the Swedish police did not. He was hoping by some miracle that Jacob's team might be about to crack the whole EIC terrorist group wide open. Mårten anticipated that if his hunch was correct, he was on track to finding and arresting Tyrone, but if the FBI had cornered other members of the group, then they could be interrogating them right now, getting answers and information as to Tyrone's plans.

"Oh, ah..." Jacob hesitated, and Mårten tensed. "That's the reason I was phoning. We've just taken a good look at the CCTV footage, and it's... Ah...not actually Tyrone who flew to Sweden."

What the fuck? Mårten slowed his car and then pulled over onto the edge of the road. This wasn't a conversation he should have while he was driving. So many questions crowded his mind.

"How can you be sure?" he insisted.

"Because the man who boarded the plane under Tyrone's name was white," Jacob replied simply.

"Holy fuck," Mårten swore. Anger and confusion warred in his chest. If it wasn't Tyrone, who was it?

"How could you have let this slip through the cracks?" he demanded. What a monumental stuff up. But then, understanding of Tyrone's rationale flooded in. "A white guy would've been less obvious entering Sweden; that's why Tyrone chose another one of his lackeys, right?"

"Exactly," Jacob said, already way ahead of Mårten. "It took us a while to find this guy on the camera footage, because of course we were looking for a Black man. Now we've pinpointed him, we think he's one of the two other integral members of the EIC."

That'd make sense, Mårten thought, but didn't interrupt. Maybe he was the other guy in Summer's photos.

"His name is Nathan Cole. But…" Jacob hesitated again. It was unlike Jacob not to just come out and say it. Which meant that whatever he was about to tell him was going to be bad.

"Spit it out," Mårten growled. There was something more his friend wasn't telling him.

"We also believe Paige Owen is alive. It seems she's joined the terrorists after all. She was also at the airport."

Mårten was speechless. Actually speechless.

Summer had been right; she had seen Paige the other day in the parking lot after all. Why had he been so eager to brush her fears aside? And why hadn't he pushed Jacob harder to follow it up? He'd been so sure that Paige was dead. And when Summer had talked about how, in hindsight, she could see that perhaps Paige's actions on their field trip were a clue to her affiliation with the terrorist group, he'd shrugged off her concerns. Because he'd been distracted. By his cock. By his need for her. Making love with Summer in the forest that night had been magical, the best thing that'd happened to him in a very long time. And so he'd buried Summer's anxiety at the back of his mind, happy to soak in their newfound intimacy. Then he'd spent the next day lost in his introspection about what it all meant. Whether he should pursue it. Or whether he should just enjoy it and let her go. A one-time thing with no commitments.

Because he'd had sex with Summer, because he'd allowed himself to be distracted, he'd dropped the ball. And now *she* was paying the price.

Mårten covered his face with his hands, letting out a low groan.

"Mårten, are you there? Did you hear me?" Jacob's tinny voice cut through the silence in the car.

He'd failed Summer. But he couldn't dwell on that right now. Right now, he might be her only chance of rescue. He needed to get his shit together. He could ream Jacob out later about why they hadn't followed Summer's concerns up more closely. About how the FBI, with all its billions of dollars and its fearsome reputation for always getting its man, could have failed in this one little thing.

"Yep, I'm here." His voice was hoarse with emotion, and he coughed once to clear it. "Tell me everything."

"She also traveled under an alias, but they flew separately; she boarded an earlier flight. One more reason it took us so long to find them."

The cogs in Mårten's mind turned painfully as he tried to switch from self-condemnation back to evaluating the situation at hand. He needed to get his head back in the game. "So does this mean Tyrone is still in America?" he asked.

"Possibly. We don't know. We're checking all the details. All his other aliases."

"But why?" Mårten queried, his mind still slow to catch

up. "Why would Tyrone want us to think he'd left America?" He'd been so fixated on the fact that it was Tyrone who had taken Summer, he now had to reconfigure everything in his head. "So if it's Nathan and Paige who've got Summer, then what do they want with her?" Mårten said, speaking his thoughts out loud. "Are they holding her as a hostage? As leverage until Tyrone can get out of the country as well?"

"I don't know. I'm as confused as you are. Look, I'm just about to board the plane," Jacob said. "I'll be out of touch for the next ten hours, but you can contact Miller; she'll answer any questions. We're throwing all our resources at finding Summer," he added. "She'll be okay, I promise."

Mårten knew the assurance was a hollow one, and so he didn't reply.

He might not know the exact reasons behind the EIC abduction of Summer, but one thing was for sure. Mårten was heading out to this abandoned farmhouse to find her. And if she was there, he was damn well going to rescue her. The rest could be sorted out later.

* * *

Mårten was pretty sure he was lost. Actually, he knew he was lost. The map app was no longer helpful because this myriad of narrow roads and dirt tracks were not even registering anymore. This was the fourth driveway he'd taken in the past two hours, but he was determined not to give up. He was in the right area; the map told him that much at least. He was close to the lake, but he just couldn't find the correct house.

A couple of the driveways had led to two occupied farmhouses—the inhabitants of which had come out of their doors to stare at him as he pulled up in the front, wondering who could be calling on them at this late hour. But they'd all shook their heads when he'd asked if they'd noticed any suspicious behavior in the area, and then pointed him further north, confirming the Neilsson place was in that direction, but he wouldn't find anyone there, the farm had been deserted for many, many years. The third driveway had taken him to a ruined building, and for a second his heart had leaped in expectation. But even from his car, he could see the property was totally empty and falling to pieces. He'd got out of his car and walked the perimeter anyway, just to make sure. But it'd been a dead end.

The light was failing now. It was after ten, and the gray Nordic twilight swathed the sky. Almost exactly six hours since he'd talked to Summer on the phone. A lot could happen in six hours. The most urgent question was, where was Summer now? Was she still wandering around in the dark, lost in the forest? Or did the abrupt end to her phone call mean that she'd been recaptured? Because they were two very different scenarios. And if she had been caught again, had they punished her for her escape attempt? Hurt her? Or even killed her?

No, he refused to let his mind go there and focused all his senses on the road in front. The only lead he had at the moment was the Neilsson house, and that was where he was going. Everything else would hopefully be revealed in time.

He slowed his car as the dirt track turned a corner, becoming even more overgrown the further in he went. Long grass bowed before his front bumper, and shrubs scraped each side of his car. But he could see that a vehicle had been down this lane recently. There were fresh tire tracks in the damp earth, and the grass was bent and broken. He sat up straighter, his senses coming on high alert.

This could be the place.

He decided to continue the rest of the way on foot. If the kidnappers were here, he didn't want to warn them of his presence with the bright headlights of his car. Finding a small gap in the undergrowth, he parked and got out, closing the door quietly behind him. Then he stood for a few moments, allowing his eyes to adjust to the semi-darkness.

He could just make out a light in the distance through the encroaching wilderness, which was fast taking back the derelict pastures. He stalked closer, eyes straining to make out the building, right hand resting on his gun holster at his hip, his body tense even as he tried to make no sound. The light suddenly disappeared, and Mårten stopped. What did that mean? If it were simply one more farmhouse stuck way out here in the isolated forest, then maybe the owners had just gone to bed. Jacob could be right, and he was on another wild goose chase. But he was here now, and he was determined to check it out, so he kept going.

After five minutes of brisk walking, the track opened up, revealing a large gravel area with the main house nestled at the back and a couple of scattered outbuildings to the rear. Mårten hunkered down behind a copse of small shrubs to survey the scene.

Tall weeds grew up around the building, and all the windows were boarded up. A large red barn stood off to the left, but part of the roof had caved in and one wall leaned precariously inward. It certainly seemed deserted. This could be the farm he'd been looking for. Then he saw it. The rear bumper of a car protruding from behind the dilapidated barn and his heart rate spiked. It was a modern vehicle, bright and shiny. Had he found the place? Was this where they'd been holding Summer? Was she inside? He'd taken two steps forward, fingers flicking open the catch on his holster, before he could stop himself. No. He needed to slow down and make a clinical assessment of what he was seeing. He couldn't let his emotions—which were screaming at him to charge in and break the door down, guns blazing—take over. This thing had to be done right, or Summer may die.

Mårten went back to kneeling in the dirt, weighing up his options. He should probably do a perimeter search first, check to see if there were any signs of life around the front of the property, as well as other exits. Make sure there was no one guarding the area, including the outbuildings.

But the decision was taken away from him when, suddenly, the rear door of the house swung open and light spilled out. A male figure stepped out carrying a couple of bags and stalked angrily across the gravel to where the car was parked. Could this be Nathan Cole? It was hard to tell in the near-dark. The guy was smallish, almost skinny. Mårten watched as he dumped the bags on the ground and then popped the trunk up. He was muttering to himself.

"Wait, Nathan, can't we just talk about this?" The plumpish figure of a woman appeared silhouetted in the doorway. That could well be Paige, if Summer's description was correct. He was on the right track. In the right place. Now he needed to confirm Summer's whereabouts.

"Please," Paige added with a pleading whine.

"No," Nathan shouted over his shoulder, clearly not worried about being overheard by any neighbors or staying quiet. "You heard Tyrone. We need to get out of here. We were compromised when *you* let her escape."

They were on the move then. It seemed as if he'd arrived just in time. They must know about the phone call Summer made, and it spooked them, forcing them to leave their hideout. He should call this in. But he was too close; they might overhear him, and he wasn't backing away. He needed to hear what they had to say.

"Me! That wasn't my fault," Paige countered. "You started it. You were the one who decided to call Tyrone and tattle on me." Paige put her hands on her hips in the age-old action of a woman scorned. The pair were arguing like a married couple, and Mårten turned his thoughts to working out if it was possible to get closer without being seen. He needed to find out if Summer was indeed inside the house. If she'd escaped into the forest, then he would have a decision to make. Stay and try to arrest the abductors, or retreat and try to find her instead. If he ducked back into the scrub, he could circle around behind the barn and come out near where the car was parked. But beating his way through the long grass and bushes was risky because of the noise he might make.

"If you hadn't been such a goddamn pussy and tied her up like I told you to, none of this would've happened," Nathan shouted back, picking up both bags and jamming them into the trunk. "And if it weren't for me, she might've actually escaped for good. And I made bloody sure that Tyrone knows that as well. He knows what a fuckup you are."

Mårten stopped his perusal of the area and stared at Nathan's dark form. The dilute light filtering from the open doorway barely reached him, so it was hard to make out his features. At least Nathan had just answered his question. They had recaptured Summer. Which hopefully meant she was inside the house.

They were still fighting like cat and dog, and so Mårten dived into the long grass, ducking down low and making a beeline for the rear of the barn, attempting to navigate as quietly as possible through the overgrown pastures.

Fuck! He swiped at his face while trying to stay quiet. He'd just walked right through an orb-weaver spiderweb. He tried not to think about whether there'd been an actual spider in the web and kept going. The pair bickering in the background was still audible, a good thing as he hoped it was masking any small noises he made.

But then something Paige said caught his attention.

"You promised you wouldn't kill her."

What? That made him stop in his tracks, straining to hear.

"I never promised you any such thing," Nathan fired back. "I said we needed to keep her as a hostage until Tyrone had completed his mission; that was all." Mårten's palms were suddenly damp as a cold sweat broke out between his shoulder blades. Did that mean Nathan meant to kill Summer before they left? Or take her with them and then dump her body in some other secluded spot? Either way, he had to move. Now. He doubled his speed, not bothering about keeping his head low this time as he continued to listen to them argue.

"No, you said we'd let her go. You said we'd let her go unharmed after we finished with her. You can't just change your mind." Paige was panicking now, her voice rising almost to a screech. And so was Mårten, the adrenaline spike at the thought he might be too late making it hard to remain still.

"No, I didn't. You've had it your way for far too long. Now we're doing it according to my rules," Nathan snarled, and Mårten heard a slam as the weedy guy closed the trunk with force.

Mårten kept going, at last reaching the cover of the rear of the barn, where he straightened and jogged down the side of the back wall, careful to avoid a stack of rotting wooden pallets, a tangle of fencing wire and part of an engine all stashed behind the barn. Reaching the far corner, Mårten stopped and peered around the edge. He could see the car parked up close to the side of the barn, with Nathan still standing behind it, facing away from him. In the distance, Paige remained a blurry shape in the doorway of the house.

"She's done nothing. She's innocent," Paige continued. "Why don't we just leave her tied up in the house? She won't be able to escape, and if no one finds her in a few days, then…" Paige was clearly grasping at straws now.

"Not going to happen," Nathan replied flatly.

Paige took a couple of steps toward Nathan, still pleading with him to let Summer go. Telling him she would make Summer promise not to tell the cops anything about them.

Nathan just laughed in her face. Mårten weighed up his options, absently stroking his gun holster as he did so.

He couldn't take on both of the kidnappers at the same time. Nathan was closest but partially obscured by the car, while Paige was over fifty meters away by the house. If he drew his weapon and took out Nathan first—and it'd have to be a bloody good shot, he wouldn't get a second chance— that'd possibly give Paige time to escape. Or he could make himself known, bluff his way through by pretending he wasn't alone and try to intimidate them both into giving up. Paige might be an ally; she was trying to save Summer's life. But he couldn't guarantee that if he stepped out into the open and declared himself, she would take his side, or at least do nothing to harm Summer. She could just as easily turn back into the house and use Summer as a shield. Hurt her or even kill her if she felt threatened. Experience told Mårten that self-preservation was a strong motivator.

Nope, he needed a plan C; he just wasn't sure what it was yet. And he needed to do it now, while they were still preoccupied with each other.

CHAPTER NINETEEN

The sound of voices drifted through Summer's consciousness. Was that her mother and father arguing again? She wished they'd stop. She just wanted to go back to sleep. Blissful sleep, so that her head didn't hurt anymore. But the buzzing noise of those infernal voices wouldn't let her be. She didn't want to, but eventually she cracked one eyelid open.

Where was she?

Walls and a ceiling floated into focus. She was lying on the floor in a room somewhere. A dim glow drifted through the doorway, which was good. She couldn't handle bright light; it hurt her eyes, hurt her head even more.

Summer tried to open her other eye, but it refused to comply. It was also hard to breathe, something was clogging her nose. But when she made an effort to open her mouth to suck in a breath, it was taped shut. Air. She needed air, but she couldn't seem to drag enough in through the one nostril that was still working. To make matters worse, when she went to lift her hand to remove the tape, she discovered her arms tied together behind her back. As she moved, a searing pain sliced through her forearm.

Summer panicked then, rolling around on dirty floorboards, trying to scream behind the gag, wanting to rid herself of these barbaric ropes. But nothing worked. She couldn't get free. Her heart was pounding out of her chest, and she felt like she was going to pass out from lack of air.

It all came back to her then. The abduction, her escape. Nathan tackling her to the ground and hurting her. He must've recaptured her and was now holding her somewhere different from the shed. Fuck, she needed to get out of here. Needed air. Needed help. In a remote part of her brain, Summer realized she also ought to calm down; that she was hyperventilating, and if she didn't stop, she might pass out.

But Summer's animal mind had taken over, and she scrabbled at the floorboards with her fingers, desperation driving her on as she rolled over and over on the floor. It was the pain in her head and her wrist that stopped her wild flailing in the end. The headache was the same as the pain when she'd woken up in the shed after they'd first seized her. They must've drugged her again. She wasn't sure what was wrong with her arm. Could it be broken?

Summer lay still, twisting to one side to ease the ache in her shoulders and wrist, chest heaving, tears of pain and frustration running down her face. As her breathing came back to normal, she tried to tune in to her surroundings again.

The arguing voices had become louder. It was her captors quarreling, not her parents after all. Paige must be close by, Summer could hear her clearly. Nathan's voice, however, was indistinct, more of a distant shouting.

Then she heard Paige say loudly, "You promised you wouldn't kill her."

Summer froze. She'd always been afraid that Nathan hadn't meant to leave her alive. But to hear Paige utter those chilling words, to know that he was going to go through with it, made her panic rise all over again. She couldn't discern Nathan's response, but the scorn in his voice was clear. She needed to get out of here. Summer struggled again with the ropes around her wrists, fighting the pain slicing up her arm. At one stage she managed to push herself upright into a sitting position with her good hand, but it was still no good. With her hands tied behind her back, she couldn't even reach the cords securing her ankles. It was hopeless. Hot tears of anger ran unchecked down her cheeks.

What she needed was help. Where was Mårten? Where were the cops? Why hadn't they tracked her down already? That was their job, wasn't it? Mårten had promised he'd protect her. That she would be safe with him. And she'd believed him. Summer's tears of frustration turned to sobs of sorrow and despair. She was alone, and she was going to die. She'd been strong enough to escape once on her own. But this time she was doomed.

Wait. She could hear footsteps coming down the hallway. Stealthy footsteps. Paige and Nathan were even now arguing, Nathan's voice getting closer now. But they were both still outside by the sounds of it. So who was walking through the house? Summer rolled over, eyes fixed on the doorway, lying completely still. A large figure loomed; she couldn't make out his features in the murky light. But she knew who it was; she would've known him anywhere. Those familiar broad shoulders that filled the door, straight-backed stance, chin slightly lowered as he trained his intense crystal-blue gaze on her.

Mårten.

She would have screamed his name if she could've.

How could she ever have doubted him?

He was on his knees beside her before she could even blink. He picked her up and held her so tight against his chest that for one second he almost squeezed the breath from her lungs as he muttered, "Gudskelov, gudskelov."

She was no genius, but if the relief she felt was half that of his, then she had a good idea of what he was saying. But his comfort was soon torn away as he placed her gently down on the floor.

"We haven't got long," he whispered urgently, turning his head to check the door. "They're distracted outside, but we need to be quick." His fingers fumbled at the ropes around her legs even as he spoke. "My car is parked a little way up the driveway. We're going to try to make it back there before they realize you're gone. Okay?"

She could only nod in agreement. All she wanted was to be held in those strong arms again. For one split-second she had felt so safe, so treasured.

When he'd finished untying her legs, she made noises from behind the tape to attract his attention. She needed this gag removed. As his gaze drifted upward from where he'd been concentrating on the knots around her ankles, he flinched.

"Oh my God, Summer, what have they done to you?" Mårten's obvious horror when he saw her face confirmed her worst fears. When Nathan had caught her, he'd beaten her senseless. She remembered the first few blows now. After he'd knocked her to the ground in the forest, Nathan had rained punch after punch into her head and body, yelling at her that she was a bitch and she deserved everything she got. Summer must've blacked out at some stage because she had no idea how she'd got back to this room, or even how long she'd been here.

It explained why she couldn't see out of her left eye; it was swollen shut. And it explained the pain in her wrist, which was most likely broken. They must have drugged her to keep her unconscious while they decided their next move. She was probably lucky to still be alive.

Mårten removed the duct tape as gently as he could, but it was nevertheless excruciating is it lifted a layer of skin from around her mouth.

"Mårten." His name came out more of a croak than a word.

"I'm sorry," he said. "I'm so sorry I didn't get here sooner." In the dim light she could see his face, a severe mask of self-incrimination. He was working on the knots binding her wrists now, and when he tugged hard on the rope, she let out an involuntary gasp of pain.

"Are you hurt?" he demanded.

She nodded and said, "I'm not sure, but it might be broken."

"Fuck! I really am gonna kill that guy," Mårten muttered as he took more care with the knots. He helped her to her feet, one arm around her shoulder to keep her steady. Which was a good thing, because she swayed dangerously as the room swirled about her. Her legs felt like they were made of lead, pins and needles shooting upward as the blood released from where the ropes had been tied too tight. "It's okay, I've got you," he said, his lips close to her ear. "Can you take a step for me?"

Cradling her broken arm close to her body, she forced herself to take one tentative, clumsy step, then another, conscious of the fact that Paige or Nathan could appear at any second. "I'm good," she said from between gritted teeth. "Let's get out of here." Leaning heavily on Mårten, she made it out of the room, but she was so slow. She knew they were running out of time. They turned left down the hallway, her shuffling steps loud in the muted silence of the old house. She was aware that she could no longer hear Paige and Nathan arguing. Everything had gone deathly quiet outside. If they'd stopped arguing…Summer tried to quicken her pace, but her legs were sluggish to respond. They were just as battered and bruised as the rest of her body.

"I picked the lock and got in through the rear door," Mårten explained, and Summer could just make out a door standing ajar at the end of the hallway. Outside was freedom.

The idea spurred her on, and she increased her hobbling pace to a shambling run, Mårten holding her by the uninjured side.

A guttural scream echoed down the hallway. Summer stopped and turned instinctively toward that terrible sound.

"Fuck." Mårten was tugging on her arm. Then he was behind her, propelling her forward, supporting her by the waist, almost carrying her.

"That sounded like Paige," she said, her mind still caught up in wanting to figure out what was going on outside. Had Nathan attacked Paige? Should they help her? But by then Mårten had half-carried her to the threshold of the door. He shoved it all the way open with one foot, and blessed cool air hit Summer in the face. Freedom. They were safe.

That thought was extinguished when there was a roar of rage from behind, so primal it could've come from a wild animal. Then pounding footsteps echoed down the hallway. Mårten thrust her outside onto the damp grass.

"Run," he screamed.

Summer collapsed to the ground. The shock of the fall jostling her arm so that pain shot up into her shoulder. It took her a few seconds to recover and then scrabble around in the dirt on her knees so she was facing the right way.

Mårten's broad back filled the doorway as he turned to face the oncoming threat. "Stay back," he warned. "I'm police, and I will shoot you if I have to."

Nathan's only reply was to yell an unintelligible stream of words as he continued to pound down the hallway.

For the first time, Summer noticed Mårten was carrying a weapon strapped in a holster around his waist. He had his right hand on the handle of the gun, and even as she watched, he drew it. But then her view was blocked by his body, so she couldn't see what was happening. She got to her feet and backed away, trying to discover what was going on, unsure what to do next. Should she help him? But she had no idea what to do. One thing was sure; she wasn't running anywhere. Not without Mårten.

There was a shout, and the gun went off. Once. Twice.

And then Mårten was stumbling backward, falling on the ground right where Summer had been kneeling only seconds before, his weapon flying out of his hands. A howling Nathan landed on top of him, flailing wildly with a large knife in one hand, trying to stab Mårten.

Summer screamed. The sight of the blade flashing again and again toward Mårten had her frozen to the spot.

Memories of the night Marco died spiraled through her head, drawing her down into their depths.

The muggers had attacked them on a dark street while they'd been walking home from the movies late one night. They'd accosted them, stabbed Marco before she even had time to react, then stolen her bag as she fell to the pavement beside Marco, begging him to keep breathing. That they'd just killed a person was of no concern to the thugs. Perhaps they were high on drugs. The sad thing was, it'd all been for nothing. Summer had less than $20 in her purse, which she would've gladly given them if they'd just asked. And the police never caught the criminals. They'd done a most perfunctory investigation, as if Marco's life was unimportant. A Latino boy and his seventeen-year-old girlfriend weren't near the top of their lists of priorities, and gang violence was rife in a city of that size.

Another wild grunt from Nathan pulled her back to the present. She wasn't on the streets of San Jose. She was in the wilds of Sweden, and Mårten was here trying to protect her; fighting for his life. And hers.

Mårten was doing everything in his power to ward off Nathan's strikes, his training helping him to block each blow, keeping the knife away from his face, grunting with the effort of protecting himself. But eventually Nathan was bound to land a strike.

She needed to help him. She hadn't been able to help Marco. But maybe she could change the outcome today. Nathan seemed to have forgotten that Summer was there. Maybe he didn't see her as a threat, or maybe he was just so blinded by his bloodlust that all he could see was Mårten. Whatever it was, it gave her an opportunity.

The gun? Where had the gun gone? She finally spotted it, a black shape on a patch of gravel a few feet from where the men were wrestling. Half-stumbling, half-crawling, she reached it and picked it up with her good hand. Checked that it was loaded, and that the safety was off. Then she turned toward the fighting men and raised the weapon.

Nathan was still on top of Mårten, who was lying on the ground defending himself as best he could. She took aim at Nathan's torso. Summer knew guns. She trained every few months at a local gun range. After Marco's death, she'd been determined never to be a victim again. So she learned how to use a gun, just in case. Kept her skills up-to-date. This would be a difficult shot, however. She was holding it one-handed, her broken left arm useless. What if the bullet went wide and hit Mårten instead?

"Nathan," she said in a strong, clear voice. "Stop, or I'll shoot."

But it was as if Nathan hadn't heard her. He was in a frenzy, desperate to attack Mårten, and he never even looked up.

She needed to get his attention to make him stop. She fired to the left of the fighting men, the sound so loud it nearly deafened her. But it had the desired effect. Nathan froze, knife-wielding arm mid-air, staring at her with glazed, red-rimmed eyes.

"What the fu—" but he never got to finish his question. In

one swift move, Mårten snapped a hand up, dislodging the blade from Nathan's grip. Before Summer could even blink, Mårten had twisted sideways and rolled Nathan onto his back, so that now he was sitting astride the man.

"It's over, mate," Mårten said, breathing heavily. "You heard the lady. If you move, she'll shoot you."

Her hand shook, and she lowered the weapon. Thank God she hadn't had to pull the trigger. She liked to believe that she would have if the need had been desperate enough. If Mårten's life depended on it. But now she would never have to know what it felt like to shoot another human being. She watched as Mårten pulled out a set of handcuffs and secured Nathan, who was still struggling hard to get free.

"Give me the gun," Mårten commanded as he stood and backed away from Nathan. Summer was only too happy to comply, limping over and handing it to him. He took the weapon, unlatched the safety and re-holstered it at his hip, watching Nathan like a hawk. "Backup will be here in a few minutes," Mårten continued, probably saying it as much for her sake as for Nathan's. At his words, Nathan stopped struggling, emitting a large howl of rage and anguish. Of defeat. Then he closed his eyes and lay completely motionless as if by doing so he could pretend that none of this was happening.

Backup couldn't get here fast enough, Summer decided. Her bones were suddenly all doughy, as if they might not hold her up anymore. It was hard to believe this nightmare could be over. Then she remembered the scream. Paige. "We need to see if Paige is hurt," she said, turning toward Mårten.

"Yep, I will, just give me a second," he replied with a grimace.

What was wrong? Why did he look as if he were in pain?

Mårten was standing in the stream of light extending through the open door. Summer took three steps nearer as

Mårten bent over and pressed a hand to his abdomen. Now that she was close, and now that he was no longer in the dark, she could make out a mysterious stain on Mårten's T-shirt.

Oh. No.

Blood seeped from between Mårten's fingers, and he winced again as he applied pressure to the wound. Mårten had been injured. He was bleeding. Now she could see how pale his handsome face had become. How he was gritting his teeth against the pain.

All Summer could do was stand and stare. She hadn't saved the day after all; Mårten had still been stabbed. He was still going to die. He was going to bleed out, and he was going to die.

"You're hurt," she whispered through numb lips.

"I'm okay. It'll be fine. I'm pretty sure it's only a flesh wound," Mårten said, straightening up slowly, and trying to smile at her.

But he couldn't make this go away with a smile. He couldn't pretend he was *fine* just for her sake. Summer took a step backward. How could he possibly know he would be fine? He wasn't fine; this was very, very bad.

"No, noooo," Summer wailed, almost beyond coherent thought now. "You're going to die. Please don't leave me."

"I'm not going to die," he replied, shock and confusion replacing his attempt at a reassuring smile.

"Yes, yes, you are. Marco died. And you're going to as well."

She needed to get out of here; she couldn't deal with this. Not again. She couldn't bear to have someone she cared about perish again.

"Summer, it's okay." Mårten reached out to hand toward her.

"No!" She turned and ran.

CHAPTER TWENTY

Mårten's gaze stayed anchored on Summer, who sat curled up in a chair in the corner of the hospital room, even while a nurse continued to fuss around him. She looked small, diminished somehow from the woman he had come to know. She kept her eyes averted, refusing to look at him.

Mårten still couldn't unravel everything that'd happened out at the farm tonight. Of course, he reported everything matter-of-factly in his statement. Stated that after he called for backup, he'd entered the building through the rear because he was afraid for Summer's life. He'd overheard the two perpetrators talking about killing her, and they were occupied out the front, so he took his chance, not prepared to wait for the other units to arrive. He'd reported that they'd heard a scream—which must have been Nathan attacking Paige—and then Nathan had ambushed him. It was with some discomfort that Mårten had also admitted to dropping his weapon. That Summer had picked it up and kept it pointed at Nathan long enough for him to subdue the suspect.

There was an entire week's worth of paperwork in just that single incident. A police officer losing his firearm was unsatisfactory and unprofessional. But a civilian picking up that same gun and using it—even if it was to help him—was not only highly undesirable, it was humiliating and humbling as well. Summer had probably saved his life, or at least saved him from serious harm, and he made sure that everyone knew that. The last thing she needed was to be scolded for retrieving the weapon, which Rydberg was likely to do. She was one brave, kick-ass woman, and needed to be reminded of that, not admonished for it.

But he left out a crucial fact. Summer had flipped out when she'd seen him bleeding, but he didn't know why. She'd run away like she'd seen a ghost. At least she hadn't gone far, only to the front of the house, where she'd stumbled across Paige, where he found her a few moments later crouched over the body.

Everything had happened quickly then, with sirens and flashing lights filling the air as first one, and then a second unit arrived, taking charge of the scene. An ambulance had shown up shortly after, paramedics fussing over him and Summer, making sure their wounds weren't life-threatening. Which he already knew his wasn't, because it was what he'd been trying to explain to Summer before she took off. Yes, Nathan's blade had punctured his skin, but he was able to deflect the blow enough that it wasn't deep, and had pierced none of his major organs. But even after this explanation, she'd refused to make eye contact for the rest of the night. It was all plain weird, and he was hoping to get the truth out of her once everyone had left. He wanted to understand how she could go from being so lionhearted one minute—ignoring her own pain to pick up a gun and point it at her abductor without a second's hesitation—to a blubbering, terrified wreck of a woman the next.

She'd refused to go into a hospital bed of her own, preferring to sit in his room with him after his wound had been cleaned and stitched, while he was being debriefed.

Rydberg had tried to have her removed, but Mårten had made it clear she was to stay; otherwise, they would get nothing from him.

At last, the nurse stopped fussing and left the room. They were finally alone. It must be nearly two in the morning. It'd been an endless day, and the pain meds were making him drowsy. But there was no way he was going to sleep just yet. Not without talking to Summer first.

She was still wearing her Lycra suit, but someone had draped a police-issue jacket over her shoulders. Summer was beautiful, despite the fact that her hair was a mess of tangles, her right eye was bloodshot, and her left eye was bruised and swollen shut where Nathan had beaten her. Her left arm was indeed broken near the wrist; it'd been splinted and was resting in a sling tied around her neck. His gaze traveled down her body, documenting her long, lithe legs pulled up into her chest as she sat staring out the window at the city lights below. No matter how damaged, she was still the most gorgeous thing he'd ever seen. He wanted to take her in his arms and hold her until the world stopped spinning. Until she looked at him like she had the other night when they'd made love under the stars.

He knew that wasn't what she wanted, however, and so he let her sit alone, lost in her own thoughts.

Jacob's flight from Seattle was due to land soon. Even though his trip was mostly a wasted one now, Mårten wanted to see his old friend, and hoped he wouldn't turn straight around and head back to America. It'd be good to talk everything that'd happened through with somebody he trusted explicitly. Get Jacob's opinion on the repercussions of this mission. Mårten knew he'd let emotions drive him tonight, and although he hadn't technically disobeyed a direct order, and the outcome had been favorable in the end, there were many, many things that he'd done wrong.

Rydberg had made it clear there would be an inquiry into his actions and his decision-making. This would be the second internal review Mårten had been involved with in less than a year. It wouldn't look good on his file. Hopefully, Jacob would be a firm ally in the coming few days, because Mårten was going to need someone on his side if he were to get through this unscathed.

Summer shifted in her seat, and Mårten's laser focus veered to her once more. "Paige didn't deserve to die," she said in a small voice.

"No, she didn't," he agreed, trying not to show how relieved he was. At least she was talking, even if her gaze remained fixed outside the window.

He was desperate to touch her, so he patted the bed hopefully. "Will you come and sit with me?"

She turned and stared at him for many long seconds, eyes hollow and unreadable. Then slowly, painfully, she uncurled her legs and walked barefoot over to his bed. He patted the bed again, and after another moment's hesitation she climbed up awkwardly so that she was nestled in the crook of his arm, resting her head against his chest. At first she was rigid and stiff, but he curled his arm around her shoulder, careful not to jostle her broken arm, and pulled her in tighter, letting her know with his body that she was safe. It took a few moments, but at last she relaxed into him, emitting a sigh of release. His heart joggled agonizingly in his chest. It felt like she'd just given him something precious, something he needed to cherish. Her trust.

"Nathan will be charged with her murder, along with your kidnapping. He'll go to jail for a long time," he mumbled into her hair. He knew it was no real comfort to Summer, because her friend was still dead. And even though the girl had had misguided intentions, she wasn't inherently evil, unlike her colleague. But at least Nathan could no longer hurt Summer;

he'd pay with the rest of his life for what he'd done.

"Hmm," she murmured in reply. "So, what happens now?" she asked, half-lifting her head from his chest.

"Well, Jacob will be here soon and we can try to figure out the motivation behind your kidnapping," Mårten replied, his mind already drifting to the questions they might put to Nathan. Why had they abducted Summer? They still didn't know how she was connected to the eco-terrorists' plans. Surely, they hadn't taken her out of pure revenge? And why had they gone to the trouble of making the FBI believe it was Tyrone who was traveling to Sweden in the first place? Tyrone who'd carried out the snatch and grab.

"No, I mean, can I go back to Seattle?" She lifted her broken arm into the air. "I won't be able to compete in the triathlon with this. So, if I'm not needed here, I may as well leave. I want to go home," she added almost in a whisper.

"Oh, right." Mårten hadn't thought that far ahead, had virtually forgotten about the triathlon. He'd been so focused on finding Summer and saving her that any future past tonight was simply not on his radar. And even then his mind was fixed on building the case against the eco-terrorist, ensuring Nathan would not get away. Catching the perpetrator was merely the start; there'd be court cases and lawyers, and media scrums, days and weeks of logging evidence and paperwork. Liaising with Jacob and the FBI, as well as the Washington State police, to make sure all the facts were airtight. There'd be month's worth of work to do yet.

The idea of Summer might leave him to go back to America hit him like a blast of cold air. It had never even occurred to him she might want to go home. It was too soon, wasn't it? They needed more time together. With the clarity born from imminent loss, he suddenly knew he didn't want her to go. He wanted her here, by his side, and the thought of not having her was too much to bear.

He'd come to care for this complicated woman deeply. She was his opposite in almost every way; they had nothing in common. She held her cards close to her chest and often kept him at bay with her thorny exterior. Her world was one of schedules and rules, and she seemed happy with her solitary existence, where she could control everything and everyone in her life.

Nevertheless, he remained drawn to her, had witnessed some of those walls breaking down in the few weeks he'd known her, and he'd liked the glimpse of the real Summer he'd seen below the surface. She had a wicked sense of humor and could light up a room with her presence when she finally let herself go. Her determination and grit were a sight to behold—the way she was dogged in her pursuit of excellence in her triathlons, and how she had used her passion to build her own successful videography business. But there was also a vulnerability, a heartbreak she buried so deep. He'd detected it more than once, and he wanted to know more, to plumb the depths of Summer and find out what made her tick. To explore whatever was developing between them; it had the potential to be something great.

Lifting a hand, he tucked a stray strand of hair behind her ear. "Do you need to go home so soon? Why don't you stay in Sweden for a while? You can live in my house, recuperate there. We can heal together." The words came out even as the notion formed in his head. It was a good idea, now he thought about it. A great idea, even.

She made no reply, lifting her dark gaze to stare at him, confusion flitting across her face. He took hold of her good hand, and she tensed at his touch. How could he convince her to stay? Perhaps he needed to tell her the truth.

"I think we have something good. I think...I might be—" the shrill jangle of his mobile cut over the top of his words.

They both stared at Mårten's cell as it vibrated on the table next to them.

"Shit." Mårten didn't hide his disgust. It was the worst timing ever, but it was Jacob, and he knew he should answer. Jacob must've just landed in Stockholm, and he'd need an update. But this conversation with Summer was important. Maybe the most important he'd had in a long, long time.

"I'll call Jacob back," Mårten said, determined to finish their talk. But Summer was already scrambling off the bed.

"No, no, you go ahead," she replied, retreating, gaze averted once more. Shit, he'd lost her; she was withdrawing behind her high walls all over again. Had she heard him? Had she realized he was about to declare that he was falling for her? Because she was acting like a frightened rabbit about to bolt. This wasn't the reaction he'd been expecting. What had he done? The last thing he wanted to do was scare her away. Damn bloody Jacob.

"Summer, I…"

"Take the call," she replied, voice deadpan. "I want to hear what he has to say."

For a few more long moments, Mårten ignored the shrill ringtone. But he knew there was no point in pushing her, so all he could do was try to read her features as he picked up the phone and pressed it to his ear.

"Hi, Jacob," he said, not taking his eyes off Summer, who'd retreated to her chair in the corner.

"Mårten, I've got news." Jacob was almost yelling down the line.

"I've got news too," Mårten said, pulling himself together. "I found Summer. She's safe with me now. We're in the hospital." He was being as succinct as possible, trying to get his words out before Jacob butted in.

"I know, I just heard," Jacob confirmed. "Congratulations, dude, you did good." Normally, Jacob's praise would've helped allay some of Mårten's fears that he'd fucked up on the job. But the thought that he'd fucked up even worse with Summer just now was overriding everything else.

"But I think I might know the motive behind the abduction." Jacob continued, his tone tight with excitement.

"Wait, can I put you on speaker? Summer is here with me, she might want to hear this."

"Yes, sure," Jacob agreed, but he was talking again even before Mårten had time to press the button. "I just got word there's been an arson attack on the gold mine at Yellowstone. The whole fucking place has been destroyed. One person dead, two others injured. There's a huge forest fire raging on the outskirts of the national park."

Summer stood, the light of something unreadable in her expression. Mårten was sitting upright in bed now, the hand not holding the phone clenched at his side. That fucker! Mårten knew immediately what'd happened.

"Let me guess, it was Tyrone King," he said, locking his gaze with Summer's. She nodded in agreement, her one good eye going wide with shock.

"That's what we suspect, yeah. They were using Summer as a decoy so he could carry out his plan while our focus was fixed on finding her."

"Wow," Mårten breathed. That was why Tyrone had tried to make them believe he was no longer in America. So he could continue planting incendiary bombs while the FBI searched for him outside the country.

"We don't believe their intention was to kill her," Jacob continued. "Just hold her until the arson attack went through, perhaps even long enough for Tyrone to then flee the country."

"So I was sort of like a hostage, and the price of my freedom was a successful burning of the mine site?" Summer had stepped forward, her poor battered face looking more animated than he'd seen all night. "And so Paige was right;

she never intended to kill me. It was Nathan who changed the plan."

He could see relief in her one good eye. Relief that Paige had been telling the truth, at least about that part. He could understand why Summer wanted to redeem the Paige in some small way.

"Yes, that's probably accurate," Jacob replied. "Although we can't be sure until we interview Nathan. I'm hoping to catch the next flight to Luleå and be there in a few hours. I want to get you as many answers as we can, Summer."

While this was all good information, and Mårten wholeheartedly agreed, he didn't want to get sidetracked and so he interrupted with another question. "Where is King now?" Because that was the next most critical item. It was important for them to know if he yet held a grudge against Summer. Because if he did, then Summer wasn't safe until they had the bastard behind bars.

Jacob's silence was all the answer Mårten needed. He must still be at large somewhere. There was absolutely no chance of his letting Summer go back to America with that lunatic on the loose. But when he opened his mouth to tell her this, the same stubborn look settled on her face as if she already knew what he was going to say. The one he remembered when he'd first met her in Seattle. She wanted to go home, and she would fight him every step of the way. His heart sank. All he wanted was to protect her, but it seemed everything he did alienated her even further.

CHAPTER TWENTY-ONE

Summer stood next to the hospital bed, only half-listening to Jacob and Mårten talk. They were discussing the finer details of the attack on the mine site and where Tyrone might be hiding out now. None of this felt relevant to her anymore, however. The only thing that was important to Summer was her urgent, undeniable need to get home. Ever since she'd seen Mårten bleeding from a stab wound, a switch had flipped inside her. It might be better to call it a panic button. Whatever it was, now all she felt when she looked at him was a terrible fear. Dread clawed at her gut, tried to climb her throat and get out of her body as a never-ending scream. It was all she could do to keep a straight face in his presence.

Mårten had come close to dying. And it was all her fault. Again. She was bad luck to have around. Cursed. She needed to get away from him before something else terrible happened. Because she couldn't watch someone else she loved die right in front of her.

Summer barely acknowledged the idea that she might be in love with Mårten. That emotion came second; it wasn't important. She wouldn't put him in danger again.

And while he hadn't actually come out and said the L word just as Jacob's phone call had interrupted him, even the suggestion had been enough to scare her. What if he was already in love with her? And what if she'd allowed herself to fall for him too? What would she have done then? If Mårten had died, her world would've been shattered once again. And she wouldn't have been able to recover this time.

It was too much for her to risk falling in love with Mårten. Sometimes the risks did outweigh the benefits. Living in Sweden with Mårten had made her forget the rules she'd used to live by for a little while. Her rules had been set in place to protect her heart. She knew what true heartache felt like, and she never wanted to go there again. Never ever. Reality could be cruel. It could crush your dreams, and hollow you out, until you were a mere shell of a human being.

Mårten finally ended his call, placing his cell back on the side table, searching her face for answers as he did so. But she refused to look at him, instead walking over and staring out the window.

"You can't go back to America. Not yet. Not until we find Tyrone. He could still be after you." It was exactly what she'd expected him to say. Mårten was a protector at heart, his profession as a police officer a perfect match for his personality. But she could no longer be his responsibility. He needed to get on with his life, and she needed to get on with hers.

But the only way to get him to listen was to tell him the truth. Mårten deserved an answer; she owed him that much. And the only way she could explain that her carefully crafted life was the best way she knew how to live—so that she never went back into that soul-crushing, horrific, dark place—was to tell him about Marco. The whole story, the unvarnished truth. The terrible years she'd spent blaming herself, so grief stricken that in the end she had to leave her family and friends so she could build a new future in Seattle, where she wasn't reminded every day of what she'd lost.

She turned and met his serious silver eyes. Eyes the color of liquid mercury, or a wild, stormy ocean. Expressive eyes that hinted at everything he was feeling.

"I need to tell you something. About my past. About a boy called Marco."

"Hmm, the mysterious Marco," Mårten said, then immediately grimaced. "Sorry. It's just that you mentioned his name last night, and I've been wondering about him ever since."

She was sure he had. The way she'd acted must've seemed crazy. But maybe after he heard her story, he would understand.

"Marco and I were in love. We were seventeen, and after we finished school at the end of the year, we planned to get married." She'd never told her parents this. No one knew; it was a secret they'd kept between themselves. Summer never allowed herself to go down the *what-if* tunnel. After Marco had died, she'd shut away all her hopes and dreams of a white wedding, of both of them getting jobs so they could eventually afford to buy a small house. Of having children together; she would've liked at least three. But just for a second as she stood in front of the hospital window, she let the images resurface.

"We could've had a perfect life together," she breathed. "But that was all taken away when we were walking home from the cinema one night and a gang of young, Black guys stopped us in the street, demanding my handbag. I would've willingly given it to them, but Marco stepped in front of me. He was trying to protect me. They stabbed him ten times. He died in my arms."

"Summer, I didn't know. I'm so sorry..." The raw empathy in his voice was nearly her undoing. He had one leg out of the bed to come to her before she held up a hand to stop him, because she needed to finish before the words stuck in her throat.

"You weren't supposed to know. Because I've put it all behind me," she said bluntly. "But you have to know this story because it explains why I am the way I am. I don't enjoy being out after dark. And I don't go into gloomy alleys or deserted places by myself. I used to suffer nightmares every night. But now, until recently anyway, I stopped having them. I'm happy with my life as it is. I have my photography, and I have my friends, and I don't have any complications."

This time Mårten got out of bed and limped toward her. His legs were bare beneath his hospital gown, his handsome face contorted with distress.

"I can't even imagine what you've been through." Mårten stopped mere inches from her, his head bent low so he could look her directly in the eyes, but he didn't touch her. Thank the Lord. If he had…

"That kind of trauma changes people," he agreed. "I'm not going to pretend I understand."

She lifted her chin. No, he would never understand. No one did.

"But what about love? What about someone to share your life with? Are you saying you don't want that? Don't need that?" he continued.

She snorted, a derisive noise meant to drive him away. "You sound like Bianca," she accused. "And yes, that's exactly what I'm saying."

"You can't mean it." He took her hand, which was now dangling uselessly at her side, his warm touch a shock to her system. "I know my dating history is not the best example." He gave a slight shrug. "But I guess a part of me always hoped that I'd find love eventually. It's what every human being wants. Needs. Someone to care for them. Someone to share their life with. The ups and the downs. The good and the bad. Isn't it?"

"Not me." Summer had to force the words past a sudden lump in her throat. It took everything she had to drop his hand, push him away. "I know you mean well. And I owe you a huge debt of gratitude for all that you've done for me. For coming to find me, for saving me." Her insides shook, as if an earthquake was erupting in her chest. She kept her chin up, ignoring the trembling inside as she stepped around him. "But I need to go home. I can't stay here, and I can't be with you. It just wouldn't work, Mårten."

She hadn't known this would be the outcome tonight as she sat in the chair waiting for Mårten to finish talking to his supervisor and then the nurses. But now, it seemed inevitable. It was for the best, she decided as she carefully opened the door and stepped through it without once looking back.

"Summer, wait," he called, but she was already walking down the hallway.

CHAPTER TWENTY-TWO

A hint of a warm breeze blew in through the open window. It was unseasonably warm today in Seattle, and Summer's small apartment was feeling claustrophobic. Unlike Mårten's little cottage in the forest, which had felt airy and light, even in the heat of the middle of the day. She tried to push that thought from her mind, refocusing on the television, leaning forward and waving her cast in the air, urging Erin Jorganson to go faster. Natascha Sodoro was catching up to her, and although Summer didn't have a preference—if she couldn't be there to compete, then she didn't care who won—Erin deserved to win this time. The women were on the last leg of the triathlon, and Erin had set a fast pace in the run. The camera zoomed out so that the image on the television was now an aerial shot of the runners strung out along the road. It looked damn hot, and all the competitors were sucking down electrolytes by the gallon.

Strangely, Summer wasn't as miserable at not attending the triathlon meet as she thought she would be. She stared at the TV screen, unable to stay focused on the drama unfolding in Pontevedra. Perhaps that was because she'd been feeling numb ever since she'd boarded the plane out of Stockholm.

It was only two days since she'd returned home, but

already she kept finding things she missed about Sweden. Sunshine through dappled birch leaves. Picking the little wild smultron berries and letting their sweetness burst on her tongue. So many birds singing in the trees that she could barely hear herself talk. The fact that the Swedish people venerated the summer months before they disappeared into the long winters.

She was flat and lethargic, could hardly raise the energy to get out of bed in the morning. It must be jet lag; that was the only logical explanation. Her wrist no longer ached non-stop. Now it was itchy and annoying, hindering just about everything she did. Summer had forced herself to go for a run yesterday afternoon, but her cast made her clumsy and unbalanced, and she turned around after only five very unsatisfactory miles.

She checked her watch. Bianca would be here soon. Her good friend had been ecstatic to hear that she was home safe and sound, as well as being back in time for Josie and Mark's wedding this Saturday. Poor Bianca had picked up most of the slack for Summer's bridesmaid duties, and she'd done it without complaint. But Summer could perceive the relief in her friend's voice when she phoned this morning to let her know she'd returned and that she could take over.

She was finding it hard to get excited about the wedding but hoped Bianca's arrival would lift her spirits. She was a little lost, that was all, yet on Swedish time, her mind still occupied by the surreal week and a half she'd spent with Mårten. All she needed was a bit of Bianca's energy and vivacity to pick her up and set her back on the path to the reality of her life in Seattle.

The doorbell rang, and Summer levered herself off the couch with a sigh as she glanced around her messy apartment. It was unusual for Bianca to be this early, and she'd meant to tidy up a little and get dressed before her friend arrived. It was also unusual for Summer to still be in her pajamas at midday, but Bianca wouldn't mind; Summer would just tell her it was the jet lag, and they'd laugh about it, and then she would get changed.

But it wasn't Bianca standing on the landing when Summer opened the door.

It was Nikki.

"Oh, hi," Summer stammered, very conscious that she hadn't even brushed her hair yet. Blast, this was embarrassing.

"Sorry to arrive unannounced like this," Nikki said, stepping into the apartment without waiting for an invitation. "Jacob told me you were home, and I wanted to come and see how you were." She engulfed Summer in a hug, and for a second, she was so taken aback she remained stiff and unyielding. She'd forgotten how warm and demonstrative Nikki was. Forgotten how much she liked the woman. Summer returned the hug, squashing a sudden urge to cry. Why on earth would Nikki's appearance make her want to cry?

"Oh, my, look at your poor face." Nikki stepped back and studied Summer. "Jacob told me that bastard beat you up, but this is worse than I imagined." "Does it hurt?" The compassion in the other woman's blue eyes made the tears threaten even harder.

"Not really," Summer mumbled. She'd almost forgotten about the bruising on her face. She had an impressive black eye now, but it looked worse than it felt. There were also contusions on her lower jaw where Nathan had hit her more than once, but again that was fading. And the slight pain was nothing compared to everything else that'd happened that night. Nothing compared to Paige's death. Nothing compared to Mårten's being stabbed. "I'll put the kettle on," she said a little awkwardly, breaking apart from Nikki's well-intentioned embrace.

"That'd be nice," Nikki agreed, taking a seat on the couch Summer had just vacated. She was dressed casually in white capris and a T-shirt, her long blonde hair left to fall over her shoulders in a silken sheath.

Before Summer could ask how the repairs were going on her burned front porch, the other woman exclaimed, "Oh, is this your world triathlon event? What a pity you had to miss it." She leaned forward to peer at the television. Summer couldn't detect any irony in Nikki's tone. Summer had used the competition as her main excuse for not wanting to go to Sweden. Paradoxically, if she hadn't consented to go and had instead remained in America under FBI guard, maybe she would still be attending the event. Summer wasn't about to dwell on the *what if's*, however.

"Yes," she agreed, forcing a cheerful note into her voice. "But it's all good. Erin is setting such a fast pace I'm sure I wouldn't have had a chance of being beating her anyway," she demurred.

Nikki frowned but said nothing in reply and lapsed into silence, which Summer tried to fill with the clatter of mugs on the countertop. Why couldn't she think of anything to say? The air was tense and awkward in her little apartment.

"Jacob is home now too. He got in last night. And he's worried about you," Nikki said, standing and walking over to the kitchen island. Here it came at last, the real reason Nikki was here. A small, traitorous part of Summer wondered if Nikki was doing Jacob's job for him, asking these seemingly innocuous questions, and then she'd then go back and report all her movements to Jacob.

And Mårten.

"Is he?" Summer replied, trying and failing to keep the sullen note out of her tone. She'd had to endure hours of Jacob talking at her before she'd left Sweden, trying to convince her it wasn't safe yet to return to America, with Mårten hovering in the background, a worried frowned creasing his brow, like he was her father or something.

"Which means I'm worried about you," Nikki added. "They still haven't found Tyrone King, you know."

"Yes, I'm aware," Summer said, taking the tea bag out of the mug and then turning her back to put it in the recycling so she didn't have to look at Nikki. "But I don't believe he's a threat anymore." She knew she was ignoring FBI advice, ignoring their reams and reams of intel because it didn't suit her. She'd had to sign paperwork stating that she was aware of the risk and she was refusing any sort of protection. "I mean, they've captured Nathan, and he's spilling the beans about the whole thing, and Paige is dead, so their little group is shattered. Tyrone is in hiding because every cop in America is out looking for him after his arson attack. And he achieved what he wanted—to evade the FBI long enough to complete his mission—so what reason could he have to come after me again?"

It was the story she was telling everyone, telling herself, so that no one worried about her. It was a plausible story, and she wasn't sure why everyone was making such a big deal about it. Even though her photo had led the FBI to him in the first place, it was no longer relevant, and Tyrone wouldn't jeopardize it all just for revenge. She didn't know the guy personally, but no one would be that stupid. Summer also conveniently ignored the fact that the police had yet to find the man who'd broken into her apartment. He was still out there somewhere, and possibly linked to Tyrone. But Summer had already decided that he'd most likely been a thug for hire, and had now just disappeared back into the underworld from where he'd come. So she wasn't worried about him either.

Nikki nodded, but her face gave away her dissatisfaction.

Summer handed her a mug of tea and then led her back to the couch, trying not to let her irritation show. She didn't want to sound ungrateful, didn't want to criticize either Jacob or Mårten for everything they'd done for her. Didn't want to undervalue how they'd gone out of their way for her, and how much Nikki had also done to help her out of a very sticky spot. Her house had been firebombed, for God's sake. She wanted to keep Nikki as a friend and didn't want to alienate her even further.

But before she could put her thoughts into words, Nikki spoke again. "What about you and Mårten?"

"What about me and Mårten?" Summer pursed her lips. She should've realized this question would come up.

"I thought perhaps something might've…happened between you two," Nikki said gently.

Summer wondered how much Nikki knew about her time spent with Mårten. It was likely that Mårten had confided in Jacob, and then he'd passed on every detail. And it stood to reason that Nikki suspected they may have become intimate anyway; she'd been the first one to pick up on their sizzling attraction when they'd been staying at her house. The woman had a knack for being candid, and she'd blatantly advised Summer to sleep with Mårten, even if it was just to get him out of her system. But Summer no longer cared for her matchmaking attempts, didn't want to be interrogated on her feelings for Mårten. She'd put everything to do with Mårten —every emotion, every sensation, every goddamn image in her brain—firmly into a steel box inside her head, and she didn't need anyone trying to pry it open. She wanted to make it crystal clear that things were well and truly over with her and Mårten.

"Look," Summer sighed. "We had a fling. And he is very sweet." That was an understatement. Sweet wasn't an adjective she would use to describe Mårten. Hot, driven, intense, fascinating, sexy as hell, distracting, frustrating, and nearly as stubborn as her were all better descriptions. "But we are two very different people, who want different things, let alone the fact we live on separate continents," she added with a smile, hoping that Nikki didn't see how hard she had to force her lips to bend upward.

Nikki studied her for a few moments. "Oh, okay then." She blew on the surface of her tea thoughtfully. And praise be, she decided not to pursue the topic when she added, "So what are your plans now? You know, after your arm heals."

Forcing another fake smile, Summer told her about the upcoming wedding in four days. She babbled, embellishing all the things that still needed to be done, all the fun they'd have, how much she was looking forward to it all. Out of the corner of her eye, she saw Nikki glance at her more than once with what she thought might be pity in her eyes, but Summer plowed on, eager to get away from the topics of Tyrone and Mårten. Eager for Nikki to see that she was fine and was diving back into her life with gusto.

They must've talked for another half an hour, because Summer was surprised when there was a knock at the door.

Feeling self-conscious answering the door in her pajamas for the second time that day—she still hadn't found the time to get changed—she was taken by surprise when Bianca pulled her in for a hug, much like Nikki had done.

"Oh my God, Summer, what happened to you?"

Summer had forgotten that she hadn't told Bianca or any of her other friends the exact reason she'd flown off so suddenly to Sweden. Instead, fabricating a story about a job coming up that she just couldn't turn down. They hadn't known her life was in danger. Or that she was with Mårten, who was actually a police officer. But maybe Bianca had guessed some of it, judging by her hard hug and her reticence to let her go, even as she studied her face.

"Did you get into a fight?" Then she noticed the cast on Summer's wrist, and her frown turned into a look of full-blown panic.

"What the fu...?"

"Come and sit down," Summer sighed. She figured she was going to have to come out with the whole truth now. "This is Nikki, by the way." Summer introduced the two women and then grimaced when Bianca looked at her with curiosity. Because she'd been out in the desert when the break-in had occurred, poor Bianca didn't even know Summer had stayed at Nikki's house in those few terrible days when she'd needed somewhere safe to hide out and didn't know how close she'd become to the other woman. Summer had mentioned Nikki as a friend of Mårten's—the man who had helped her after the burglary—but that was all. She was going to have to start at the very beginning.

"You didn't just go to Sweden for a job interview, did you?" Bianca accused.

"No," Summer replied, shooting a quick glance at Nikki from beneath lowered lashes. This would not be easy. Bianca was going to flip out, as were the rest of her friends when they found out. And Bianca would read her the same lecture she always did, about how she refused to let her friends in, refused to accept help. Only this time, Summer would agree; she'd been a terrible friend. But that would change; she was going to be more honest and open now. If this event had taught her one thing, it was that she couldn't do everything alone, and it wasn't a sign of weakness to ask for support.

Nikki gave her an encouraging smile, and Summer knew the other woman would have her back if need be.

"Was your unexpected trip something to do with the break-in at your apartment?" Bianca asked as she sank onto the couch beside Nikki.

"Yes. It turns out it wasn't just a random crime," Summer

began, taking the armchair opposite. "The guy was after my camera and my laptop. Or rather, what was on them. An incriminating photo."

"Wow," Bianca breathed.

"And he didn't get what he was looking for the first time, so he came back. Remember, I told you Mayte, Trent, and Serena helped me clean up. Then we went and had dinner?"

Bianca stared at her open-mouthed, eyes wide with disbelief, nodding her assent.

"Well, he was waiting for me when I arrived home," Summer said, adding a slight pause for effect.

"Fuck," Bianca whispered, hand over her mouth.

"But when he chased me, he fell down the stairs, and I got away. So then I ran to Nikki and Jacob's residence around the corner, friends of Mårten's." She inclined her head toward Nikki. "They offered me a safe place to stay a second time, for which I am forever grateful."

"God." Bianca swallowed, her face a mix of confusion, surprise, and fear. "That must've been awful." But then, the light of a different emotion crept into Bianca's eyes. "And so what did the sexy cop have to do with all this?"

Nikki laughed loudly, surprising them both. "He is rather sexy, isn't he?" she agreed, and Bianca swiveled to look at her.

"I never met him," Bianca admitted. "But from what everyone has told me, he sounded very nice."

"He is quite yummy," Nikki replied, shooting a subtle glance at Summer. "Some people don't seem to see that, however."

Now, wait just a second. Summer would not allow her story to be derailed like this. This wasn't about her and Mårten, or how sexy he might be. It was about how her life had been in unspeakable danger. "Anyway," she began. "I'll get to Mårten's part in the whole thing shortly."

"Good, because I want to hear everything." Bianca leaned

back on the couch, looking as if she was settling in to watch a captivating movie.

Summer detailed how Jacob was an agent for the FBI, and how she and Mårten had found the incriminating photo later that night when she couldn't sleep. Bianca interrupted, wanting to know exactly where they were sitting on the bed and whether Mårten was wearing all his clothes. Summer became increasingly frustrated as Nikki began filling in particulars that she believed Summer had left out, and soon it was Nikki and Bianca doing most of the talking, while she could barely get a word in edgeways.

Even though this was the first time the two women had met, they seemed to click instantaneously. Maybe it was their shared concern over Summer that drew them together, because they were now discussing her as if she weren't there. Summer sank back into the armchair, wondering if her newfound promise to be more open with her friends was actually a terrible idea. So much for Bianca flipping out; she was doing the exact opposite. As she and Nikki bonded, it felt like they were ganging up on her, trying to force her to rethink everything she knew about Mårten. Well, it would not work.

CHAPTER TWENTY-THREE

Mårten pulled his car up onto his curved driveway and turned off the ignition. But instead of getting out, he remained sitting, staring out the windscreen. The leaves of the birch trees in the little copse beside his cottage shimmered in the summer sun, bright-green and vibrant, but he barely noticed. He didn't want to go into his empty house. Didn't want to see the single coffee cup sitting in the drainer where he'd left it this morning. Didn't want to be reminded that he was alone again. A flock of robins arrived in the branches overhanging the driveway, twittering and fluttering, their little red chests flashing in the sunlight; they were the sound of summer to Mårten. But they also brought to mind the woman with the same name. The woman he couldn't seem to get out of his soul. She had so loved watching the little birds as they came to his feeder, taking so many photos and then exclaiming over their beautiful colors.

He'd been cleared to go back to light duties, which meant sitting behind his desk all day, but surprisingly it'd been an exhausting today, and he hadn't stopped to eat lunch, so he was ravenous. But when it came to the thought of cooking dinner for one, he balked. Nothing seemed to taste the same. His fridge was empty anyway; Mårten had had no urge to go back to the little gourmet supermarket because it also reminded him of Summer. She'd been so incredulous of all the unique items on the shelves, commenting on all the wonderful fresh vegetables, some of which she'd never heard of before. How she'd wanted to savor everything—cheese from a tube, the big round rye crispbread, knäckebröd, that everyone in Sweden took for granted, even the pickled herring, which was definitely an acquired taste.

Summer had been gone for five days now, and it felt like a lifetime. He shouldn't have let her go. Should've been able to stop her. But she was so bloody stubborn. And when she told him about Marco, he hadn't known what to say. He could see how someone might not recover from such a trauma, and it explained a lot about her. Things that he'd half guessed already, such as the way she was always so guarded, especially around him, kept her life so rigorously controlled, and was terrified of commitment. He'd wanted to comfort her —a small part of him had stupidly hoped that maybe he could help her heal—but she'd turned her back on him, shut him out, and even though he had tried to reach out, she'd rebuilt that indomitable wall between them.

The wound in his side ached annoyingly the longer he sat here, but he still couldn't force himself out of the car. His phone rang out of the blue, and Mårten stared at it blankly for a few moments.

At last, he hit the answer button. "Hey, Jacob." Mårten knew his voice came across as flat, but right now he didn't care.

"Hey, bro. You sound shit. Bad day?" What was this *"bro"* thing? Jacob sounded more American every day. The thought almost made him smile. Almost.

"Yep." Bad week if the truth be known, but Mårten didn't elaborate. "Have you got any more news?" He cut to the chase instead. The FBI was still trying to track down Tyrone

King, and until they did, Mårten wouldn't rest easy, and Jacob knew it.

"I'm not sure. Nothing concrete anyway. But..." Why was Jacob hedging? Mårten sat up straighter in his seat.

"But there's something. Tell me," he demanded.

"This is not official," Jacob warned, then drew a deep breath. "One of our IT guys found some chatter on a dark web message site that we've been monitoring. He can't find a solid link that connects it to Tyrone, but someone with a profile that matches our eco-terrorist was reaching out to a contact in Seattle. Asking for information about the city and details of where he could hire a photographer for a particular wildlife project he had in mind."

The hair on the back of Mårten's neck stood on end. "Fuck," he whispered.

"Miller asked if we could follow it up, but the boss say's there's not sufficient detail to make a solid connection. Many groups use this message board, a lot of them are suspected hard-core terrorists. He argued it could be anyone making this request, but he didn't believe an eco-terrorist was radical enough to be taken seriously on this site, and so while we should continue to monitor it, he doesn't think it should be given priority." Mårten swore under his breath as Jacob went on. "He needs more convincing intel before he'll commit to spending more manpower on it."

"So you're saying that he won't agree to putting a guard on Summer without some proper proof." Mårten gripped the steering wheel with one hand, his knuckles going white.

"Yeah," Jacob replied unhappily. "Miller has put as much pressure on him as she can without getting both of us fired," Jacob gave an ironic laugh. Mårten was sure Jacob would've argued until he was blue in the face, or he was ordered out of the room, and he didn't blame Jacob or his partner for the leader's lack of action. He didn't blame the team leader either. He had superiors to answer to higher up the food chain, and it was a lot harder to take risks when you were accountable for every dollar you spent, as well as a duty to protect the agents under your command. Mårten and Jacob had railed against Rydberg's inaction on a case more than once back when they had been partners. Both Mårten and Jacob had been known to act without direct permission more than once, had taken risks that'd paid off in the end. But things were different now. Jacob couldn't jeopardize his brand new position at the FBI to go chasing ghosts.

"What do you reckon we should do?" Mårten asked.

"That's the problem. I don't think there's anything we can do. Not in an official capacity anyway."

"Hmm," Mårten replied, his mind whirling with possibilities. Jacob might not be able to act officially, but perhaps he could. Which was probably why Jacob was telling him all of this. He couldn't come right out and say it, but was he hoping that Mårten might do something?

"Nikki went around to see Summer the other day," Jacob said just a little too casually into the silence.

"How is she?" Mårten blurted the words before he could stop himself.

"Nikki said she seems fine. She has a wedding coming up tomorrow that's keeping her occupied."

"Oh, yeah. That's good." Mårten remembered it was one reason she hadn't been too happy to come to Sweden because she would've failed in her bridesmaid duties. It was good that she could now attend her friend's nuptials. He wondered what sort of dress the bride had picked out for Summer to wear; she'd look stunning in just about anything, he imagined.

"Nikki also thinks that Summer is missing you, but she's too stubborn to admit it," Jacob added.

Mårten made a scoffing sound. He should be grateful that

Jacob was trying to make him feel better, but he was a realist. And while Nikki had high empathy and was good at reading other people's feelings, Jacob's words didn't comfort Mårten in the slightest. He would only believe it if he heard it come from Summer's mouth. And that wasn't likely to happen.

"Anyway," Jacob said into the silence. "I just thought you'd like an update on what's going on over here. Let me know if you come up with any solutions," he added, but then left it at that and they ended the call. It wasn't Jacob's place to tell Mårten to come back to America, but Mårten knew his partner well enough to understand that was the purpose of his call.

He sat in the car, drumming his fingers on the steering wheel, Jacob's words echoing through his head. Was Summer still in danger? If that message on the dark web had been from Tyrone, was he planning a trip to Seattle? And for what reason? Some kind of stupid retribution? It wasn't beyond the scope of plausibility; criminals often did things with very flimsy motives that most normal people wouldn't understand. And Tyrone King definitely wasn't most normal people.

He knew Summer wouldn't appreciate him turning up on her doorstep. But what else was he to do? The FBI didn't think the intel was strong enough to act on. And even though Jacob would offer to stand guard outside her house if Mårten asked him to, he couldn't do it 24/7. He'd need backup.

Rydberg would be indignant if Mårten asked for more leave so soon after his last holidays. But then he had just solved a major case. He should be given brownie points for that. And he'd returned straight back to work without taking the few days sick leave the doctor had suggested. Maybe he could take that prescribed leave after all.

Dammit. Damn bloody Summer for being so contrary and not taking her own safety seriously. Damn bloody Tyrone

King for holding some sort of personal grudge. But if there was even the slightest risk that Jacob's intel was correct, he couldn't leave Summer unprotected.

He knew he had to get on the next flight to Seattle.

His heart pounded painfully at the thought of seeing Summer again. But that wasn't the reason he was going, he told himself. Things were over between them, if they'd ever really started. He needed to keep reminding himself of that. He was going there to protect her, that was all. He'd initiated this whole thing, and now he would finish it.

Mårten punched Rydberg's number into his phone and waited for his supervisor to answer. Mårten was going whether or not Rydberg agreed, but it would be better to have a job to come back to, if he could wrangle it.

* * *

The road was deserted as Mårten strode down the quiet, leafy pathway. Saturday morning in this part of Seattle, and there was not much going on. As soon as his flight had landed, he'd gone straight to Nikki's place and dropped off his luggage, hugged her hello, and then without even waiting to have a coffee, headed off to walk to Summer's apartment. He was hoping to catch her before she left for the wedding. Otherwise, he might be stuck, because he had no idea where it was being held. He had no contact details for any of Summer's friends, so he might well have to Google every marriage ceremony taking place in Seattle that day if he missed her, which wasn't ideal.

Nikki hadn't been surprised to see him, telling him that Jacob was expecting him, but had popped into work even though it was a Saturday to check on something, and would catch up with him this afternoon.

She also understood that Summer was Mårten's priority. "Go and talk some sense into that woman," she'd said, and then wished him luck. He was going to need it.

He rounded the corner onto Summer's street, the entrance to her apartment now visible a few hundred meters away.

Wait. Was that her standing on the sidewalk? He couldn't be sure. There was a lady in a shimmering, silvery, full-length dress with long dark hair hanging down her back struggling with a large duffle bag right at the edge of the curb. It had to be her. Yes, now he could see the cast on her left wrist. She must be waiting for a taxi or for someone to come and collect her. He'd just made it in time. Mårten lengthened his strides, wondering if he should call her name. But he was still too far away for her to hear unless he really shouted, and he didn't want to scare her away when he was so close to seeing her again.

All of a sudden, a dark sedan pulled up beside her. Shit. Mårten ran. He was going to miss her after all. But then something happened that took Mårten a few seconds to comprehend. A tall man wearing a black balaclava got out of the car and grabbed her by the arm. Summer struggled against him, shouting incoherent words as her dress swirled around her ankles. But then the thug shoved a weapon in Summer's face, and she stopped fighting, becoming compliant as he forced her into the backseat.

What the fuck was going on?

"Stop. Police," Mårten yelled, sprinting down the street, but it was too late. Without a backward glance, the man got into the car, and it took off at high speed down the empty road, leaving the black duffel sitting alone on the side of the curb.

Mårten had his phone out of his pocket and was dialing Jacob's number within seconds. He glanced about in a panic. What to do? He needed to follow that car, but how? To his utter relief, a taxi appeared around the corner, and he flagged it down, his cell still held to his ear as he kept one eye on the disappearing car.

"Follow that car," he yelled as he jumped into the taxi. "I'm a police officer pursuing a felon," he added, pulling his badge out of his shirt pocket. It was a Swedish police badge, which was gold instead of silver like the American badges, but that didn't seem to deter this guy, as after one quick glance, he floored the gas pedal.

The driver was Black, in his mid-twenties, and he seemed to relish his role. "Cool, man. I ain't never been involved in a police chase before."

Mårten leaned forward, his eyes fixed on the black car ahead of them, which was no longer disappearing, as the driver kept up and they perhaps even gained on it. It had to be Tyrone in that car, didn't it? No one else would have a reason to snatch her off the street. Or if it wasn't him, could he have sent some of his cronies to do his dirty work?

Jacob finally answered his phone.

"I need you to track a car," Mårten yelled. "I got a partial. It's a black town car. A sedan—I'm not sure what make. The first three letters are BZN." Mårten hadn't been sufficiently close to get a good look at the full registration plate, and he knew his partial probably wouldn't be enough. "I'm following the car in a taxi down Summer's street. Someone just snatched her off the curb right in front of my eyes."

Jacob had the wisdom not to ask stupid questions. Instead, he said, "Stay on the line. I'll get someone on it right away. And I'll send any available unit to your location."

Mårten merely grunted. Then he pointed a finger at the windscreen. "He's turning," he said roughly.

"I see it," the taxi driver replied. The dude was good. He wasn't panicking, remaining calm and in control; in fact, he was enjoying it.

Mårten stayed on the line with Jacob as they followed the car, twisting and turning through the streets. They seemed to be heading out of town, and at one stage they drove over a long bridge, which took them off the main island where the city central was located, and began moving east through the suburbs and then into the mountains. They caught up with the car when it had to slow for the city traffic, and Mårten could give Jacob the full registration plate. He talked to the driver, making him stay well back, so they weren't noticed. He exchanged names with the guy, who was called Rishi, and Mårten told him he was doing a great job.

"Where the hell is this guy going?" Mårten muttered to himself. He still didn't know if it was Tyrone driving, but he was feeling more and more confident that it had to be.

"Are you sure you want me to keep following him?" This was the first time the driver had shown any signs of nerves.

"Yes, yes." Mårten ground his teeth together, then said more slowly. "Yes, please, you're doing a great job." But Mårten knew he needed a plan. These abductors could be driving all the way to Chicago for all he knew.

They'd stopped a few cars back from the town car at multiple sets of traffic lights now. Should Mårten take the chance next time and jump out and confront the men in the car? There had to be more than one, because the guy with the gun had got into the back with Summer when they took off, which meant there was at least also a driver, perhaps even a third person in the vehicle. But if the signals went green before he reached the car, or things didn't go according to plan and the thug fired his weapon, Summer could be hurt or even killed.

Mårten worried at his lower lip as he discussed options with Jacob, who was still on the line.

"I've got a match for the car," Jacob said, cutting into their tactics discussion, and for a second Mårten held his breath. "But it won't help right now. It's registered to a hire company. I'm looking for the rental contract to see if I can get us a name."

"I think he might be heading to Cougar Mountain Park," said Rishi, interrupting his conversation with Jacob.

"You think so?" Mårten was quick to jump on the idea.

"I mean, this road could take us anywhere outside Seattle, like Boise or even as far as Spokane, but I know Cougar Mountain is coming up ahead on the right. My friends and I like to walk out here. The forest trails are amazing."

Rishi could be onto something, and Mårten felt a spike of adrenaline at the mention of the park. If Tyrone were indeed inside the car, then it'd make sense he'd take her somewhere isolated, somewhere that resonated with him, where he might feel at home. Like the closest piece of wilderness to the city. He relayed the information to Jacob, who said he'd send out a couple of units to the area.

"Where could he take her in the middle of the day where no one else will see them?" Mårten pondered to himself. If he were going to kill her, then he needed to have no witnesses to his crime. The location would have to be isolated.

"It's a big place," Rishi supplied. "I know of quite a few bodies that've been recovered from the park; some had been there for years. Hikers just found the bones. There was even one tourist who was killed by a wild cougar." Rishi smiled, seeming to get caught up in all the ghoulishness of it all.

"Shit," Mårten swore, that was the last thing he needed to hear.

"Wait. Drop back a little," he commanded. The car was turning off onto a minor road, and the forest crowded in on the narrow trail, making it hard to see around the next corner. Mårten was regretting the use of a taxi. In city traffic, the bright yellow car would blend in, but it'd stand out on this road.

"It looks like he might be heading toward a place called the abandoned clay pits," Rishi said as the road continued its winding course. "Few people go there. It's not nearly as picturesque as Coal Creek Waterfall or the peak of Cougar Mountain. And even less so now that they've closed part of it off." Rishi made a disgusted face. "The government, in all its wisdom, is going to allow fracking in the park. After so many years of our mayor being dead against it, all it takes is one stupid policy change from the new president and whammo, now the miners are granted free access to the park. Personally, I think it's disgusting. I would…"

"Wait." Mårten held up his hand. "Did you say fracking?"

"Yep."

"That's it. That's got to be it." Mårten felt a familiar tingle, the one he got when he knew he was onto something when he was running a case. Hadn't Tyrone's family lost their dairy farm due to some unscrupulous miners setting up fracking wells around their ranch? "Did you catch that, Jacob?" he said into the phone.

"Sure did. I'll get backup out there as soon as possible."

CHAPTER TWENTY-FOUR

"Tie her up nice and tight, Diego," Tyrone instructed. The other man pulled even harder on the ropes so that they cut into Summer's skin on her arms, and she whimpered through the duct tape that was covering her mouth. He'd already hastily tied her ankles together, her long silver dress caught up in the knots at her feet, dragging it down so that the shoestring straps dug painfully into her shoulders. She recognized the guy from his beady eyes and hooked nose. He was the one who'd broken into her apartment and stolen her camera. Who'd accosted her in the stairwell, and scared the shit out of her.

Summer didn't know where she was, but they couldn't be too far from the city. By her reckoning, she'd been in the car for less than an hour. After Tyrone had forced her into the back seat at gunpoint, she'd been gagged and blindfolded and left terrified and shaken, curled in the fetal position in the corner against the door. Neither of the men had spoken as Diego had driven them out of the city. She'd known it was Tyrone as soon as the car pulled up in front of her, even though they were both wearing balaclavas; it could be no one else. All of Jacob and Mårten's warnings had rung through her head like a sledgehammer. They'd been right, and she'd been terribly, terribly wrong. For whatever reason, Tyrone had appeared to exact vengeance on her.

Diego was strapping her to a tall metal contraption that towered tens of meters above their heads. They were on a construction site within a small clearing deep inside a forest somewhere. She could see there'd been recent earthworks, with fresh piles of dirt heaped around them, and a couple of what she assumed were storage sheds set into the encroaching trees on one side of the glade.

Summer stared directly at Diego, pleading with her eyes for him to let her go. But his swarthy face remained impassive. Both men had dispensed with their balaclavas once they arrived in the wilderness, which she knew was a bad sign, because it meant they were confident she would not leave here alive, and therefore couldn't possibly identify them.

"Those idiots think that one little fence is going to keep people out," Tyrone scoffed. "Well, it might keep normal, law-abiding people out, but not me." He flashed his teeth—so white against his Black skin—in a predatory smile and pointed at the chain-link fence through which Diego had cut a hole with wire cutters and then forced her to clamber through the break. Surprisingly, Tyrone was very good-looking. Tall, athletic, with high, strong cheekbones and piercing dark eyes. He was also terribly charismatic, his voice smooth as velvet, and his smile beguiling. She could see why Paige had found him so attractive. And why others might follow his teachings, however psychotic they might be.

Diego finished his task and went to stand next to Tyrone.

"Did you know the Northern Spotted Owl breeds in this forest? It's highly endangered, too," Tyrone said casually.

What? Summer was struggling to follow his lightning-fast changes in conversation.

"Yeah. So if they're allowed to continue building these

fracking wells, not only will they destroy all the surrounding creeks and rivers, making them too toxic for anything to survive, but the noise and the pollution will drive away any owls in the area." Tyrone raised his palms toward the sky. "Where are these poor birds supposed to go? Tell me, because I'd love to know. Paige told me you're an environmentalist, just like she was. So tell me, how are we going to save the owls if all we ever do is demolish their habitat?"

Summer didn't have an answer, and she had no idea what he was talking about with his reference to fracking or endangered owls. But casting her gaze around the area, she could see what he meant about habitat. This mine site—if that was indeed what it was—was in the middle of a dense, old-growth forest. And now she remembered something about Northern Spotted Owls; they inhabited wild places surrounding Seattle, such as the Cascade Ranges and Cougar National Park, as well as other mature coniferous forests. But she didn't have time to figure out if she knew where these woods were, as Tyrone began speaking again.

"You look mighty pretty in that dress; it's a shame you're gonna have to die in it. Paige would've been mad at me for killing you, especially when you look so beautiful." Tyrone stared at her impassively, but her head was spinning with yet another topic change. How did anyone keep up with his quicksilver mind? "Ironically, she's the reason that I have to kill you now. An eye for an eye, and all that sort of thing. If she'd survived, then maybe so would you. Paige looked up to you, idolized you, did you know that? She thought you might even be persuaded to join our cause. But she was clearly wrong on that count." He made a scoffing sound, and Diego gave him a sympathetic glance.

Summer struggled to get her head around all this new information. Uppermost in her mind was the fact that he meant for her to die here. But why? It wasn't her fault Paige had ended up dead. It was his right-hand man, Nathan, who'd killed her. This was completely fucked up. It was Tyrone who'd sent Paige and Nathan to Sweden in the first place to kidnap her. Maybe his intention hadn't been to kill her once they finished with her, as Paige had always declared. But then Nathan had gone on a rampage and lashed out at Paige because she'd questioned his authority. Nathan was the one Tyrone should be taking his rage out on, not her. But Nathan was locked up in a jail in Sweden, and Summer had no way to defend herself, because the duct tape stopped any form of two-way communication. She made desperate grunting noises, hoping perhaps he'd remove the gag and let her speak, let her tell her side of the story, but Tyrone ignored her as he continued to drone on.

"I loved Paige, and she loved me. We were seeing each other in secret for months, did you know? That stupid fiancé of hers didn't have a clue. He was an ignorant dolt with no backbone or passion. Paige deserved so much more in a man."

Summer wasn't surprised to hear the pair were in love after the way Paige had talked about him. But she would've snorted in derision if she could have at the fact Tyrone obviously considered himself as a *better sort of man*. He was a criminal, hiding in the shadows, using violence and intimidation to make his point. There was no honor in that.

"When you took that photo of me and Nathan in Yellowstone, I was furious," Tyrone went on. "I thought you'd jeopardized everything, months of planning down the drain. But Paige calmed me down, assured me you didn't even know what you had; persuaded me you hadn't seen us on the mine site that day because you'd been so fixated on the dreaded company buildings and the damage they were doing to the pristine forest. But I still believed it'd be better if there were no evidence. So I sent Diego to retrieve the photos, but he couldn't complete the mission. It was nice of your lovely neighbor—Tad, was it?—to let him into the building. Seems like Tad had a bit of a grudge against you, because he even showed Diego where your apartment was. Nice of him, hey?" Tyrone cocked his head and gave her a cheeky smile, as if this was all some huge game to him. "Diego got your camera, but alas you had your computer with you. And then you got away."

"I did my best," Diego replied sharply.

"Yeah, that's all we can ever do," Tyrone agreed as he cast Diego a sideways glance. But there was indulgence in his eyes, a certain warmth that made Summer think these two had known each other for a long time. This guy wasn't just a lackey; he was a confidant and possibly even a friend, which was surprising to learn. Perhaps there was honor among thieves after all. Or at least a strong loyalty. Not that it rendered these men any less brutal or desperate in her eyes. And now at least she had an answer as to how Diego got into her building. Blast bloody Tad, she'd let the cops know about his deceitfulness when she got out of here. If she got out of here.

"But it didn't make our lives any easier," Tyrone continued. "And by then we assumed you'd probably already found the photo, and we worried the jig was up. We couldn't complete the mission with the whole of the fucking FBI after us, could we now?"

Summer widened her eyes at him. What was she supposed to say? All she could do was listen to his monologue and hope and pray that the longer he talked, the more chance someone might notice she was missing. Bianca, at least, would be worried by now. Summer was scheduled to meet her at the church so they could put the finishing touches on the interior and then wait for the florist to deliver the bouquets for decoration. The big duffel bag that she'd abandoned by the side of the road when Tyrone had abducted her contained all the ribbons and gauzy fabric meant to be draped across the entrance, along with the wedding ceremony cards that would be placed on each seat for the guests. Bianca might phone Trent or Mayte to see if they knew where she was, perhaps even send one of them around to her apartment to make sure she hadn't slept in. But she probably wouldn't have thought of calling the police yet. Nikki had made sure Bianca had Jacob's number as well as her own, just in case. But Bianca wouldn't have reached that level of panic yet either.

So, it was up to her to get herself out of this mess. Yet again. She tested the rigidness of the ropes against her wrists as she half-listened to Tyrone as he continued with his story. They were so tight that even the slightest movement caused pain in her right wrist as the rope bit into her skin, but the plaster on her left wrist was much smoother and bulkier to bind. She felt it give a little as the ropes slipped against her cast when she twisted her hand. Stealthily, she flexed her fingers trying to get a purchase on the steel framework. Maybe if she could reach one of the knots…

"Then you disappeared to Sweden," Tyrone said, bringing her focus back to him. "And that's when Nathan came up with the bright idea of using you as a decoy. Take you as a hostage so that everyone's eyes were turned to you, and not on what me and Diego were up to. Pretty neat, hey?"

No, not neat at all. Not when she'd been on the other end of that kidnapping. Not when she'd been the reason that Tyrone had carried out his attack and one person had been killed because of it, and not when Paige had paid for it with her life. She barely stopped herself from shaking her head. Instead, she tried to make her eyes look interested. Keep him talking. He could sermonize and pontificate as much as he wanted as long as it gave her extra time.

Tyrone lapsed into silence, tipping his head back as if studying the deep blue sky of the summer day. "But there is a lovely kind of symmetry to all of this," he finally said, returning his dark gaze to her. "When I found out about these new fracking wells, I knew exactly how you were going to die."

Summer watched with increasing trepidation as Tyrone began to pace across the broken earth in front of her. At least he'd given her a hint of what was going on here. This metal contraption must be part of the equipment used to extract the gas from deep underground; perhaps even the drill rig itself. She racked her brain to see if she could remember any recent media reports about fracking wells being built on the outskirts of Seattle. There'd been something about Cougar Mountain now she thought about it. Was that where she was —somewhere in Cougar Mountain Regional Park?

"You see, I'm the son of a dairy farmer's daughter. I know, I know, I don't look like the stereotypical farm boy." He gave a cheerful wave of his hand as he paced. "But the story is quite beautiful. My father, who was Black, obviously, fell in love with my mother, who *was* a stereotypical Pennsylvania white dairy farmer's daughter. Of course, her parents were against the marriage, but eventually they came to see that apart from the color of his skin, he was a good man at heart. He was a hard worker. He gave his life to that farm, and he loved my mother fiercely; did right up until the end. But that's not the true tragedy. The real tragedy is how that farm was taken away from us slowly, piece by piece, bit by bit, over many years. It was steadily destroyed when the gas companies were allowed to drill nine fracking wells around the farm on government-owned land. They told us there was nothing to worry about; that it was all completely fine and harmless. But then we started losing the newborn calves. A few in the first year, more in the next, until our losses were over fifty percent."

Summer stopped her covert struggling for a second and focussed on Tyrone's words. She had a bad feeling she knew where this was going.

"Then, my mum got sick. Little things at first, like she would get lightheaded and have trouble breathing sometimes. Now, she can't even walk without a frame and is in constant, irrepressible pain. We tried talking to people, to the mining company itself, to the county statesman, to the mayor, and even the governor of Pennsylvania, but no one was interested because they were all getting kickbacks from the corrupt mining companies. Eventually, it was all too much, and we lost the farm. My parents had to move into town, and then my father committed suicide." Tyrone said this in a bland monotone, as if it had all been inevitable, but Summer caught the hint of anguish in his eyes. "There is only one way to make these people understand, and that's hitting them where it hurts, take their livelihood away from them. Talking is no good; they won't listen to words. All they care about is money."

She already knew most of this, but Tyrone had added his own personal pathos to the story. It was terribly sad, and it explained a lot about him. She already knew this was where his hatred for mining companies had started, and recognized that now it was festering like an open wound. Past trauma always affected your life; she understood that better than most. And afterward, you did what you had to do to survive.

Tyrone stopped his pacing, his eyes glazing over, as if lost in memories.

"Come on, man, stop your yakking, let's get this over with," Diego said impatiently into the silence; he'd clearly heard all this before. "The cops could be here any moment."

"Yeah, yeah," Tyrone growled, his head snapping up as he refocused on the present. "Keep an eye out while I finish the job, then will you? Make sure there are no witnesses."

Diego did as he was told, heading toward the perimeter fence, replacing his balaclava as he did so. Shit, she needed to act now. Whatever Tyrone had planned was gonna happen soon. She wriggled her hands again, her broken wrist protesting as she twisted it inside the cast. But something moved, she felt something slip.

"It'll be over quick, don't worry," Tyrone said in a soothing tone, perhaps noticing the anxious lines creasing Summer's forehead. "Once the flames reach the gas and that pipe blows, it'll burn for ages. It might take them a few days to identify your body. The heat will be so intense it'll char the flesh from your bones, so there'll be hardly anything left. That should give us time to disappear."

Shit, he was going to blow up the gas rig and her along with it. She should've expected something such as this. Her heart was already pounding so fast she could feel it fluttering like a bird inside her rib cage, but at his words, it increased tenfold and she could now hear her own blood surging through her veins. She began to hyperventilate. Did he really expect to get away with it? If she could speak past the gag in her mouth, she would've said that the FBI would be onto him like a rash. He wouldn't get far because Mårten would figure it out and track him down. Too late to save her, but not for Tyrone and his lackey to end up in jail for the rest of their lives. She struggled some more, vainly trying to break free.

For the first time, Summer noticed a small container resting at Tyrone's feet as he picked it up and walked toward her. He splashed the liquid all over her, and she gagged at the overpowering smell of fuel. Then, he held a lighter aloft in his hand.

Oh, fuck.

He was really going to do this. He was really going to set her alight. She didn't want to be burned alive. She didn't want to die. Summer shook her head violently, willing him not to do this, at the same time pulling frantically at the ropes around her wrists, ignoring any pain.

Suddenly her cast arm came free, and she swung it forward, waving it defiantly in Tyrone's face, screaming at him from behind her gag, almost hysterical now.

Air, she needed air. She was going to pass out if she didn't get this thing off her face. Awkwardly because of the plaster, she ripped away the duct tape from her mouth. It hurt as it shredded skin from her face, but she didn't care, dragging in great gulps of wonderful air. She screamed, but it came out more like a strangled cat sound.

Tyrone smiled, a twisted smile, half pitying and half triumphant. "Sorry, darlin'," he said, flicking the lighter so that a flame appeared. "Screaming ain't gonna help you now."

She brandished her cast like a weapon, waving it at his face as he came closer. But Tyrone merely ducked and then stood tall to face her again, the lighter still held family in his hand.

"You asshole," she yelled.

All of a sudden, her other hand slithered free, and she glared in victory at Tyrone as she brought it around to the front. With both hands loose now, she could… But she'd forgotten her feet remained tied together at the ankles, and with nothing to hold her upright, she lost her balance and toppled forward. Her palms landed in the damp earth, and she cried out in pain as her broken wrist took most of the brunt of her fall.

The smell of fuel assaulted her nostrils, it was all around her, on her clothes, in her hair, saturating the sparse grass growing at the base of the drill rig. Her legs, she needed to get her feet free, and then she'd be able to run.

"Oh no you don't," Tyrone said, and she twisted her face up to see him staring down at her. She began to tremble uncontrollably. He was going to do it; she was going to burn alive. There was no time to contort her body to reach her feet before he dropped the flame.

"Paige wouldn't want this," she beseeched, locking her gaze with his.

Out of nowhere, there was a loud crack, and a crimson bloom appeared in the middle of Tyrone's forehead. He fell to the ground, the flaming lighter still in his hand; the grass catching alight as it touched their stalks.

It took her a few seconds to figure out what'd happened.

Then Mårten broke from the cover of the trees and began sprinting toward her.

CHAPTER TWENTY-FIVE

"Summer," Mårten screamed at the top of his voice. He was still one-hundred meters away when he saw the first bright lick of flame. She looked up at her name, confusion and then relief flashing across her face, but she lowered her gaze and went back to trying to put out the growing blaze.

Fuck. Fuck Fuck. His aim had been true. He'd killed the guy, that was for sure, but it hadn't stopped Tyrone's lighter from igniting a flame as he fell. Mårten had taken the opportunity as soon as Summer had dropped to the ground and was no longer in the way. The arsonist had been a couple of meters away from Summer when Mårten shot him, at a far enough distance not to have set the grass on fire. Or so Mårten hoped. But Tyrone must've accidentally splashed fuel on the dirt around his own feet as well, and when he'd fallen, the lighter had set that fuel blazing.

Mårten put on an extra spurt of speed, running faster than he'd ever run before, the broken earth and piles of dirt hampering his effort. His stab wound pierced him with excruciating pain at every step, but he ignored it. Nothing was more important than getting to Summer.

Summer was trying to flick sand over the encroaching fire with her hands, but it wasn't working. The puddles of liquid had well and truly caught now, and the flames were spreading fast toward her. He couldn't understand why she wasn't getting up and running away? Was she hurt or injured somehow? When he'd first arrived, creeping through the forest like a wraith, hoping against hope that he wasn't too late, he could see her standing with her hands tied behind her back, bound to a metal structure, and he'd moaned in frustration. He'd watched Tyrone speak to Summer almost as if he was on a stage giving a sermon, and Mårten had waited —his gun trained on his target—for exactly the right moment. The other man by Tyrone's side was a complication, and he was another reason Mårten waited.

Jacob had assured him backup was on the way. If they arrived in time, then he wouldn't need to take down two targets simultaneously.

He'd watched with relief as Tyrone sent the other man back out through the fence, leaving him unguarded and a single, clear mark. But then the terrorist had splashed gas around Summer's feet, he knew he had to act. Summer had begun gesticulating at Tyrone with both her hands, so she must've freed herself somehow. She'd been so magnificent, shimmering like a goddess in her silver dress, long hair flying about her face as she snarled at him like a wildcat. He'd never seen anything more beautiful, and he'd never wanted a woman more than in that moment. In that second, he'd understood completely that she was the one for him. He was in love with her, and he'd been stupid to let her go. Now, he might lose her all over again.

Summer had suddenly fallen to the ground, and she was no longer in danger if his bullet missed its mark. So he took his shot. And his aim had been true, because Tyrone had dropped like a stone.

But if she'd been free, why hadn't she taken her first opportunity to flee from the encroaching flames? Instead, she was trying in vain to dampen the fire with handfuls of sand.

Then he understood; her legs must be bound. "Untie your feet," he yelled frantically. "You need to free your feet."

Summer didn't look up at him this time, but she must've heard, because she stopped flicking dirt over the blaze and curled her body toward the metal contraption.

Mårten's breath rasped in his ears, and his chest pounded so hard as his legs pumped up and down, up and down, carrying him ever closer to Summer. Even though he was doing the best he could to ignore the pain in his side, he knew it was slowing him down some. As he got closer, so did the flames. Now, it was no longer a small lick of light; the fire was growing quickly, racing from one clump of grass to the next, all of which had been soaked in the highly combustible fuel. Mårten weighed up possible scenarios in his head as he ran, trying not to stumble; if he fell now he would never get to her in time.

Finally, he reached the fire, skidding in the dirt as he came to a stop. But the smoke was billowing so thick he could barely make out Summer as she lay on the ground just beyond the conflagration, still clawing at the ropes around her ankles. He began kicking dirt over the burning grass, trying to put it out with his boots. But it soon became obvious that he needed to get between Summer and the flames to give her any chance of untying herself. Leaping over the wall of fire, he landed near Summer's head.

"I'm here," he shouted. A ring of flames had virtually enveloped her now, and he could feel the searing heat even through his jeans and shirt. Summer's bare shoulders and arms must be sizzling from the radiant intensity of the fire. Oily smoke roiled around them, forming a thick black cloud that made it hard to breathe, and even harder to see. Using the side of his boot as a makeshift shovel, he dragged it through the broken ground, trying to make a sort of firebreak around her to stop the flames spreading. It seemed to work for a moment, but he couldn't circumnavigate her body fast enough, and the blaze spread past the back of the metal tower before he could stop it. Soon they would be encircled, with no way to get out.

"I can't get them free," she wailed. "Mårten, I can't get free."

Shit. Mårten left his futile attempt to divert the flames and instead dived toward Summer's feet, landing in the dirt on his knees, his fingers fumbling with hers as they both attempted to untie the knots. He could feel the encroaching heat on the back of his neck. That's when he saw she'd nearly done it. There was just one more knot to go, but it was tight and her hands were shaking uncontrollably. He worked at it feverishly with his strong fingers, tugging, pulling.

"I got it," he crowed, flinging the rope aside and lifting her feet—which he now noticed were bare—up and away from the metal. Summer sat up, and then he helped her to stand, wanting to hug her to him and never let her go. But Summer sagged against him, as if all her strength was now gone. The heat was almost unbearable. A ring of flames surrounded them. The only thing stopping the fire from overtaking them was the small break he'd dug in the ground with his foot. They'd have to jump over the conflagration to escape. And she wouldn't be able to run through the fire, not without shoes on. Without a second thought, he picked her up, grunting as he took her weight and she put pressure on his wounded side. Her arms wound instinctively around his neck, and she buried her face in his chest. The smell of gas assaulted his nostrils; she must be covered in the stuff, that fucking bastard. She wasn't heavy, but this maneuver would still be dicey.

"Hang on," he called. "I'm going to jump through it."

She said nothing, merely buried her head deeper against

his chest. She was traumatized; her whole body was trembling like a leaf, all her energy spent. It was up to him now. She'd saved his life back at the farmhouse, so it was his time to return the favor.

He took two steps backward, surveyed the spot where he thought the flames were lowest, held his breath, and ran.

One. Two. Three steps, and he was through to the other side. But the heat had been almost unimaginable, singeing the hairs on the backs of his hands, his eyelashes, the tips of his hair.

Then Summer screamed, and he looked down to see the hem of her dress had caught fire, and it flared hot and bright. He hadn't been quick enough after all, and because her dress was splashed with lighter fluid, it'd ignited as they passed through.

The only way to put out the flames was to smother them. Stop, drop, and roll. So that's what he did. He dropped to his knees and placed Summer on the ground, then he leaped on top of her, covering her body with his. Using his body as a shield, he rolled them over and over, beating at the fire with his bare hands. He needed to stop the sparks from reaching her upper body. Fuel also soaked her hair. If the flames caught in her hair... he didn't even want to think of the consequences.

At first, Summer tried to fight him, but then she realized what he was doing, and she went with him as they rolled together. Eventually, he could see only smoke, as the last remnants of the flames were doused. The bottom third of her dress was gone, the edges of the fabric singed and blackened. But he didn't let her go; couldn't let her go. He held her to his heaving chest, not wanting to give the sparks even the smallest chance of reigniting.

The last thing Jacob had told him before Mårten had put away his phone and lined Tyrone up in his gun sight was that a Seattle police unit had arrived and parked behind the taxi, with two more on the way, and they should be heading in his direction at any moment. It was a five-minute run from the car park down the secluded path to the clay pits. So where were they? Why weren't they here already?

As if in answer to his thoughts, a few moments later, someone dropped a piece of heavy clothing over the top of them and began wrapping them in it, making sure all the flames were indeed out. Mårten glanced up and saw a uniformed cop using his police-issue jacket as a fire blanket.

"Stay on the ground," the cop ordered. "We need to make sure it's completely out." Another cop was making his way across the clearing, removing his coat as he came. The first officer took the jacket and said, "Tell Harman and Tarismin to bring as much water as they can find. Then, call in the paramedics. I'll check on the other guy." Mårten assumed the cop meant Tyrone, but they would find him dead. He knew his aim had been true.

Summer whimpered and pushed him away. "It's okay, baby," he soothed. "Just lay still. We'll get you some help as soon as we can." Mårten knew he hadn't been able to protect her completely, and now he needed to check how badly she'd been burned. He braced himself and gently rolled her onto her back, using the police jacket to keep her off the earth. First, he checked her feet and her lower legs, which were most affected by the burning dress. He winced, but forced himself not to look away. All of her lower limbs were an angry lobster-red, with some blistering around her ankles, but none of the skin was broken or blackened. He was no doctor, but these looked like second-degree burns at worst, and he drew in a deep breath of relief. They were bad, and she would need hospitalization, but it could've been a lot worse.

Working his way up her body, he lifted what was left of her

charred dress at around mid-thigh to check that the burns didn't extend further up her torso. Then he checked her bare arms, which were singed and red, but the skin wasn't even blistered here. He wasn't proud of himself—he hadn't been able to protect her absolutely like he'd wanted to—but she was alive and she would make it through, hopefully without too much trauma and scarring. Finally, he let himself look at her face, smoothing the hair away from her brows, and brushing the dirt from her tear-stained cheeks with his thumb. He stared deep into her eyes. God, she was beautiful. Alive and beautiful.

"You came," she said simply. "You're supposed to be on another continent, and yet when I needed you…" More tears brimmed in her eyes. She sat up and threw her arms around his neck. He didn't know what to say, so he just held her.

A few moments later, an officer arrived with bottles of water and began fussing over Summer's legs, pushing Mårten out of the way. "I'm Constable Harman," she said. "We need to get these burns cooled," she added matter-of-factly, as if treating someone who'd been set on fire by a madman in the middle of a national park was an everyday occurrence. "Paramedics will be here soon."

"Oh, Mårten, your hands." Summer's exclamation took him by surprise, and he glanced down at his palms, astonished to find they were red, raw and blistered. He hadn't even noticed he'd been burned, had felt no pain at all, because he'd been so worried about Summer. It must've happened when he'd beaten the flames out around her legs.

"Looks like you're going to need treatment too, sir," Constable Harman said, opening another bottle of water and handing it to the first cop to pour over his palms. He knew he'd also need treatment for his stab wound; it felt like the stitches had busted open as he leaped over the flames, but that could wait. He wasn't going to traumatize Summer again by lifting his shirt and letting her see the blood that was certain to be there. Instead, Mårten sat back and let the police officer administer to him, locking his gaze with Summer over the top of Harman's head. There was relief, and gratitude, and something else in her dark brown eyes.

There was so much he wanted to convey to her. So many things he wanted to explain. But he had time now. Tyrone was no longer a threat, and Mårten was determined he was staying in America until Summer heard what he had to say. Heard him and, hopefully, felt the same way.

CHAPTER TWENTY-SIX

Nikki came bustling into the room carrying two blankets and two glasses of water. She put the water down on the side table nearest to where Summer was sitting on the couch and then proceeded to flap around with a blanket, placing it gently over Summer's lap. Then she did the same to Mårten, who was ensconced in the single armchair next to her.

"Is there anything else I can get you?"

"You've done more than enough, thank you," Summer said with a genuine smile.

Jacob came to stand in the doorway, a big grin on his face. "Look at the pair of you, like an old married couple of invalids," he joked, but Summer could see the affection hovering behind his eyes. It was his way of telling them he was glad they'd both survived.

Nikki was still flitting around them, repositioning Summer's blanket and opening the window a crack to *'let in some fresh air'*.

"Come on, we're going out. These two will cope for a while on their own. They need some space," he added, gently taking Nikki by the arm and leading her out of the room.

Mårten and Summer sat in silence as they listened to the other couple fuss about getting shoes on and grabbing handbags in the hallway, before Nikki called out, "See you in a couple of hours. Text us if you need anything."

"Will do," Mårten replied. Then the front door clicked shut and they were finally alone together.

"It was so lovely of Nikki to let us stay for a few days," Summer commented into the silence.

"I'm not sure we had any choice in the matter," Mårten replied, tilting one corner of his lips up in a sardonic grin. "I think if you'd insisted on living at your place, she would've just come around and kidnapped you in the middle of the night."

"Either that, or she would've moved in and slept on my couch," Summer agreed, also with a twitch of her lips. Nikki's heart was in the right place, she hadn't wanted Summer to spend her first few days out of hospital alone in her little flat. And so she had presented the idea that the spare bedroom Summer had used earlier was still vacant, and she would be nursing Mårten with his bandaged hands anyway, so she may as well look after both of them at the same time. Jacob had backed her up, agreeing that the best place for Summer while she was recuperating would be at their house. Summer was still struggling to get around with both legs bandaged, and she was also taking some powerful painkillers. Who knew burns could be so painful?

Summer could barely walk from one end of the house to the other, and she certainly wouldn't be jogging or riding a bike any time soon. But it could've been much, much worse. Mårten was nearly as badly off as she was; he had very limited use of both hands. Nikki had demanded that he stay in Seattle with her and Jacob for the next few weeks. Until he could prove that he was mostly independent and could handle everyday tasks, like getting dressed by himself, or even the simple task of using eating utensils. So they were both spending their invalid days being pampered while

Nikki waited on them hand and foot.

While Nikki was doing this out of the goodness of her heart, sometimes Summer wondered if the other woman didn't also have an ulterior motive. Such as keeping Mårten and Summer under the same roof for as long as possible. Summer suspected that Nikki was still playing matchmaker, even now.

"How are you feeling?" Mårten asked, rising from his chair and coming to sit on the couch next to her. His leg brushed hers as he sat, and the little hairs along her arms and on the top of her thighs rose to attention. His touch still caused an electric charge to run through her every single time.

"Better today," she consented. "The nurse said I'm healing well. She said I might start using the waterproof bandages in a day or two." Which would be great, because it meant she could at last shower herself. Having to take a bowl bath every day to get clean was not Summer's idea of fun. Nikki had arranged for a nurse to visit once a day to check their wounds and make sure they were on the path toward healing quickly.

"How about you?" She pointed to Mårten's hands. It was still a struggle to see his poor hands and not feel terribly guilty; he'd been burned trying to save her. If she'd just listened to him in the first place and stayed in Sweden, none of this would've happened. Mårten had never once said *I told you so*, however, and she was grateful for his lack of righteousness. He'd also re-opened his fresh stab wound in his rescue attempt, and it had to be stitched again, with the doctor giving firm instructions not to exert himself in any way for at least two weeks. Mårten had given the doctor a rueful smile and made the promise, but Summer had her doubts about whether he would keep it. The man was infuriating sometimes.

Mårten lifted his left hand. "This one is good," he said and flexed his fingers to show her the movement he now had in that hand. Only two of his fingers remained bandaged, with a thin white swathe still covering the flashy parts of his upper palm.

"This one is going to take a little longer." He grimaced. Mårten was right-handed, which made his injury all the worse.

Summer hadn't viewed the damage to his hands since Saturday, four days ago, when they'd been blistered and an angry red. If they were anything like her burns, the blistered areas would still be weeping, and the red areas would be peeling as new layers of skin were laid down.

They'd been kept apart in separate rooms at the hospital and had only seen each other fleetingly over the past few days. She'd given her statement to the police, and that was the end of it, but Mårten had been inundated with interviews from both the FBI and the local police, defending his actions. A Swedish cop shooting an American citizen—even if he was a wanted felon—on American soil was a tangled web of legal and operational hurdles that they had to unpick very carefully to make sure Mårten wasn't charged with any offenses. It'd been a tense few days, and for a while, Summer had been petrified that Mårten was going to be thrown in jail for his actions—all because he'd come to save her life. But Jacob and his partner Miller had been instrumental in making sure Mårten had been cleared of any wrongdoing, and as of yesterday, the FBI had declared Mårten was free to go home to Sweden.

Mårten reached over and took her hand in his less damaged one. She tried to withdraw it, afraid she was going to hurt him. "No." He shook his head. "I need to feel you, to touch you. I've missed you."

"Me too," Summer admitted, raising her gaze to meet his. She'd been craving his touch the whole time she'd been cooped up in hospital, dreaming of his powerful arms around her, like they'd been all too briefly after he rescued her from the flames.

"Actually, I've more than missed you," he amended. "I'm in love with you." He let the words hang in the air, fixing her with his steady ice-blue gaze. His abrupt declaration hit her hard in the middle of her chest. Oh, blast. She wasn't ready for this conversation, not just yet. Of course she'd considered where this relationship would go next while she'd been ensconced in a hospital bed—it'd been just about the only thing she'd thought about. And she was sure she loved him too. But there was so much at stake here. If she revealed she was in love with him, what did that mean for her? Her carefully crafted, safe life would be in jeopardy. Was she ready to throw that all away? Mårten deserved to know the truth about how she was feeling.

"I'm scared," she admitted at last, her voice coming out in a croak.

"So am I," he conceded. "But I'll do anything to make this work. I'll even move to America if that's what it takes. If Jacob can do it, so can I." His silver eyes fixed intently on her face, and she knew he meant every word. Wow, Mårten was prepared to uproot his life and move. For her. That was big. Huge. He had a career and a life over there. As did she here in Seattle.

She gave a weak laugh, and suddenly her mind went to images of her and Mårten living in the house next door, with the white picket fence and the wide veranda out the back, waving to Nikki and Jacob from their front garden. They could be friends, go on double dates. But something about it felt wrong, and the image was quickly replaced by her and Mårten sitting on his small porch sipping red wine and contemplating the birch forest full of birdsong. She suddenly realized she'd been at her happiest when she'd been with him in Sweden.

Could she do it? Could she move to another country for Mårten? For Love? If she didn't do it now, she knew she'd most likely end up miserable and alone. She wanted Mårten in her life. Needed him like she needed air to breathe. Her answer had to be a resounding yes.

"Well, I've been thinking." She raised an eyebrow and looked at him from below lowered lashes. "I don't need to stay in. Seattle," she mused. "I mean, I could easily run my business from anywhere else in the world."

She didn't tell him this, but she'd already looked up possibilities for extending her environmental videography business in Luleå. The university there had just opened a new research center focusing on the Arctic and Antarctic polar regions. The online blurb said it was a hub bringing together various researchers and their expertise on different projects, such as climate change and sustainability in areas affected by human habitation and even by global wars such as the Russia and Ukraine conflict. It sounded impressive, to say the least, and more than one project had piqued Summer's interest. Even if they didn't need an experienced environmental photographer, Summer didn't doubt there would be plenty of other opportunities in the area.

Mårten's grip tightened on her hand, and she almost winced for him. "What do you mean?"

"I mean, Sweden is so beautiful in the summer. In my line of work, I could find plenty of assignments on offer in Europe, or I could even fly back and forth to America if need be."

"Summer," Mårten breathed. "Would you really do this? What about your friends? Your family?" He twisted on the couch so his knees thrust up against hers, a spark of something elemental and hopeful in his eyes.

It would be hard to leave her friends, but her family were all the way down in San Jose, and she could just as easily visit them from Sweden as she could from Seattle.

She wouldn't be giving up anything career-wise. Wouldn't need to renounce any of her grand passions. She may even be enhancing her opportunities to grow her photography business if she could get her foot in the door of some of the world-class institutes in places such as Finland or Germany. The Nordic countries were years, if not decades ahead of America when it came to sustainable living and their care for the environment. And she'd have her pick of triathlon events to choose from; the European competitions were robust and even more competitive than the American ones. Perhaps moving to Sweden was the answer she'd been looking for all along.

And then there was Mårten.

For the past twelve years, Summer had held herself separate from love. Had never allowed herself to dream—not even for a second—that she might be worthy of love. That if she let it in, then something good might come of it.

"I realized something on the day Tyrone tried to kill me," Summer said, pursing her lips and reaching up to touch the cross sitting in the hollow at the base of her neck, its familiar shape giving her courage to continue. Marco had given her this necklace for her seventeenth birthday, and now it felt as if he were speaking to her through the warm metal, giving her permission to let him go at last.

Mårten nodded, waiting for her to talk, but she could feel the slight tremble of his hand in hers.

"I realized I was wrong. I can't escape pain and heartache by building walls to avoid those emotions. They'll come for me anyway. So I may as well embrace them, embrace all that life offers, and take the good along with the bad. As long as I'm with you, I can bear any adversity, overcome any difficulty." And who knew, maybe one day her love for Mårten might even help to reverse the damage all those years of trauma had wreaked on her soul.

"I love you," she said. "And I want to come and live in your cottage in the forest, if you'll let me."

He cradled her chin with his thumb and forefinger and brushed his lips against hers. "Let you? Of course I'll let you. I'll even pack your bag for you. We could go right now. Right this instant. Come on, I'll carry you to the airport." He stood, tugging her up with him so she had no choice but to be pulled into his chest.

"Slow down, Inspector Viskten," she laughed. "We have plenty of time." His eagerness was infectious, and she stood on tiptoe so she could reach his mouth, ignoring the twinge of pain in her legs.

"I want to take you back to my home," he murmured against her lips. "I want to make love to you, over and over, in the grass in the meadow. I want to show you with my body how much you mean to me."

"I want that too," she agreed as a twist of desire unfurled in her gut. She cursed her damaged flesh, and his damaged hands, and kissed him again, harder this time, letting her desire run away with her. "And I'm sure if we're very careful…we might work something out right now," she said with a seductive tilt of her hips against his.

"Damn right we can." Before she could stop him, he'd picked her up, cradling her against his chest, careful not to touch her bandages, and headed down the hallway. "Let's go and celebrate in the best way possible," he said, almost banging her shoulder on the doorframe in his hurry to get them into her bedroom.

Summer kissed his cheek; her heart almost exploding with emotion. This man was everything, and she couldn't wait to start their new lives together. In some peculiar, perverted way, perhaps she owed Tyrone King her thanks, because if he hadn't sent his lackey to burgle her apartment, she would never have met this amazing man, the love of her life. Never have discovered she was capable of giving love and receiving love, so that she was finally free of her demons. Without a moment's hesitation, she knew she would go through everything she'd endured over the past three weeks all over again if it meant she could give Mårten her heart.

"I love you so much," she whispered in his ear as he closed the door behind them and laid her reverently on the bed. Then she took his mouth with hers, and everything else was forgotten.

CHAPTER TWENTY-SEVEN

THREE MONTHS LATER

"Don't move," Summer hissed out of the side of her mouth, not daring to turn her head even the smallest bit. Mårten's body was pressed up against hers as they lay on their stomachs together, hidden in the long grass. Mårten never even blinked an eyelid in response, just kept staring through the waving fronds. He was good at this; she had to give him that much. Her muscles were so tense from lying still for so long, they were almost cramping. But he lay calm and motionless, cool as a cucumber.

Summer refocused on the small forest clearing just in front of them. This was the moment she'd been waiting for. Three days of preparation and tracking, following false leads, biding their time patiently beside a small lake or hunkered down behind a copse of young birch trees watching a trail for fruitless hour upon hour. Three days of wondering if Petar's information had been wrong, and he'd sent them on a wild goose chase. But then today they'd spotted the fresh footprints in the mud, and she knew he was really here.

Jacob's friend, Petar, knew how badly she'd wanted to capture a photo of a wolverine in the wild and had sent her a message a few days ago telling her one had been spotted near his home town of Jokkmokk. After a quick deliberation, Summer decided she might never get another opportunity like this and when Mårten had also elected to come with her, the deal was sealed and they'd driven the two hours out from Luleå to start the search. Petar had taken them out to where the animal had last been seen, helping her track it for the first day, showing her the signs she needed to look for before he had to return to work the next day. She owed Petar more than one drink when they got back to town tonight because he'd just made it possible for her wish to come true.

Slowly, ever so slowly, she used her thumb and forefinger to readjust the focus on her telephoto lens, moving the camera a few millimeters to the right so that a dark head filled the middle of her viewfinder.

The wolverine stared directly at her, its coal-black eyes alight with a mixture of intelligence and watchfulness. God, he was so beautiful. His fur was thick and wiry, a blend of rich dark-brown and chestnut, and his small ears flicked forward and back. He was an adolescent male, probably yet to mate, on the move, looking for females. It wasn't unheard of to find a wolverine this close to Jokkmokk, but Summer knew she was extremely lucky, nonetheless, as their preferred habitat was to the north, in the untamed mountainous regions, away from all habitation. Not many people had seen this rare animal in the wild; the largest member of the weasel family, with a reputation for being fierce and tenaciously strong.

The click of her shutter as she took the photo sounded incredibly loud in the silent woodlands. The animal froze, its entire attention directed to the small clump of grass where she and Mårten were hiding.

Blast! He was going to run. Summer took a burst of ten more photos, knowing she might lose her subject at any second. The wolverine stood up taller, sniffed the air and then bared its teeth, turning to slip back into the undergrowth without a trace as she clicked and clicked in a frenzy to capture her target. Then the animal was gone, leaving nothing but cold air in its wake. But even though she'd had him in her viewfinder for less than twenty seconds, Summer was left with a feeling of complete elation.

"Oh, my God, he was stunning," she said, at last turning on her stomach to look at Mårten.

"Yes, he was." The look on Mårten's face told that he was just as awestruck as her.

"Do you know how extremely lucky we were to see him?" She exhaled the words on a sigh of delight. "There are less than 700 individuals left in the wild, and we just saw one of them." She couldn't keep the grin off her face, even as she carefully tucked her brand new Nikon back into its protective bag.

"I do know," he replied. "I've lived my whole life in this country and never had the privilege of seeing one. Until now. And if it weren't for you, I probably never would have," he added, rolling onto his side with a groan as he stretched out rigid muscles held immobile too long.

Summer stared at the spot where only a few seconds ago the wolverine had stood, reliving every moment. Then, her joy turned suddenly to worry. "God, I hope I got at least one good image. We need to get back to town so I can download them all. Quick, come on." She went to push herself up to her knees when Mårten's low growl and his hand on her waist stopped her.

"There's no hurry," he said into her ear, pulling her down onto his chest, nuzzling his lips against her neck, his short beard tickling her skin. It was late September, and while winter was still a month or more away, there'd been a significant change in the weather over the past week, with temperatures dropping quickly. And out here in Jokkmokk it was colder still, so on Mårten's suggestion, Summer was rugged up in a thick puffer jacket and a knit cap, with warm thermals underneath her jeans.

No, she guessed there wasn't any hurry to get back; they could enjoy their moment of triumph for a little while longer. So, in spite of the cold and the fact the light was fading, and they should probably make their way back to the main path before it got dark, she let her jubilation at finding the wolverine bubble to the surface.

The whole experience had been extra special because she'd got to share it with Mårten. He looked so endearing, lying there with his knit cap slipped sideways, almost covering one eye, tufts of silvery hair protruding from the exposed side. Those full lips puckered into an inviting grin as she continued to stare down at him, his silvery gaze darkening as he considered her. He was so damned good-looking, and she was so damn much in love with him. Could hardly believe he was hers.

Frigid air nipped at her nose and bare fingers, but she ignored the chill as she lowered her head to kiss Mårten firmly on the lips. These past three months had been the best months of her life. She loved living with Mårten in Sweden. It was a much simpler life here, but she was so happy, it felt like a small miracle. Because she'd never dreamed she could ever be this happy. Living in Mårten's small cottage suited her immensely, she'd decided.

After she'd been released from Nikki's care and her burns had healed enough for her to travel, Summer had flown down to see her family, to explain the whole sordid situation in detail and assure them all that she was now fine, and there would be no more danger for any of them. And to tell them the truth about how Marco's death had affected her. Had turned her into a recluse, afraid to really live. Her parents had been shocked to hear how badly the trauma had impacted her, but none of her sisters seemed terribly surprised. They had seen beneath her veneer of self-sufficiency and her eldest sister, Jasmine was especially glad to hear when Summer told them about Mårten. So happy she'd been brought to tears when Summer announced she was moving to Sweden. But they were happy tears, delighted as she was to know that Summer had finally found love.

Summer had left her family with a promise that she would bring Mårten back to meet them all soon, perhaps for Thanksgiving.

Her friends in Seattle had been shocked at first to hear that she was moving away. She'd invited them all out to dinner at her favorite little cafe right before she flew down to see her family, deciding it would be better to get it over with and tell them all at once, asking Mårten to join them once she'd broken the news.

Bianca had tried to talk Summer out of such a rash move to start with. But then she'd laid eyes on Mårten when he arrived and her mood had changed, deciding that the way he looked at Summer was *panty-melting*, and perhaps Summer was right to take the chance at love with such a hot—if not slightly serious for her liking—Swedish cop.

Mayte and Serena had both squealed with delight when she'd haltingly told them she was in love, nearly deafening her. And Trent had told her to *"Go for it, girl."* embracing her in such a giant hug, it left her with tears filling her eyes. Then when Mårten had arrived fifteen minutes later, Trent had also embraced him in another of his enthusiastic squeezes, wiggling his eyebrows in delight over Mårten's shoulder at Mayte and Serena, who were waiting their turns to get in on the cuddle-fest, clearly approving of Summer's choice.

Summer was still mortified that she'd missed Josie and Mark's wedding—even though she had the *best excuse ever*, as

Mark put it—but her friends had both been delighted that she'd found someone and wouldn't stop hinting that she would be next on the list to get hitched, and they couldn't wait to travel to Sweden for a summer wedding. And while Summer acted horrified at the thought, on the inside she was surprisingly unperturbed by the idea.

She missed her friends; she would be the first to admit it. But they had all promised to visit when they could get some free time, and Summer was due to fly back to Seattle in October to help Nikki complete the project she and Tammy Pittman had started on the orca whales, and she couldn't wait.

And now she was making new friends in Luleå. Summer really liked Mårten's police partner, Aurora, and they had become good friends over the past months. She often invited Aurora to dinner, along with a few of Mårten's other friends. They would sit outside on the porch and drink wine as Mårten and the men grilled salmon or chicken, talking quietly together; there was something about Aurora that Summer found appealing. They had similar values and laughed at the same jokes, and she was easy to be around. The policewoman was younger than Summer, but that didn't seem to be an issue, and while Summer was trying to break her need to always be in control, she could understand that in Aurora's field of work a lack of spontaneity and recklessness might be a good thing to help keep her safe.

Mårten had confided that he thought Aurora might have been sweet on him for a while. Summer didn't disagree—it'd take a hard woman not to be a little starry-eyed around this irresistible man—but as soon as Mårten revealed Summer was coming back to live with him, Aurora had cooled her enthusiasm, becoming completely professional around him, making it clear, to Summer at least, that she would not be a threat. Aurora clearly had strong morals, and lusting after a man who was rapturously in love with another woman was not something she would ever do.

Thinking about Aurora, Summer lifted her head, breaking the kiss so she could stare down into Mårten's clear-blue eyes, a question on her lips.

"What?" he asked, his hungry gaze never leaving her mouth.

"I was just wondering how Aurora is going today? You haven't had a single phone call from her? Should we be worried?" Aurora had one bad habit, and that was she would call Mårten constantly, peppering him with questions. She was a rookie and still on probation, and paired together with her need to be a stickler for the rules, she didn't like to make a decision without first consulting Mårten. Which drove him mad at times. Summer knew that Mårten and Aurora were working on something big, but neither of them would give her the details, and Mårten had probably had to push the boundaries with his boss and Aurora to get these few days of leave approved. It was a little odd that Aurora hadn't been in touch with him even once today.

"Why are you thinking about Aurora? She's the last thing on my mind right now. In fact..." He rolled her over so that he was on his knees, pulling her up to a sitting position next to him. "I have something I want to ask you." He tugged her up, so they were both standing, leaned in and kissed her achingly tenderly on the lips, pulled his gloves off and tucked them into his pocket, then dropped to one knee in the dirt in front of her.

What the hell...?

"Oh." It was the only sound Summer was capable of uttering before she covered her mouth with both hands. Was Mårten about to do what she thought he was going to do?

* * *

"Summer," Mårten said, looking directly up into her eyes.

"This might seem an odd place to do this, but I believe I fell completely and utterly in love with you that first time when we made love out in the forest, so it feels fitting we keep the magic going out here amongst the trees."

Summer made a small squeaking sound, her eyes so big and round they almost filled her entire face. Mårten hadn't known he was going to do this until this very moment. He'd been carrying the ring in his shirt pocket for a few weeks now, unsure how to make the perfect proposal, hoping that inspiration would hit. And now it had. They'd just shared an extraordinary moment with a beautiful, wild animal, and his heart was still beating fast in his chest at the majesty of the wolverine, its eyes so fierce and arresting he couldn't look away. The sun was setting low on the horizon, the sky turning indigo, and the cold air was so hushed and crisp. They were completely alone, just the two of them in this heavenly landscape.

But he had to get this right. He knew they were awesome together, but God, he hoped she felt the same.

Reaching up, he touched the necklace at the base of her throat. "I love that you continue to wear this," he said. "Because Marco will always be a part of your life, a part of who you are."

"Oh." Summer seemed taken aback, as if she wondered where he was going with this. But Marco needed to be acknowledged. Summer had been in love with him, and his untimely death had colored the rest of her life. In many ways, Marco had helped shape Summer into the woman he loved. Now, he hoped that Summer could finally let Marco go, and give her heart wholly to him.

"And I want to make a promise to Marco that I will love you as much as he ever did. That I will hold your heart safe within mine, keep your soul protected forevermore." As he said this, he touched the necklace quickly once more. Then he pulled the ring out of his shirt pocket and held it up for her to see. The solitaire diamond sparkled in the soft evening light.

Tears sprang to Summer's eyes, and she got down on her knees beside him, so they were now face to face.

"Will you let me do that, Summer? Will you marry me?" He clasped both of her hands between his. Her fingers were cold, but he barely registered the fact as he stared into her eyes, liquid pools of emotion, waiting for his answer.

"This is so unexpected," Summer replied, her gaze never leaving his. "But you're right; you couldn't have found a more perfect place." She tilted her head back so she could stare at the heavens. He did the same and saw a single pinprick of light—the evening star—high above in the pastel sky. "And I know Marco would give me his blessing. He would never have wanted me to shut myself away from love," Summer continued, lowering her head as he did the same, so that their noses were almost touching. He could feel her soft breath on his lips, see the pumping vein in her neck giving away how fast her heart was beating. "So, my answer is yes. Yes, I will marry you, Mårten."

Her mouth collided with his and they were lost in each other for moments of ecstasy. When at last she broke away, he fumbled with her left hand, holding his breath as he slid the ring on her finger, praying he'd got the size right and it would fit her small hands.

It did. They both looked down as she wiggled the ring, making it sparkle, and Summer seemed completely entranced by it; unable to look away. "It's gorgeous," she murmured.

"You've just made me the happiest man on Earth," Mårten whispered.

"Ditto," Summer whispered back. "I feel like my heart is going to burst."

"Come on," he said at last, pulling her back to her feet. "While I'd love nothing more than to lay you down in the grass and have my wicked way with you, I think we should get moving." The air was growing colder with every minute they spent here, and it was a half-hour trek back to where they'd left his car. They had torches and a GPS, so they couldn't get lost, but he wanted her back in their hotel room, warm and safe where he could make love to her properly. He made her put her gloves on, even though all she wanted to do was keep staring at the ring, and he replaced his. It felt like he was barely touching the ground as they worked their way back through the undergrowth to the small animal track they'd followed to reach the clearing. Once they attained the small rise, they turned as one to look back at the spot where they'd seen the wolverine. This place would live forever in their hearts now.

"Now Nikki and Jacob have an extra reason to come and visit. To attend our engagement party," he said, grabbing her hand and leading her up the path.

"Yes. Oh, yes." Summer did a little skip and a hop. "Let's make it soon, then. I can't wait to see them. Although I'll have to put up with Nikki lording it over me, because she knew we'd end up together all along." Summer did a good imitation of Nikki's pretty pout, one eyebrow raised in a knowing glance, exactly the way Nikki would've done. Mårten laughed. He'd like to see Jacob again, too. Couldn't wait to share the news with his friend. If it hadn't been for Jacob, Mårten might never have met Summer, so he had a lot to thank him for.

Summer meant everything to him now; he couldn't imagine never having met her. It must've been fate, or kismet, or karma. Whatever it was, he was so glad that he now held Summer's heart. It was the most precious thing he could imagine.

Also by Suzanne Cass

NEW

The Three of Hearts Series
Nordic Romantic Suspense
Books can be read as stand-alone
Winter's Heart
Summer's Heart
Aurora's Heart
Women's Mystery Romance Fiction
Single Title

Finding Kait

Dark Tides Series
Mystery and Romance collide.
Books can be read as stand-alone
Into the Rain
Rain Washed
The Clearing Rain
Stormcloud Station Series
(A Stargazer Spinoff Series)
Small Town Romantic Suspense
Books can be read as stand-alone
Clear Skies
Starlit Skies
Crystal Skies
Dawn Skies
Tangled Skies
Outback Skies
Stargazer Ranch Romance Series
Small Town Romantic Suspense
Books can be read as stand-alone
Combustion: Prequel Novella
Wildfire
Firelight
Snowbound: A Christmas Novella
Snowfall
Cloudburst

Silverstorm
Island Bound Series
Mystery Romance (on an Island)
Books can be read as stand-alone
Bound by Truth
Bound by Silence
Bound by the Stars
Colors of the Earth Series
Small Town Romantic Suspense
Books can be read as stand-alone
Shadows in the Dust
Shadows in Deep Blue
Shadows of Red Earth
Romantic Suspense
Single Title
Island Redemption
Glass Clouds
Chasing Bullets
Love in the Mountains Novella Series
Small Town Short Romance
Novellas can be read as stand-alone
Rain on a Tin Roof
Lost and Found
Rescue his Heart

Please Leave a Review

The greatest gift you could ever give an author is to leave a review. You will be helping other people to discover this book and making a difference to me as an Independently Published Author. If you liked this book and want other people to read it to, please leave a review.

About the Author

Suzanne Cass is an Australian author who writes rural romance and romantic suspense abounding with passion and danger.

Her debut novel, Island Redemption, won the Romance Writers of Australia Emerald Award in 2016. Suzanne was also a finalist in the 2019 Romance Writers of Australia RUBY award.

She had always had a fascination with the tough resilience of people who live in our amazing red-dirt outback country. When not writing about the characters that inhabit her head, Suzanne can be found roaming the Perth beaches with her border collie, or encouraging from the sidelines as her two sons play sport.

Facebook: www.facebook.com/suzannecassauthor/
Instagram: www.instagram.com/suzanne.cass/
Pintrest: www.pinterest.com.au/suzanne_cass/

9 780648 643074